I DO

NOT

TRUST

YOU

ALSO BY
LAURA J. BURNS & MELINDA METZ

SANCTUARY BAY

LAURA J. BURNS & MELINDA METZ

I DO
NOT
TRUST
YOU

WEDNESDAY BOOKS
NEW YORK

I DO NOT TRUST YOU. Copyright © 2018 by St. Martin's Press. All rights
reserved. Printed in the United States of America. For information,
address St. Martin's Press, 175 Fifth Avenue, New York, N.Y. 10010.

www.wednesdaybooks.com
www.stmartins.com

The Library of Congress Cataloging-in-Publication Data
is available upon request.

ISBN 978-1-250-05230-8 (hardcover)
ISBN 978-1-4668-5391-1 (ebook)

Our books may be purchased in bulk for promotional, educational,
or business use. Please contact your local bookseller or the Macmillan
Corporate and Premium Sales Department at 1-800-221-7945, extension
5442, or by email at MacmillanSpecialMarkets@macmillan.com.

First Edition: September 2018

10 9 8 7 6 5 4 3 2 1

To our editor, Vicki Lame,
who loved the idea of ancient Egypt as much as we did

The Boston Record

Gregory A. Engel, an influential scholar of archeology and linguistics, was killed Thursday, in a small plane crash northeast of Mumbai, Maharashtra, India. He was 46.

Dr. Engel received his doctorate in linguistic anthropology from the University of Sheffield in 1994. In 1996, he traveled to the Upper Nile Valley to study the transliteration system used by Egyptian priests after the invasion of Alexander the Great, beginning the work he would continue until his death.

A research paper Dr. Engel published in 2017 posited that the language of the Horus priests lasted at least 500 years after the last known appearance of hieroglyphic script. His hypothesis was based on his discovery of writings in the secret language of the priests on paper carbon dated at approximately A.D. 900. Dr. Engel received the R.R. Hawkins Award, which recognizes outstanding scholarly works in all disciplines of the arts and sciences, for the paper.

Dr. Engel was preceded in death by his wife, Dr. Daisy Leong, a physician with Doctors Without Borders. He is survived by his daughter, Memphis Leong Engel.

CHAPTER 1

The lotus flower was wrong. Its loop bent down where it should bend up. No matter how she translated it, the phrase didn't make sense with the lotus that way.

Sorry, Dad, M thought. *I know you wanted it to mean the Nefertum temple, but it's not. The flower just isn't right.*

"Memphis? Are we boring you?"

M's attention snapped back to her teacher, who wore the same slightly exasperated expression she had every time they interacted. Ms. O'Malley was cool enough, and pretty smart. But she didn't know history like M knew history—and that was the one thing they both knew.

"Nope. Rome is my second-favorite empire," M replied.

Ms. O'Malley narrowed her eyes, trying to figure out if this was scolding-worthy behavior. M held her gaze.

"Just make sure you're listening while you doodle," Ms. O'Malley finally said.

"Always."

She went back to her lecture and M went back to her hieroglyphs. Her *doodles*. They had helped win her father the R. R. Hawkins Award a few years ago, and they would be the subject of the first scholarly article M published once she got her doctorate. But there were only two people left in the world who could read them. To everyone else, they were just doodles.

Maybe the lotus flower wasn't *actually* a lotus flower and the phrase didn't mean the little shrine to the god Nefertum. It had been a long shot anyway. She and Mike had only taken up this part of the translation because M's father had started it already, so they had something to go on. If only she could sit in a room with Dad like always, puzzling over the tiny pictograms together with a bowl of M&Ms nearby. But that part of her life was over. She would have to finish translating the map without him.

M shook her head. Wallowing didn't get work done, that's what Mom always said. Or at least what Dad had told her Mom said. The memories of Mom weren't as strong as they once were. Now she was mostly someone M remembered through Dad's stories. Who knew where the line was between truth and memory? Mike said it didn't matter—that love was the only part of the story that mattered.

"That's ludicrous," Nick Washington's voice broke into her thoughts. "You're assuming the Church didn't know exactly what they were doing."

"They were missionaries. Their whole job—" Brianna Lin started.

"They were conquerors!" Nick's face was smug. His voice was smug. M was pretty sure his soul was smug too. It was his defining characteristic. "The Church didn't take over the world by being tolerant. They wanted everyone to think like them, so they made everyone pray like them. You can't keep your local god unless you start calling it your local saint."

"The Church isn't an empire. Rome was an empire," Brianna argued, sounding more on edge. Nick had that effect on people.

"In fact, there is little evidence the Church appropriated pagan gods," Ms. O'Malley pointed out.

"Oh *everyone* knows it. Even the holidays used to be pagan holidays," Nick said. "Like Christmas, or Easter. They were pagan festivals before the Church took them over. You want to talk imperialism? *That's* imperialism. The Roman Empire let people keep their own gods. They were tolerant."

Brianna didn't answer. She looked ready to cry. M sighed. Nick's debating style was basically to be a bully. M didn't like bullies.

"They weren't tolerant. You're just ignorant of their worldview," she said calmly.

All eyes in the room went to her. Nick's face lit up. He loved a new victim. Or a new sparring partner. He only cared about fighting. He didn't have to believe what he was fighting for.

"I don't think I've ever been called ignorant before," he drawled. He was going to Yale in the fall and worked it into conversation at least once a day.

"Not to your face, maybe," M replied, earning an "oooh" from her classmates. "The Romans didn't give a crap about the gods of their conquered territories. They were polytheistic. They simply did not have the concept of 'my god is the only god, so all other gods are false.' To them, it didn't matter if their conquests worshipped other gods. All that mattered was that they paid taxes. Meanwhile, the Catholic Church held a monotheistic worldview, so they rejected other gods. They didn't view it as imperialism, they viewed it as doing God's work."

"It doesn't matter why they did it, they still stamped out native religions," Nick argued.

"The why is the only thing that matters. If you don't understand how people thought at the time, then you don't understand history," M told him. "The Romans weren't being nice. If they saw a local god as a threat to their power, they stamped out that god just the way the Church did. But they did it for financial reasons, for security reasons, not for theological reasons. But that doesn't fit your narrative, I guess."

Nick's eyebrows drew together, and for a moment he seemed at a loss. Ms. O'Malley pounced.

"Okay, enough debate. We were talking about the expansion of the Roman Empire, not the implications of their religion." She shot Nick a frown, while Brianna smiled at M.

Nick gave an unconcerned shrug, but M knew he hated when he didn't get the last word. Almost as much as she hated when clueless people tried to show off.

"You should've seen Miss Memphis here get into it with Nick last period," Brianna said, squeezing in between M and Inez at their usual spot in the cafeteria. "She shut him down with her crazy ancient cultures voodoo."

"He's an ass. He's lucky he's hot," their friend Ayana commented, waving her spork in Nick's direction.

M shrugged. "I wouldn't try to debate him in Physics. I just know more about Rome than he does."

"What about AP Chem? Would you debate him in that?" Inez asked in a fake-serious voice. "Would you debate him in German class?"

"She'd debate him in German, in *German*," Brianna joked. "And if he tried to fight back, she'd switch to Greek."

M threw a French fry at her. "I can't help it. I grew up speaking different languages."

"And learning about pharaohs. And becoming well versed in the history of the Etruscan people," Ayana said, putting on a fake accent that was probably supposed to be British. "Oh, and setting broken bones in the bush."

"That only happened once," M muttered. Her friends laughed.

"Anyway, it was epic. Thanks," Brianna said. "I can't stand fighting with people, and Nick always goes after me."

"He knows you hate it," M pointed out. "That's why he does it."

"An ass, like I said." Ayana shrugged.

"You think he's coming to the party tonight?" Brianna asked.

"Probably. Everyone else is," Inez replied. "Even Memphis."

M made a face. "Anything to get out of the house. Bob and Liza would expect me to play board games with them otherwise." Her friends exchanged a glance. M winced. "No offense."

"Oh, were you offending someone?" Nick piped up from behind her. "Good girl."

Immediately Bri looked down, while Ayana rolled her eyes. Inez just smirked, glancing back and forth between M and Nick.

"I was not offending anyone. I only meant I don't like parties," M said. She didn't bother to turn toward him. It didn't matter; he inserted himself onto the bench next to her anyway. A little tingle ran up her spine as the scent of his cologne hit her nostrils, spicy and warm.

"Mmm, they're boring. Everyone talking about the prom or the senior trip or whatever. I'm over it," Nick said.

Me too, thought M, wishing she didn't agree with him. She loved her friends, but even they were all about high school. M just didn't care. High school was nothing more than what she had to get through before she could leave. After the crash, after the shock of Bob and Liza becoming her guardians, she'd asked if she could go off to college early, either Boston University or the University of Sheffield in England. Both had the kind of archeology program she wanted and would've let her in with no questions. They knew her father. They knew high school was a waste of time for someone like her.

But her guardians said no. They said she needed stability and normalcy after losing her dad. Never mind that traveling the world and taking care of herself *was* normal for her. While she and Dad technically lived in Boston, she'd never spent more than a few months there during the school year. They traveled. Half the year spent on digs. She missed it.

"What's with this thing, anyway? Is it to fight off bad guys?" Nick teased, finding an excuse to touch her. He reached for M's collapsible bo staff, tucked in the inside pocket of her jacket like always. But before he touched it, before his flirty smile registered in her mind, M had already grabbed his hand, twisted it back to the breaking point, and used the pain to push him off the cafeteria bench and onto the floor. With her other hand, she whipped out the stick and shoved it up against his throat.

M froze. *He's just hitting on you.* Her friends were aghast, and everyone nearby watched, openmouthed. Nick's eyes were wide with panic.

"Sorry." M stood up, leaving Nick on the floor. "I'm really sorry."

"Freak," he muttered, climbing to his feet. He glanced around, noticing the barely concealed laughter from onlookers. "Jeez, I just wanted a fry," he joked, as if he hadn't been humiliated, then hurried out of the cafeteria.

"What. The. Hell?" Inez asked. "He was flirting with you and you beat him up!"

"I know." M groaned, shoving her staff back into her pocket. "I didn't mean to. It was just reflex."

Her friends were silent. She'd freaked them out. Should she explain the years of self-defense and martial arts training? That she and Dad ended up in some rough places? Her friends lived in a city, they understood danger. Sort of. In a nice, upscale Boston kind of way.

M sighed. There was no point in trying to explain. Nobody understood her life.

"You kinda push all the guys away," Brianna pointed out quietly. "Maybe not like *that,* but still . . ."

"I don't do romance," M replied. She was done with love, period. She'd loved her parents, and they were both gone. Love hurt too much. It was better to steer clear of it.

They all ate in silence for a minute.

"I mean, he *is* an ass," Ayana said finally. And everybody laughed.

> **M:** You up?
>
> **MIKE:** It's a 12 hr time difference. Of course I'm up.
>
> **M:** Like you never sleep in on weekends.
>
> **MIKE:** Fine, your text woke me.
>
> **M:** I don't think that glyph is a lotus. It's bending the wrong way.
>
> **MIKE:** It has to be a lotus. If it's not, the whole phrase is wrong.
>
> **M:** The rest of the phrase never sat well with Nefertum anyway.
>
> **MIKE:** Your dad said it was a lotus.

MIKE: M?

MIKE: ??

MIKE: Sorry.

M: Just cause he's gone doesn't mean everything he ever thought is true.

MIKE: I know.

M: If I assume all of his translations were right, I'm closing my mind. He would hate that. If I think he was always perfect then I'm not thinking of him as a real person anymore.

M: Sorry.

MIKE: And he feels too far away. Like he's really gone.

M: Yeah.

MIKE: We don't have to finish the map right now. It's been around for a thousand years. It can wait a little longer.

M: No.

M: It's the only thing that makes me feel close to him.

MIKE: OK. We'll do whatever you want.

M: But I can't work tonight. Just wanted to tell you about the lotus.

MIKE: Friday night plans?

M: Party at Tyler's. Bob and Liza threatened to send me to a shrink if I didn't start acting like a "normal teen."

MIKE: It'll be fun.

M: Doubt it.

MIKE: Well, try.

M: I wish you were here.

MIKE: Me too. I miss you.

M leaned back in her chair, her hand finding the small glass pendant around her neck. Why did Mike have to live so far away? They hadn't seen each other since the memorial service, and who knew when they would again. Bob and Liza were determined to keep her trapped in Boston. "No more of this unsettled living" was Liza's favorite refrain. It was hard to know why her parents had chosen guardians with a worldview so opposite their own. They'd all been friends at the University of Sheffield, but obviously Bob and Liza had changed since then.

If only her parents' will had been changed too.

"Wallowing doesn't get work done," M whispered, turning back to the hieroglyphs she'd painstakingly copied from the parchment map so they'd be easier to work on. As long as she focused on the tiny pictures, she didn't have to think about Dad. Or Mom. Or Mike being a world away.

If it wasn't a lotus, what could it be? An axe, maybe? The hieroglyphs had been written in ink, so it was also possible the scribe's hand had merely slipped.

"Memphis! Pizza's here," Liza called from downstairs.

M winced. She hated that they lived in her house. It didn't make things normal like they thought. Instead it made her home feel less like one. They tried. Liza got pizza every Friday because when she'd moved here from England, she heard Friday night pizza was normal for Americans. But Friday was Thai night for M and her father. And every time she saw Bob sitting in her father's favorite chair, she felt a wave of misery.

"I'm going to a party," she called. She shoved the hieroglyphs into her desk drawer, grabbed her jacket, and trotted downstairs. Even the lamest party was better than another fake-happy fake-family pizza night.

"Whose party?" Liza asked, her eyes bright with curiosity.

"My friend's."

"Which friend?" Liza sounded thrilled, as if M were a three-year-old who'd just found her first playmate.

"Max Devilmann," M told her, straight-faced. It was the joke name Mike always used when making reservations at questionable hotels. "I'll be out late, don't bother waiting up."

"Be home by midnight," Liza said.

"Liza. I'm eighteen now, remember?" *You're lucky I didn't skip out entirely the day I stopped being a minor.*

Liza pursed her lips and tried to stare M down.

"See you tomorrow." M forced a smile and headed out, pulling on her jacket to ward off the April chill. Out of habit, she checked for her bo staff as soon as she heard the door click shut behind her. An image of Mom's long, surgeon's fingers demonstrating how to properly hold the staff flashed through her mind. They'd been in Nairobi then. M was seven.

She broke into a jog, pushing the memory away. Brianna had offered to drive her, but the party wasn't far. M liked feeling the air on her cheeks, liked breathing in the city's scent of early spring blossoms mixed with the smell of the swamp Back Bay was built over.

A shadow flitted past her, and she slowed to a walk. Across the street, two women were walking a yellow Lab. Twenty yards ahead a guy in a suit bounded down the steps of a brownstone and came in her direction, giving a vague smile as he passed her.

Something was wrong.

Another shadow darted between the pools of light under the old streetlamps. The guy in the suit kept walking away.

M pulled out her phone, stopping, as if she needed to check something. A quick glance over her shoulder revealed a young guy dressed in all black from his leather jacket to his motorcycle boots. He had a shock of thick dark hair and wore a bracelet of twisted thread on his right wrist.

He didn't even glance at M as he passed. She let him get in front of her, then started walking again. After half a block, he headed up the steps to a brownstone with a Valentine's Day heart wreath still hung on the door.

M kept going, the itchy sensation in her hands growing stronger. The neighborhood seemed normal, but in her gut she knew something was off. Her gut was never wrong. The first thing—the most important thing—her parents had ever taught her was to trust her instincts.

The party was at some lacrosse guy's house five blocks away. She needed to keep going straight.

She turned right at the next corner.

Somebody was behind her, walking slowly, unthreatening.

The guy dressed in black.

M broke into a jog.

His pace picked up behind her.

She broke into a run. Up ahead was a wrought-iron fence surrounding a small side yard. M reached for one of the bars, swinging herself up and vaulting over. She hit the ground running, her Chucks pounding the cement walkway, then the grass in the yard as it opened up behind the brownstone. A short stone wall separated it from the next yard.

M jumped it and kept going.

His footsteps echoed hers. She could hear his breathing.

Another wall. Another backyard. He kept coming.

Enough. Time to go on offense.

A quick scan of the next yard showed a small deck built onto the back of the house. She ducked under the row of evergreen bushes growing along the wall, before jumping the wall and climbing onto the deck, giving her a five-foot advantage on her pursuer.

The guy in black vaulted over and paused, looking for her.

M pulled the bo staff from her jacket and flicked her wrist, causing the ends of the staff to snap into place so it was three times longer. His head turned at the sound. M jumped, landing in front of him before he could react. She circled the staff above her head and brought it down in front of her into ready position.

"Memphis," he said.

M moved into horse stance, legs wide, knees bent, preparing to attack.

"I'm not here to hurt you."

She brought her arms up. Before she could execute the rib strike, he jumped back, scrambling to get away.

"Stop!" he cried. "M, stop!"

Shocked, she paused. Nobody called her M except her family. And Mike.

"Your father sent me," the guy said.

M adjusted her grip, keeping the bo staff poised over her head. "My father is dead."

This time he didn't flinch. "That's what they want you to think."

CHAPTER 2

The fluorescent lights of the diner shined down on his bracelet. It wasn't regular thread, but some kind of flax woven together in an unusual design. His dark hands curled around the coffee mug, dwarfing it. His fingers were long, elegant, his nails perfectly buffed.

"My name is Ashwin Sood." His accent was British, posh. The motorcycle jacket looked beat-up but obviously so, as if he'd bought it already distressed. "I know your father."

M sipped her coffee. The world was buzzing somewhere at the back of her mind, thoughts and emotions, questions and sobs, all fighting for her attention. Instead, she focused on him. His hair was black with a wave. His eyes hazel, beautiful against his dark skin.

"I'm sure it sounds—"

"He died in a plane crash. They brought me his wedding ring from the wreck." M replied coldly. The coffee felt like it might come back up. M closed her eyes, willing it—and her feelings—back down.

"I don't know anything about that."

He was lying.

"I only know he is alive and I saw him last two days ago."

She broke.

"This is a cruel fucking joke," she spat, opening her eyes. "I don't know who you are or what you're trying to accomplish, but I hope you rot in hell."

But her anger couldn't keep the worst emotion from bubbling up anyway, despite her defenses. Hope.

Ashwin seemed taken aback. He stared at her, then looked down at his hands. M wanted to storm out, but hope kept her rooted in place. She had to know, even though it was a lie.

"He said to give you this." Ashwin pushed a scrap of paper across the table. On it, sketched in small hieroglyphs, was a message. M felt as if her heart stopped. She'd know her father's writing anywhere. His slanted, careful rendering of pictograms that looked like Egyptian hieroglyphs, but weren't, not exactly. His use of standard symbols intermixed with the strange, off-kilter signs used only by the priests who served Horus thousands of years ago. It was a language her father had devoted his life to deciphering.

"He said you could read it. Can you?" Ashwin watched her intently.

"I learned these signs along with my ABCs. It was our secret language," M whispered. She wanted to question him, doubt him . . . but couldn't. She could barely breathe. The hope was getting stronger. It sat there like a lump, constricting her throat.

No. Her father was dead. He'd been dead for almost a year. It was insane to think anything else. Hope was useless and wrong. It would hurt her. If this turned out to be a lie, it would be like losing Dad all over again.

"What does it say?"

M's attention snapped back to him. "He didn't tell you?"

He shook his head, expression worried. Why worried? M narrowed her eyes, filing his reaction away for later. She looked at the paper, running through the glyphs in her mind, translating images to words. Her father may have been the official expert, but she'd grown up with these little pictures. He'd always said she would be more fluent because she learned it all at a time when her brain functioned like a sponge.

"Do you call yourself Ash?" she asked.

"Yes." He narrowed his eyes. "Why?"

"It says to trust you."

She saw him relax a bit, the muscles in his jaw unclenching. "Anything else?" he asked.

M considered not telling him until she could figure out her own thoughts. The note didn't make sense. It was about Dad's work. It didn't say: "I'm alive!" or "Help!" It was just a message about Ash and about the map. Nothing more.

"It says I should give you the map," M said slowly.

Ash smiled, relief washing over his face. She knew there was something about him that just wasn't quite right. But her mind was still spinning.

"But I'm not giving you anything. I don't believe a word of this," she added. She sat back and waited for his reaction.

Ash held her gaze. "Dr. Engel assured me he put proof in his message to you," he said at last.

Proof. M immediately flipped the paper over. The cult of Horus was big on secret messages. Dad had always loved that. There would be hidden keys in their correspondence, double meanings in their pictograms, even outright tricks to fool non-priests. There would be important clues hidden in different places.

On the back was one tiny picture. An owl—the ancient Egyptian hieroglyph for the letter "M." But instead of the typical face, this owl had a small smile. It didn't mean the letter "M," Dad had always said. It meant the girl M. It was how he'd started writing her name when she was little. She hadn't seen this smiling owl in a year.

Her eyes grew wet with tears, the diner blurring around her. She wondered if she would faint. Then the anger took back over.

"Where is he?" she demanded.

"He's being held prisoner," Ash replied. "By a group of archeologists."

M snorted. "I've spent my life surrounded by archeologists. They're not the taking-prisoners type. They're not generally the knowing-which-end-of-a-gun-to-hold type. My father was unusual that way. *Is* unusual." There it was again, the hope. Could her father really be alive? M pushed her giddiness away and focused on Ash. "He taught me well. I can take you down before you know what hit you. So tell me again, where is my father?"

He sighed. "You're correct. These archeologists are more like . . . zealots. When your father published that article about his map, it caught their attention."

"Why?"

"Dr. Engel's article was widely circulated because of the map's inconsistencies," Ash said. "The paper and ink dated to the Middle Ages, but the language was that of a cult gone for over three thousand years. People wanted to know how such a thing was possible, as I'm sure you're aware."

M felt a stab of panic. "Are you saying conspiracy-theory nutbars have my dad?"

"No. These archeologists found it interesting for a different reason. They recognized what the map was for."

"What it was *for*?" M frowned. It wasn't really a map at all. Her father hadn't wanted to call it one, but he'd lost that fight with his editor. It was more like a list of descriptions, attributes. Dad had called it a "word map." That the random hieroglyphs described certain locations had been his first big breakthrough. Until then, the scroll had sat untouched in the British Museum for a hundred years. Early archeologists had thought it a practice paper for an Egyptian scribe learning how to write. The glyphs on it didn't say anything when strung together, they seemed like nonsense.

Only after realizing that the words described specific places did he get a grant to take the scroll for further study. And then, once carbon dating put the paper so much later, it was clear no Egyptian scribe had been involved.

Dad hadn't cared much about the places, or the dating inconsistency. He cared about the language. He was a linguist before he went into archeology, and the unique tongue had piqued his interest. He hadn't known what the word map was for, and he hadn't cared. All that mattered to him was translating what it said.

Mike had asked, once, why these locations would be listed all on one scroll. But Dad didn't know. M hadn't thought about it since.

"The people who have your father believe this is the map they have been searching for," Ash told her. "One that will lead them to an ancient artifact that was divided into five pieces and hidden."

"What artifact?" M asked. "I've never heard anything like that."

"A figure of the god Set." Ash sighed. "They took your father because he is the only one who can read the map. They plan to hold him captive until he can translate the entire map, and they can recover the pieces."

M couldn't stop staring at the scrap of paper in her hand. Dad was alive. He was still here in the world with her, writing to her in their secret language. A sob escaped her lips. "Is he okay?"

Ash looked surprised. "Your father? Yes. They are treating him well. Although . . ."

"What?"

"He fears his time is running out. That's why he sent me to find you."

M couldn't think about her father in danger. If he was alive, he needed to be here with her, safe, right now. "Where is he? Why didn't you call the police?" she demanded.

He hesitated. "It is a complicated situation."

M stood up abruptly. "Your story doesn't make sense. If these archeologists want to locate an ancient artifact, why wouldn't they just ask for my father's help? Surely it would be worth enough money that they could cut him in instead of committing a felony."

"Please. Listen," Ash said quickly. "I promise I will explain."

M sat back down. "You have five minutes, then I go to the police."

"Very well. What do you know about the god Set?"

"Are you kidding me?" M asked.

He didn't answer.

"Fine. He's the Egyptian god of chaos and war, usually depicted as a strange-looking animal," M said. "He killed his brother, Osiris, chopped up his corpse, and scattered it throughout Egypt. Then Osiris's wife, Isis, found the pieces and restored his body. Or she restored it enough to conceive a child, who became the god Horus, ruler of Egypt. Osiris went to the underworld and ruled there."

Ash nodded. "Right. So this is a representation of Set that has been chopped up and scattered, just like what he did to Osiris."

M rolled her eyes. "Except it's a statue, not a person. What does any of this have to do with my dad?"

"These people don't want to sell the artifact. They want to use it," Ash said. "They believe that if the pieces of the Set artifact are rejoined, Set himself will rise, like Osiris did. They worship him. They think they're doing his will."

Silence. M took a long sip of her now lukewarm coffee, then set it down carefully. "Let me get this straight. When you said archeologists took my father, you meant zealots. And when you said zealots, you meant a bunch of crazy-pants cultists who think they can resurrect an ancient god of the underworld."

Ash blinked, his eyebrows drawing together. "Well . . ."

"It sounds bananas, and you sound like a liar." M leaned toward him. "Am I also supposed to believe that these cult members told you this whole story and let you come find me even though they apparently faked my father's death and kidnapped him?"

"No!" he protested. "I'm a student, an anthropology major. I got a job working with their group, doing grunt work, barely even a research assistant. For months it seemed normal. I would see Dr. Engel in the study, working on his translation. I assumed he was one of them. But one day I saw them bring him back to his room. They locked the door from the outside."

M felt a chill run through her. Even the idea of Dad locked up, controlled by strangers, made her panicky. She had to help him.

"I began slipping him notes," Ash said. "He told me the truth. He asked me to get word to you."

M frowned. Dad's note didn't ask for help. It didn't even say "I love you." It only said to trust Ash and give him the map. It was the type of thing you might write if somebody put a knife to your throat and told you to.

"He asked you to get the map from me? Not to call the cops. Not to rescue him."

"He thinks the only way to gain his freedom is to find the artifacts," Ash said. "He's confident in his translations, but his captors haven't discovered any of the Set pieces at the sites he sent them to."

"Meaning his translations don't point to the correct locations," M said, doubtful. Dad had previously translated two lines of glyphs pointing to specific archeological sites. There was no way those translations were wrong.

"He now suspects it is a cipher. He hopes there is a decryption key of some sort on the original map that he did not notice before." Ash cleared his throat. "He has not told the archeologists his map is not the original."

M raised an eyebrow. "They're archeologists and they didn't notice he's using a copy?"

That didn't make sense, though to be fair, her father's copy was fairly authentic looking. He liked getting the feel of the original without compromising its integrity by exposing it to the elements. And besides, the original was nearly impossible to read. M felt a little dizzy thinking about Dad's copy of the map. She'd assumed it was gone, consumed in the flames of the plane crash. She had been working from the original, taking pictures with her phone so she could blow them up and copy the glyphs. She only took it out when absolutely necessary.

"Memphis, he needs the original map," Ash said. "If he can figure out the true locations, they will release him."

"Okay." M put on a smile. "Let's go."

Ash stared at her, uncomprehending. "Go?"

"Yes. Let's take them the map."

As she'd expected, he instantly began to backtrack. "You don't understand. You are to give the map to me and I'll bring it to them. Isn't that what your father's note said?"

"It said to give you the map," she agreed. "But I'm not going to do that."

"What . . . why?" he sputtered.

"An hour ago my father was dead. Now he's alive. So I want to see him. Now. If you're going back to where he is, I'm going with you."

"But . . . no, he wants me to bring back the original, not you," Ash said.

"Where did you tell your employers you were going? Do they know you're here for the map?" she asked. "When you show up again and give him the original, do you really expect them not to notice?"

"I . . ."

"You're obviously not telling me the truth," M said. "If you want me to turn over the map, I'll only do it when I see my father's really alive."

Ash dropped his face into his hands. "I cannot bring you to your father."

"Why not?"

"It's too dangerous," he finally said, looking at her. "These people are violent. It wouldn't be safe."

Violent. M pushed the thought away. "You said they were treating my dad well."

"For now," he replied. "It won't last. They are organized and powerful. They will hurt him. They will hurt you." He leaned forward, staring intently into her eyes. "You should know . . . your guardians, they are part of this. They arranged a fake plane crash. They produced a falsified will. Memphis, they never even knew your parents."

"You told me you didn't know anything about that," M pointed out.

"I'm trying to protect you," he insisted. "They watch you, don't they? If you give them any reason to think you're aware of this, they'll hurt you."

That's why Dad is cooperating, M realized, a sick feeling settling into her stomach. *Because they're threatening me.* She pulled out her cell. "That's exactly what I'm going to do then."

Ash's eyes widened. "Excuse me?"

"I'm going to call Liza and tell her everything you just said," M replied. "I'll offer her a deal: she can have the original map as long as she lets me stay with Dad while he translates it."

His upper lip was sweaty now. Panicked, his eyes darted to her hand, calculating whether he could snatch her phone away.

"Or, you can tell me the truth," M said. "The actual truth."

CHAPTER 3

The moment stretched out, frozen in time. Philip had taught Ash to do that, to focus so completely on each passing second that even the briefest instant could seem long. Long enough to make an impossible decision? Ash closed his eyes, opening his mind to his god.

"Fine." The girl pulled up a contact on her cell.

"No!" he barked, all the stillness of reflection gone. "Stop. Fine. I'll tell you."

With a satisfied smile, she put her phone down in her lap where he couldn't reach it. "Who are you really?"

"Everything I've told you is true," he insisted. He simply hadn't told her all of it. He couldn't. Still, she was threatening to reveal his presence to her guardians. He had to give her something more.

"You just announced that the person I love most in the world is alive and in danger. I'm not really in the mood to be patient," she said, tapping her fingernails on the table.

Ash felt jumpy, confused. This girl set him off-balance in a way he thought he'd outgrown. "I told you about the cult of Set," he said slowly. He could tell her enough of the truth without revealing anything sacrosanct, but he must choose his words carefully.

"They're an actual cult?" she asked. "Not just a few crazies feeding off each other?"

Ash shook his head. "The worshippers of Set are an ancient sect. They have remained true to their god for millennia." Her eyes narrowed, skepticism on her face. "I'm using the word 'cult' in the scholarly way, to mean a group specifically devoted to one deity. Not the way it's used now, to signify unhinged devotion to a nonsensical belief. You must set aside your preconceptions. What you consider mythology, other people considered religion. For thousands of years, ancient Egyptians believed in their gods much like you believe in your god."

She laughed right at him.

Ash blinked, surprised. He hadn't spoken to Dr. Engel much about his daughter. There hadn't been time. That she knew martial arts, that she could read the note he sent, those were things Dr. Engel had found pertinent to mention. Ash was beginning to wish he'd asked for more information. He hadn't expected a schoolgirl to be such a challenge.

"It isn't a joke," he told her. "To the followers of Set—"

"*You're* the joke," she cut him off. "Mansplaining religion to me. You know who my father is, yet you think I don't know what the word 'cult' means? I learned about Egyptian mythology before I could talk. Other mythologies, too. My mother made sure I understood that it wasn't just stories people told, but a way of life, a method for applying order to a chaotic world."

"Yes, well . . ." Ash wasn't sure what to say.

"The point is, any Set worshippers today would be cobbling together a religion based on a tiny percentage of what original acolytes would've known. We've unearthed plenty of ancient artifacts, but that doesn't mean we have even a tenth of what existed. So, are they an actual cult with coherent beliefs, or are they just reading Wikipedia and making it up as they go?"

Ash stared. He'd been expecting a bored teenager constantly taking selfies on her phone, someone who would simply hand over the map and believe whatever he told her. Perhaps his idea of American girls had been wrong.

"They are the original cult of Set," he said without thinking. "They have a greater knowledge of their god than any archeologist, because their beliefs have been handed down in secret. As have those of the cult of Horus."

Now it was Memphis's turn to look surprised. "Horus?"

"It is said that the battle between Set, god of discord and mischief, and Horus, god of kings, will continue until the end of time, when chaos will overrun harmony and the waters will swallow the earth," Ash told her. "From our earliest recorded history, there have been worshippers of Set and worshippers of Horus. The cults of these two gods have spread throughout the world, and the cults are locked in an endless battle. The followers of Set have pledged to resurrect their god, and the followers of Horus have pledged to give their lives to stop Set from rising. They believe if Set becomes incarnate, destruction and death will follow."

Memphis let out a low whistle. "You're one of them."

"Yes. I am a member of the Eye."

"The Eye of Horus," she murmured. "The sign of protection and health."

"Right." He had to stop being surprised and find his balance in this conversation. "The priests of my religion have a mission, passed down for thousands of years. We are to guard the pieces of the Set artifact. Whenever a piece is threatened—in any way—the Eye is to move all of the pieces to new hiding spots. We cannot let the pieces join. We must prevent Set from rising again."

Ash hadn't been raised by Philip. He'd spent long enough on his own to realize how insane he sounded right now. He could speak freely of his god with the rest of the Eye, but out in the world it sounded . . . odd. But when the girl spoke again, it wasn't about the lunacy of his beliefs.

"And you want my father's map. You think it's a map to the pieces of the Set artifact."

"Yes."

"So this Eye group of yours hid the pieces . . . but you don't know where they are?"

Ash felt a wave of embarrassment as she fixed her critical gaze on him. He spoke of knowledge handed down for millennia, but more had been lost than kept. "We have forgotten many things," he admitted.

"Like where you put the most important statue ever?"

"Yes," he snapped. Memphis smiled, and Ash's cheeks grew warm. "And also how to read the map that tells us where they are," he added, rushing to get it over with.

"Holy snakes!" she cried, laughing. "You can't read the language of Horus?"

"It's not funny."

"No, it's sad," she chuckled. "It's really sad."

"The tongue became mixed with the Coptic language during the Ptolemaic period, and eventually the symbols used by the priests were corrupted. There was a . . . divide . . . between the written language and the spoken one. By the time the Eye realized it, we'd lost the knowledge of our written tongue." That was how Philip had explained it at least.

Memphis was still grinning. "No need to be defensive."

Ash attempted to regain his stillness. "When we read your father's article about the map, we hoped he might help us regain what we'd lost. But the cult of Set got to him first."

Instantly her smile vanished. She toyed with her necklace,

blinking back tears. "So you were planning to ask for his help?" she said, clearing her throat.

"More or less." They had planned to ask his help, yes, but never to let him know what the locations meant.

"But you really just want to find the pieces of the artifact, not relearn your old language," she went on.

"We want to find them so we can move them. Each time the pieces are moved, a new map is made," he explained. "It is a great horror that the cult of Set has gotten their hands on a map. Our only defense now is that they can't read it."

"And neither can you." She studied him. "Did the Eye even know about this map? It was in a museum vault for a hundred years."

He shook his head.

"You forgot your language, you forgot where the pieces were, and you even lost the map that would tell you." She sounded appalled. "I'd say your cult isn't doing the best job keeping up with your ancient mission."

Ash sighed. "All of these things are shrouded in history. We know of the cult of Set, and they know of us, but it's been many generations since any of the knowledge was needed. Your father's article took us by surprise."

"You want to prevent them from finding the pieces," she said thoughtfully. "So all you need is to get rid of the one person who can translate it, or get rid of the map itself."

He froze.

"You went to the cult of Set to find my father. You lied to them about being a grunt. So you could rescue him?" she guessed. "But that didn't work, so you came up with a backup plan."

Ash desperately tried to think of a good story, but the girl was ahead of him.

"A plan to get the original map from me to keep it away from the Set group. My dad's map is missing vital information, so it's useless. But as long as you get my map, you can prevent the Set people from finding the pieces, right?"

"Memphis—" he started.

"But it's also the same thing as murdering my father," she interrupted. "Once he's sent them to too many wrong places, they'll realize his map is wrong. They'll kill him."

Ash looked down at his coffee. He couldn't bring himself to meet her gaze.

"See, if you hadn't told me they were dangerous, here's where you could've tried to convince me they'd let my father go if he was useless to them," she said.

"You must understand what we are talking about here. If the pieces of the artifact are reunited—"

"I don't care about your religious nonsense," she hissed, all pretense gone. "You're here to steal my map." The bo staff was in her hand again, though he wasn't sure how it had gotten there.

"If there was another way, I would take it," he said, meaning it more than she could realize. "But I need you to give me the map."

"You'll have to kill me first," she said. "Oh, wait, that won't help! You don't know where the map is."

He gave her a hard look. "And you don't know where your father is."

He saw a flicker of pain in her green eyes.

"Refill?" The waitress appeared, oblivious, pouring coffee into their mugs without waiting for an answer. She pulled the bill from her pocket and slapped it between them. "Whenever you're ready . . ."

When she was gone, Memphis suddenly smiled, put down her staff, and picked up her coffee. "You didn't know what was in the note my father sent. You didn't read it?"

"It looked like hieroglyphs, but most of it was nonsense," Ash replied warily.

"That means you never got a good look at the copy of the map he was working from, huh?" she asked. "You didn't realize it was the same language."

He felt stunned, stupid. *Their secret language . . .*

"Yup. I can read the map, too," she said. "So I guess you'll need to kill me after all. In addition to stealing my map, that is."

Focus on the stillness, let the god move through you. It didn't work. This entire encounter had gone wrong from the very start. "I am not a murderer," he whispered.

"I'm glad to hear that. So, no hard feelings? Just because I know your ancient language and you don't?" Her voice was still cheerful, but now there was a sharp undercurrent to it. "I'll make you a deal. I will find whatever decryption key is on the original, and I'll translate the locations correctly. Then you and I—*together*—will use it to find the pieces of the Set artifact. And when we have them all, I'll give them to you."

Ash's breath caught in his throat. To have the pieces, all of them together, was a tantalizing thought.

"Just as soon as the Eye rescues my father," she added.

"I'm going to bed!" M called the instant she got home. She headed straight for the stairs. The last thing she wanted was a conversation with Liza or Bob. She just might snap and attack them.

"Memphis?" Liza appeared in the kitchen doorway. "I thought you said you'd be home late."

M looked at her blankly.

"Wasn't the party fun?" Concern flashed across Liza's pretty face. "Did you have a fight with your friends?"

The party, M thought, remembering it for the first time in hours. "No, I'm just tired," she said. *Bri is probably mad I bailed on her.* It didn't matter, though. She wouldn't see Brianna again for a long time.

"Why don't you come have some popcorn with us?" Bob called from the living room. "We paused the movie."

M's heart slammed against her ribcage. How could they pretend to be so normal, so infuriatingly boring and nice, when they'd been lying to her for almost a year? When they were holding her father captive?

I could pin Liza before she even knew I was coming. If I had her in a vulnerable position, I could force Bob to make them release Dad.

"Memphis?" Liza said again, searching M's face. For the first time, M noticed the calculation in her foster mother's eyes. When Bob appeared behind her, his hand was in the pocket of the giant Red Sox hoodie he always wore. Did he have a gun? Had she been a prisoner this whole time and never noticed?

"What's wrong?" Bob's mouth smiled even as his eyes grew cold.

"Have you ever thought you were really good at something and then realized you're not?" she asked.

Liza tittered in her usual insipid way, but now it sounded fake. "I thought I was a good cook until that day you made us Vietnamese food!"

And I thought I was an expert at observing human behavior until I realized you were an evil fraud, M replied silently.

"Is this about school?" Bob asked.

"Yeah," M lied. "I got a bad grade on a quiz today and it's been bothering me. I couldn't enjoy the party."

"Well, I'm sure you'll do better next time," Liza said. "Maybe if you study a little before bed, you'll feel better."

"You're right." M forced a smile. She'd never gotten a bad grade in her life. "Good night."

"Night," Bob called.

"See you in the morning," Liza added.

No, you won't. You will never see me again.

Upstairs, she locked her bedroom door, propping a few barbells against it to make it extra hard to open. It was bizarre, feeling afraid of her guardians—she'd barely given them five minutes of thought before. But now that she knew she'd been living with the enemy this whole time, she felt as if they were watching her.

After a minute, she heard voices in the living room, and her heartbeat slowed. M sat at her desk, finally doing what she'd wanted to do ever since Ash mentioned a decryption key: she unclasped her necklace, slid the small glass pendant off, and opened one end. With a pair of sanitized tweezers she gently removed the tiny, ancient scroll of parchment inside. Pulling her magnifier lamp down, M slowly unrolled it, scanning for anything she hadn't spotted before—a glyph out of place, a mark she'd thought was a blot, anything. Maybe the lotus that bent the wrong way?

But she had to admit, the map looked the same as it always had. What was she supposed to tell Ash? How could she claim she'd find the pieces of the Set artifact when she couldn't find a key? Maybe Dad was wrong. Maybe there was another reason the cult hadn't found any pieces at the locations he'd sent them to.

"Maybe because the whole thing is absolutely insane," she whispered. "And there are no pieces of an ancient magical statue hidden anywhere, and this is a wild goose chase."

She sat back and closed her eyes, letting the familiar sounds of her room surround her. The soft irregular clanking of the radiator. The ticking of her old-fashioned clock. The whirring of her laptop. It still smelled like home in here. Her quilt was the one Mom had bought in Jakarta. The photo on her bulletin board was one Dad had taken of M and her friends making faces at the junior class picnic last year, one of the only school events she'd made it to. She could picture the whole room without looking at it. It would have to be enough from now on. Home hadn't really been home since Dad died, anyway.

It was time to leave. When she had her father back, she'd be home.

If there was a decryption key, she didn't have time to find it tonight. She'd just have to keep bluffing for now. The important thing was to stay with Ash and con him into telling her where Dad was. If she figured out how to find a piece of the statue first, all the better. It would give her a bargaining chip.

M opened her eyes and stood up. She turned off her laptop, sliding it into its carrying slot in her backpack, followed by her passport. A pair of jeans, three shirts, a couple of bras, some socks, underwear. Her bo staff. Everything she needed she had packed in less than thirty seconds. The scroll took longer, she had to be gentle. But soon enough it was returned to the safety of her glass pendant. She clasped it around her neck and pulled on her jacket.

Her room had casement windows that opened wide and silent, a bonus. She flicked off the light switch and parted her curtains, letting cold moonlight fill the dark bedroom. Bob and Liza weren't so overbearing that they checked on her at night, so they wouldn't realize she was gone until tomorrow.

M hesitated. She turned back and grabbed the picture of her and her friends. Next to it was an old shot of her with Mike. She took that, too. Putting both photos carefully into the inside pocket of her jacket, she climbed up on the windowsill and swung onto the sycamore tree in the backyard. She used the end of the bo staff to gently push the windows closed, then climbed down. M vaulted the back wall into old Mr. Hannesy's yard, then headed for the street. Ash was waiting at the corner like she'd told him.

"We're going to Italy," she said. "You're paying."

CHAPTER 4

"So . . . Naples," Ash said.

"Mm-hmm." Memphis was gazing out the plane window, ignoring him. She had said only the bare minimum since they had gotten in a cab near her house. She was infuriating. Her father had been friendly, always polite, even to his captors. Perhaps she took after her mother.

"Why there?" he pressed.

She gave a heavy sigh. "Uh, because it's the closest airport to where we need to be?"

Be still, be like still water. This was the attitude he'd been expecting originally. "Yes, I know," he said patiently. "And where do we need to be?"

The silence stretched out between them. Most people were uncomfortable with long pauses. They became restless, nervous, they needed to fill the quiet.

Memphis was not one of those people, apparently.

Eventually, Ash gave a sigh of his own. "If we are going to find the Set artifact, I will need to know where we are going. Keeping me in the dark isn't an option." Just saying the words sent a shock through him—*find the Set artifact.* Was such a thing possible?

An image of Hugh came to him. They were sitting at the lunch table as children, Hugh whispering about the pieces of Set. The statue had been lost for centuries. Finding any of the pieces was nothing more than fantasy. But Hugh had been convinced it would happen, that he would somehow locate the pieces.

Now Ash was the one about to do it. He was living Hugh's lifelong dream, and it gave him a queasy feeling to know he couldn't share it with his best friend.

Focus. He pushed the thought away. The girl's plan was still a fantasy. Even if she could translate the map, even if she could find the artifacts, he had to stop her before that happened. His mission was to retrieve the map and bring it to the Eye. That was all. And it was proving more difficult than expected. Now he would have to leave her someplace safe once he retrieved the map. He couldn't keep her around. But he didn't want to abandon her in a foreign place without help, either.

I'll slip money into her bag, he decided. She seemed savvy enough to know how to navigate an airport. If he got the map during the flight, he could ditch her in the airport at Naples. All she'd have to do was buy a ticket home.

"Baiae," Memphis said, jolting him out of his thoughts.

Ash blinked, confused.

She smirked. "You asked where we're going?"

"Baiae," he repeated, trying to place it.

"The ruins, near Cumae." Memphis yawned and pushed the button to tilt her seat back. "Happy now?"

"That's not one of the locations your father gave the Set followers," he said, his pulse quickening. "Did you find a decryption key?" If she had, then she really did know where to find the statue. It was almost impossible to believe.

Memphis turned in her seat and stared at him. Her light green eyes were clear and intelligent, and Ash found himself feeling as if she could see through all his lies. Her father had the same eyes, the same way of making Ash squirm. But her father had decided to trust him. She would too.

He kept his face neutral and held her gaze.

"So," she finally said. "Ash, short for Ashwin. Hindi name. I'm guessing some mix of Punjabi . . . second generation? . . . and straight-up Brit. Your middle name is probably something like William or Henry, right?"

Ash swallowed hard. "Edward."

She took the sleeve of his linen shirt between her fingers. "Your parents have money. Grunts don't wear bespoke clothes."

Don't look away. Remain still, Ash told himself. She continued to caress the fabric, leaning uncomfortably close to him.

"You grew up somewhere nice. Someplace like Sutton Coldfield?" Her eyes were still on his, unwavering. "But you wanted to get to London the minute you were old enough."

Ash nodded. Why bother pretending otherwise?

"You had a year of university. Maybe two. Then you quit. You figured you could be an archeology grunt without a degree. You'd get to see the world, slum it a little, have some adventures, get laid in exotic places." She chuckled, but there was no warmth in it. "You're like a thousand other guys I've met."

"I doubt that," Ash murmured.

"True. Because unlike them, you're insane," she replied. "Somewhere along the way, you got brainwashed into joining a cult."

She abruptly let go of his sleeve and turned back to the window. Ash took a shaky breath. She'd gotten a lot right. His parents, their money . . . even Sutton Coldfield. It was unnerving to know somebody could read him so easily. Had her father seen him the same way?

Still, there were things she didn't, could never, know about his background.

Memphis sighed and shifted, eventually settling into a position she was comfortable with, long legs curled up underneath her, head leaning against the window. She closed her eyes.

Ash glanced around the cabin, not really seeing the others in first class with them. This girl irked him. She was entirely too sharp.

Baiae. Why there? Did she have a key? Could she read the priests' language so easily that she'd decoded a location in the half hour she'd spent at home without him? If so, she was taking him to an actual piece of the Set statue his people had been trying to find for ages.

No amount of mental control could still his heartbeat. To find a piece and see it with his own eyes, to be the one who achieved that goal before the other devotees . . . the idea made him giddy. And if this girl could make it happen, why not take advantage? Even Philip would have to admit the pieces would be safer rehidden. Ash and Memphis could find them. That way, it didn't matter if the cult of Set had a map.

This was a much better plan than simply stealing the original.

Once he had all the pieces, he would take them straight to the Eye. Memphis's deal was that the Eye would get them only after they'd rescued her father. But Philip would never agree. It was too dangerous.

Maybe after the pieces are rehidden, we can save her father, Ash thought, his eyes moving over her. Without her, they'd have nothing. At least they could try to help. She was right that Dr. Engel would be dead as soon as his usefulness was over.

Still, the consequences of the Set cult rejoining the pieces of the artifact were too great. Her father might need to be collateral damage.

Ash eased his phone out of his pocket and texted Philip, keeping one eye on the girl.

> **ASH:** The girl has the original & can translate. Will lead me to pieces in return for her father's rescue.

> **PHILIP:** No.

> **ASH:** We can move the pieces, make a new map. This is the safest way.

> **PHILIP:** Under no circumstances are you to hunt for the pieces. Stick to the plan. Contact me when you have the map.

The plan. Ash sighed, deflated. His opportunity to find the Set artifact didn't matter. He'd been so thrilled at the prospect. But Philip spoke for the god, and the god wasn't concerned with Ash's feelings.

He stared at Memphis, watching her back slowly rise and fall. Her long hair fell over her face, but he could still see her eyes were closed. She was asleep. Ash leaned forward, reaching for the backpack she'd stashed under the seat. She had refused to check it or to let him put it in the overhead bin. Even now, one strap was wound loosely around her ankle, which dangled from the seat.

Ash moved with excruciating slowness, pulling the strap off her, one inch at a time. The map had to be in the backpack—it was the only thing she'd brought. Once he'd freed the strap, he carefully slid the pack toward himself.

Her foot came down hard on his hand.

Ash gasped and looked up at her.

Her eyes were still closed, her breath still slow. But she wasn't asleep. She pushed her foot down on his hand once more for emphasis, and a small smile spread across her face. "Dream on," she said.

The car was a new, low-slung Ferrari. M really wanted to make fun of Ash. Who rented a Ferrari? But she had to admit it was nice to go flying down an Italian road in luxury. She and Dad had never traveled like this—it was always beaten-up old Jeeps for them.

She shifted her gaze from the landscape to Ash. He was undeniably gorgeous. Rich, well dressed, well spoken. And, apparently, batshit insane. Why had Dad trusted him? Maybe there'd been no other choice. The idea of her father being so desperate made her stomach churn. She needed to focus. On Ash. On his lunacy.

"What?" he asked, not taking his eyes off the road.

"You can't really believe all that stuff. You don't, right?" M asked. "That a bunch of cultists can glue a few pieces of rock back together and—bam!—an ancient god will pop up and destroy the world?"

A muscle in his cheek twitched, but he didn't say anything.

"It doesn't even make sense," she went on. "Why would he destroy the world when he just finally got back into it?"

That one at least got a frown from him, but still no answers. She shrugged. "We need to stop on the way for spelunking gear. And snorkels. I reserved some at a shop on the coast."

"*Spelunking* gear?" Ash sounded appalled. "Why?"

"It's good to have when spelunking," she replied. If he was going to be silent and obtuse, she would be too.

He sighed. "I thought we were going to some Roman ruins. Are there caves involved? Water?"

"Both."

"Well, how do you know there's a piece there?"

"I read the map."

"And what did it say?" The impatience in his voice was increasing. Good.

"It said a bunch of stuff in a language you don't know," M replied.

Suddenly Ash cut the wheel, veering off the road and onto a rocky shoulder before jerking to a stop. "Why should I follow you anywhere if you won't tell me the reason we're going?"

"Why should I lead you anywhere if you won't tell me where my father is?" she countered.

The anger in his eyes evaporated. He stared out the window. Silently.

Were they going to sit there all day? M gazed across the landscape, watching a wisp of steam rise in the distance. This area had a lot of volcanic activity; even with the car windows closed and the AC on she could smell the sulfur in the air.

"I'm not the one who took your father," Ash finally said.

"But you're not helping me get him back, either," she said.

"I don't have a choice!" he burst out. "I'm already going against orders by even being here with you. The least you can do is tell me why we're here."

M turned to look at him. "Do you think I don't know that you'd knock me out and steal the map if you only knew where I hid it?"

His perfect nose wrinkled in disgust. "I don't use violence to get my way."

"Good for you," she murmured. He did appear to be shocked. An image of Nick on the cafeteria floor flitted through her mind, and she winced. "I do, sometimes. By accident."

Ash's baffled expression made her laugh.

"Okay, look, I don't trust you and I know you only want my map. But the place we're going is probably dangerous. We need to use the buddy system," M told him. "So can we agree to be a team for today?"

"Yes," he said. "But I'm not going anyplace dangerous without knowing what brings me there."

M paused. "Fair enough. I'll explain while you drive."

He managed to hide his satisfaction, mostly. They pulled back onto the road. She ran over the translation in her mind, trying to remember everything her father had worked out about this location. Ash was assuming she'd found some hidden clue, but the truth was she'd gotten lucky when she picked this place—lucky the Set cult hadn't already come to Baiae on her father's recommendation. Why hadn't he sent them here? Was he lying to them about his translations?

What if I never find the decryption key? I can't keep bluffing forever.

"There are hieroglyphs," she said. "That's what the map is, just a bunch of glyphs. It describes locations, it doesn't show them on a map the way we think of it."

"Yes, I know." His tone was dry.

"Well, sorry, genius, I didn't think you'd seen my father's copy," she retorted. "Anyway, the glyphs for this one were *goddess, cave, dead,* and *tree thief.*"

"Tree thief?"

"It's a weird one," she said. "And there was also a phonogram. You know what that is, of course."

He smirked. "A group of hieroglyphs that symbolize a sound. We *do* study the ancient texts. It's just the hidden meanings that have been forgotten."

"By *you*." She smiled. "Anyway, this phonogram is for *Vesuvius*."

"The volcano?"

She nodded. "It's right over there, you know." She pointed out the window.

"We're not spelunking in lava, are we?" he asked. "Because that equipment would be *quite* expensive."

M laughed, surprised he had any sense of humor at all. "Not lava, but the water might be hot."

"Really?"

"Yes. Listen. Vesuvius means it's in Italy. So we start with that. Then the glyphs for *goddess* and *tree thief* obviously lead to a sibyl."

"There is nothing obvious about that," he said.

"Well, goddess means goddess," M replied. "Tree thief was harder to understand." It had taken her father more than a year to figure it out. "You've read *The Aeneid*, right?"

"I read the CliffsNotes . . ."

"Aeneas visits an oracle, the sibyl of Cumae, and she tells him the future," M said. "She also tells him to offer the Golden Bough to the goddess Proserpina. The Golden Bough was mistletoe."

"It was?"

"It was. It's a very sacred plant," M said. "But I'm telling this backwards. There is a type of oak mistletoe called Phoradendron. Tree thief."

Ash frowned. "You've lost me."

"In Greek. 'Phoradendron' means tree thief in Greek. Mistletoe is a parasitic plant that grows on trees."

"How did Greek get involved in this?"

"Whoever wrote this map didn't have a hieroglyph for mistletoe—such a glyph wouldn't have existed in the language of the ancient Horus priests, because mistletoe never grew in Egypt."

"But by the time they were making this map, they had left Egypt," Ash guessed.

M nodded. "They spoke Greek, of course. It was the tongue the last pharaohs of Egypt used," M said. "So they did the best they could. You know, use glyphs to say tree thief, assume your descendants will still know Greek, and hope they figure it out. Like we figured it out."

Ash looked at her with fresh interest, but didn't say anything. M supposed he was embarrassed he didn't even speak Greek, let alone the Horus language.

"Anyway," she went on, "a goddess that had something to do with mistletoe, and was in Italy. Initially Proserpina seemed like the clear answer."

"She's the queen of Hades," Ash put in. "I know that one. Hades kidnapped her and she ate a pomegranate."

Pomegranate seeds. M rolled her eyes. "She's a goddess of the underworld, so that would explain the glyph for *dead*. And we know she liked mistletoe because that's what Aeneas gave her as a gift. So it made sense."

"But?" he prompted.

"But the glyph for *cave* didn't fit. There are no Italian caves that were really sacred to Proserpina. So it had to be the sibyl."

"The sibyl who talked to Aeneas?" Ash sounded skeptical. "But you said he visited a sibyl in Cumae. We're going to Baiae."

"Right. But from other myths, we know there were two sibyls in this area. One in Cumae, one in Baiae. Or maybe it was always just one and the locations got confused. Who knows? Over time, stories get twisted so much that their real meaning is lost." M smiled. That was her father's favorite warning when he spoke of mythology.

"I don't understand."

"The sibyl in Baiae supposedly lived in a cave that hid the

entrance to the underworld," M explained. "So, dead and cave. Simple."

He snorted. "Convoluted."

"Well, let's hope it's right," she muttered.

By the time they reached the ruins, it was midafternoon. The place was nearly deserted—most tourists went to the nearby archeological park instead, since it had an entire underwater town to explore. These ruins, in contrast, were crumbling and overgrown, and had never been properly excavated. Baiae had been a resort town once, full of villas and enormous bath houses, during the Roman Republic. But M wasn't looking for those. Dad's translation of the glyphs meant "the sibyl cave at Baiae," and that's where she was going.

"Wikipedia says Cleopatra was in Baiae when Julius Caesar was murdered," Ash commented, looking at his phone instead of the ruins.

"Guess he should've gone with her," M said, scanning the stone walls for the entrance. Other than a half-asleep guard near the road and a couple of Japanese tourists eating a picnic lunch, they had the place to themselves. M knew what the tunnel entry looked like, but it was small and hard to find.

"Mistletoe," Ash said. "I hope this means we're in the right place."

M followed his gaze to a scrubby tree that had seen better days. Half of it was covered with oddly shaped balls of leaves, almost like tumbleweeds stuck in the tree branches. One or two had sprouted small yellow flowers shaped like berries. On impulse, M went over and broke off a sprig. "Can't hurt to bring the golden bough with us," she commented.

Ash nodded. "It worked for Aeneas."

M stuck the branch in her jacket pocket, telling herself it was good luck. A minute later, she broke into a smile. She found it: a tall, narrow crack in an ancient wall abutting a hillside. It was half hidden by a pile of boulders. A thick, rusted chain stretched across the opening.

"It's off-limits," Ash said.

"You're right, there's no way we can step over the chain," M deadpanned.

"Or limbo under it." He winked.

M grinned, catching his eye a second too long before glancing quickly back at the guard and climbing over the chain into the darkness beyond. Ash followed.

Inside, the tunnel was barely wide enough for her shoulders to fit. Ash had to turn and walk sideways. When they were far enough in that nobody would see, M snaked her hand up and turned on the small head lamp she was wearing. The light illuminated the tunnel about three feet ahead, but there was nothing to see.

"Does it open up soon?" Ash asked.

"Nope," she said cheerfully. "It stays narrow the whole way down. Why? Claustrophobic?"

"Well, I'm not a fan of being squeezed like a tube of toothpaste," he said. "How could anyone think this was an acceptable tunnel?"

"It's the sibyl's cave," she said. "She was probably smaller than you."

"How did Aeneas fit?" he complained.

M sighed. "You know he's a fictional character, right?"

"You said he visited the sibyl."

"In the story he does. Stories are based on truths, so you can use them as a guide. But you can't take them literally," she explained, talking to keep her own panic at bay. Between the dense blackness ahead, the stone walls pressing in on her, and Ash completely blocking the way out, she was anxious. "Nobody really thinks Aeneas existed. He was a way for the Romans to say they were descended from the Trojans.

Aeneas was from Troy, and after his journeys he founded the city that later became Rome."

"But not really."

"No, not really. Probably not really." She tried to shrug, but the tunnel was too narrow. "No one can be sure. Welcome to archeology."

They inched along the dark tunnel for another minute.

"Does it actually stay this narrow the whole way?" Ash asked. "Because I'm thinking about getting claustrophobic."

"Look up," M told him. "There's plenty of room above us. Focus on that." She looked toward the ceiling to point her lamp up. The top of the tunnel could barely be seen. "It's eight feet high. Apparently, whoever made this place was super skinny and really tall. Maybe the sibyl was a supermodel."

Ash took a deep breath, and coughed. "You're right, that does help. The fumes don't, though."

"Sulfur," M said. "That's probably why they don't want people in here."

They went on in silence. The tunnel sloped at a gentle pace, but always downward, deeper into the rock. There were alcoves carved into the walls every twenty feet or so meant to hold candles or oil lamps. M found herself thinking about the workmanship of it, how smooth the walls were, how perfect the arches of the alcoves. It was solid rock, tufa. Carving out this tunnel wouldn't have been easy . . . so why do it? Had there really been some kind of priestess living here, pretending to tell the future?

"Here," she said, stopping. "The tunnel splits." She used the slightly wider area to shake out the tension in her shoulders, and Ash let out a groan as he straightened himself after walking sideways for so long. He tossed his pack of spelunking gear onto the stone floor and flexed his fingers. "Have you been dragging that this whole time?" M asked.

"I had no choice. I couldn't fit through with it on my

back," he said. "I'm lucky I didn't have it on when we came in or we'd both be trapped, with me jammed between the walls."

He cracked his neck. Then he squatted and began rooting around in his pack, nearly knocking M over in the small space.

"Pro tip: put your head lamp on *before* you go into a dark cave," she said, shoving him.

"Somebody forgot to tell me it was going to be like going through the birth canal the whole way and I wouldn't have room to get my equipment," he pointed out.

M turned away, purposely leaving him to root around in total darkness. She shone her light into the tunnels ahead. On the left, the narrow hall continued at the same slight downward slope. But on the right, the second tunnel took a sharp turn downward at a much steeper angle.

"Which way?" Ash asked, turning on his head lamp.

M's gaze raked over the dusty walls, the nearest alcoves, the blank rock on all sides. There was nothing in the tunnel on the left. "Down."

This passage wasn't as narrow, and they were able to go much faster. The alcoves in the walls were more closely placed here, and the thick smell of sulfur stronger. M had forgotten her anxiety by now. She always did on a dig. There was so much to wonder at that she had no time for worry.

From the sound of Ash's strained breathing, he didn't feel the same. Still, he was right behind her and not complaining. She'd met a lot of archeology grunts who wouldn't have held up as long.

M could hear the water now, and her mind was spinning. Where was she supposed to look for the artifact piece? Dad had been convinced his translation was correct. But now that she was here, deep underground in what was clearly a Roman structure, she couldn't help feeling how wrong it all seemed. A Set animal from ancient Egypt wouldn't be found here. It was the wrong civilization, the wrong time period, even the wrong mythology.

"I hear something," Ash whispered, close at her back.

M nodded. "Keep going."

A bend in the wall hid what was next. M stopped briefly to wipe the sweat off her brow. Ash's face was dirty, his expensive T-shirt stained with sweat. She found herself weirdly thinking it was a good look on him. His eyes were lively. Excited, even.

"You want to go first?" she asked.

He didn't hesitate. He stepped around the bend and disappeared into the darkness. M followed.

It was a small room, but it felt like a huge cavern after the narrow tunnel system. The sulfur smell reached a new pungency here, and the heat was almost unbearable. Across from the entrance, bubbling and popping, hissing with steam, ran an underground stream.

"What is that?" Ash asked.

"That," M told him, "is the River Styx."

CHAPTER 5

The water stank. Sulfurous steam rose to the stone ceiling and then dripped back down in tiny, rank droplets. M stood on the small landing that stretched out over the river, pointing her lamp toward the depths.

"I thought it was a myth. The river you cross to get to the underworld, yes?" Ash said. "There's a ferryman and you have to pay him . . ."

"Which is why a lot of ancient Greeks and Romans were buried with a coin in their mouths." M squinted at the landing. There was an iron ring driven into the rock, and the tattered remains of a rope. Nothing more than a few threads, really, but she knew what it had been. "Someone tied a boat here once."

She didn't think it had been Charon, the ferryman of myth. Hopefully it had been one of Ash's cultish ancestors, using a boat to hide a piece of the Set artifact someplace downstream. Just seeing evidence that someone had been here made her more hopeful.

"I don't see a ferryman," Ash said.

"That *is* a myth," M told him. "But all myths—"

"—are true," he cut in. "And all myths are false."

M's heart gave a strange, painful thunk as her father's words left Ash's lips. That was one of Dad's favorite lines. It had been the original first line of his article about the map until his editor had changed it. She raised her eyes to Ash's.

"I listened when your father spoke," he said softly. "Did you think I didn't?"

I thought you were lying about even knowing him, she thought, only just realizing it was true. She hadn't believed a word he said. She hadn't admitted it to herself, but she'd been far too scared to trust Ash. She'd come along on this crazy quest just in case. Just in case Dad was alive, just in case Ash wasn't a con man, just in case the impossible could happen and someone you loved could come back from the dead. But she hadn't truly thought any of it was real. Until now.

"Which part of this one is true?" he asked, oblivious to the emotions running rampant through her. "Not Aeneas, you already mocked me for believing in him."

"Not—" Her voice broke, and she cleared her throat. "Not the underworld, either. If you cross this stream you'll find another tunnel up and a chamber likely used for rituals."

"Do you think the Set piece is hidden there?" he asked, his voice quiet.

M forced her mind away from her father. If Dad was really, truly alive, she needed to have laser focus to get him back. They were here to find the artifact.

"No," she said. "The chamber has been clear for decades and nobody found anything Egyptian there. If they had, this place would be a tourist attraction, not an abandoned maze." That much was true. If they were looking for something purposely hidden, she had to think like a hider.

The Styx flowed sideways through the small chamber. If you crossed it, there was a room on the other side. But where did it flow from? And where did it flow to? She pulled out her flashlight and pointed it upstream, where the river flowed from a hole in the rock not much higher than the water. Then she looked downstream, where it disappeared into another hole, this one a few feet taller.

"That way," she said, dumping her pack on the ground.

In a few minutes, they'd put on their spelunking gear. Ash seemed nervous.

"First time cave diving?" M asked, lowering herself into the stream.

"First time doing it in any official way," he admitted. "I've gone swimming in strange places on a few occasions. Accidentally."

M raised an eyebrow, but further questions would have to wait. The current was stronger than it looked.

"This is really hot," Ash gasped.

"Yeah. Nearby volcano, remember? Let's just hope it doesn't reach boiling point." She stuck her snorkel in her mouth and let the stream take her through the exit hole. *Maybe we should've gotten scuba gear,* she thought as she went under. The stone roof was inches above her here, and water filled the snorkel. M felt a flash of panic, then anger. How could she be stupid enough to come unprepared? She'd known there was water. It should've been obvious that the entire cave might be filled. It was completely unlike her to do something this dumb.

She tilted her head up so the lamp would show the ceiling. It was close enough to make her eyes cross trying to focus on it.

Then it vanished.

Instantly M blew out the snorkel and sucked in a lungful of air. She reached for Ash, hauling him to the surface. He sputtered, then shook her off, treading water. Their lamps hit on a ceiling about five feet above them here, and the river widened. Seconds later M felt her feet scrape ground.

She got her footing and stopped in waist-high water.

"It's more like a lake here," Ash said, pulling off the snorkel.

M nodded. "There's a beach thingy." She waded out onto a stretch of rock at the edge of the water. The air felt cool, though it had to be at least a hundred degrees. Anything after that scorching water was a relief.

"You need to visit more beaches," Ash commented, tossing his water-laden pack onto the ground beside her.

"I said *thingy*," M pointed out. She took her pack off and shook it to get some of the heavy water out. She pulled the small flashlight from her pocket and switched it on. "It isn't a lake. It's more like a braided river. It splits here." She bounced the beam of light over the shallow streams that crisscrossed the ground, each carving its own path across the rock. The main river rushed on behind them, but three separate rivulets ran off about ten yards from where they stood, heading into the darkness of the cavern.

"This part isn't carved. It's natural," Ash said. "Are you sure we came the right way?"

Nope. M glanced around, desperately searching for a clue. Finally she noticed another iron ring, this one half buried in the wall of the cave. "Yes. See? There's a hook to hold a lantern." She grabbed her pack and waded across one of the smaller streams to get a closer look. The cavern was natural, but it had been visited before. Along this particular wall she counted three fissures, and one of the rivulets went into each opening.

"Are we supposed to explore them all? How do we know there's anything other than water on the inside?" Ash asked, following her gaze. "I don't want to go through *that* again."

M watched the running water, hoping for an idea. Nothing came.

"Are you sure there wasn't anything else to the translation?" Ash pressed. "Some other hint?"

"Tree thief," M murmured, her hand going to her jacket

pocket. It hadn't been meant as a hint, but it might work just the same. She pulled out the good-luck sprig of mistletoe and held it up.

"What exactly are you doing?" Ash asked.

"Making an offer of the golden bough. Maybe Proserpina will help us." M waded back to the main river, stopping at the place where the three streams split off. She dropped the branch into the water. It danced and spun for a moment, caught in the conflux. Then, slowly, it drifted off into the rivulet on the left. M pointed her light at it as it gained speed.

Suddenly the branch took a turn into a tiny, narrow channel they hadn't noticed in the darkness. The mistletoe inched lazily along in a small trickle of water at the bottom, making its way across the cavern. M hurried after it, but the little branch disappeared before she could reach it.

"What happened to it?" Ash asked.

M crouched down and turned so her head lamp would illuminate the situation. "The wall doesn't go all the way to the ground over here. There's kind of a ledge, an overhang a few feet above the water. The water flows under, but I can't see what's on the other side. If there is another side."

"Lovely," Ash muttered.

"There's room for us to squeeze through," M said. "If we're following the mistletoe." She didn't really think the little branch had any power, of course, but this was the best hidden riverbed. And the overhang hadn't always been so high off the ground—the edges were straight. Carved by a human, not by the water.

"We're going through blind?" Ash asked, incredulous.

Without answering, M began to shimmy underneath the overhang, trying not to think of the weight of the rock above her. Her head was pointed in, following the path of the mistletoe, but she couldn't turn. The space was too tight. A rope around her waist was attached to her pack, pulling it behind her. There wasn't enough room to crawl, so she had to drag herself bit by bit. Even when she was completely underneath the overhang, her head lamp still didn't show anything on the other side except darkness. Would she even be able to get back out if she needed to? It would be harder to move backward. Had Ash been sensible enough to wait, or was he jammed behind her?

When your brain is anxious, give it something to do, M thought, one of Dad's favorites. She thought about the map. There wasn't a decryption code. She'd been so busy trying to process everything that she'd let herself have doubts. She'd even taken the scroll out to study it, which was dangerous—any contact or exposure to air was dangerous for such old paper. *That was stupid. I know every millimeter of that scroll, every glyph on it, every inkblot and tear.*

There was no decryption code.

Had Dad really thought there was? Or was he buying himself time? Was it his way of telling her there was a problem he couldn't solve?

The fingers on her outstretched hand felt a breeze. M's whole body relaxed. There was new air in front her. She wouldn't die wedged beneath this overhang. Soon her whole body was out of the tiny space, and she had room to sit up and stretch. Ash was nowhere to be seen.

"I'm through!" she called. "It's about ten feet. You'll have to suck it in if you want to fit."

"Not bloody funny," he called. She heard him moving around, starting his journey through.

She turned her attention to the new cave. It was narrower than the cavern they'd just come through, but longer. And louder. M pulled out her flashlight and shone it around. The trickle of water she'd followed in widened into a creek a few paces away. But that wasn't where the noise came from.

All through the room—more of a hallway, M could see now—were other slots in the walls like the one she had crawled through. And each one issued another stream of water. Some were near the ground, like hers. Others were high up, creating mini-waterfalls. There were small rivulets and gushing streams, all coming together into a river near the other end of the long room.

"A little help?" Ash called from behind her.

She stumbled over to him, pulling on his arm to help him squirm free of the overhanging rock. "It's an antechamber."

He blinked, uncomprehending.

"A hallway leading somewhere! Look! That little trickle turns into a river and there are a bunch of others, too. They're all going that way." M didn't give him time to get his bearings. "It's clearly ritualistic, maybe even entirely manmade. See?"

She went over to the wall and placed her flashlight standing up in an alcove carved into the rock. "Picture oil lamps in all of these alcoves," she said. "They're all over the walls, each near one of the water outlets. It would be beautiful. And weird-looking. Otherworldly. And do you hear the noise?"

"Water?"

"Different water sounds! Drips and roars and bubbles all at once. Like voices. You hear it?"

Ash frowned. "I suppose. Some are howls, others are whispers."

"Exactly! The myth says the sibyl's cave has a hundred mouths. Each mouth was supposed to have a voice the sybil could understand. This is the cave."

"So we're in the right place." His eyes shone.

"Yes!" she answered gleefully, fighting the urge to hug him; it was hard to remember he was the enemy right now. "Let's go."

She swung her pack onto her shoulders, grabbed her flashlight, and headed down the hall. The various sounds magnified, getting louder and louder as they approached the far end, the slots for water coming closer together now. By the time she spotted the arched doorway, the roar was loud enough that she had to shout, and the water was a river, wide enough that it filled nearly the entire cave, leaving only a small walkway alongside.

M shone her flashlight through the doorway. This was a little room, no more than ten feet wide. The alcoves for lamps were stacked on top of one another in vertical lines—she couldn't tell if there were three or four alcoves in each wall because the ceiling was so high that her thin beam of light didn't reach. The acoustics of the room amplified the already loud water, making it sound as though they were underneath a waterfall.

"This room seems awfully small after all that buildup," Ash said, putting his mouth close—too close—to her ear to be heard over the roar.

"There would've been a chair here," M told him, pointing with her light. "Right in the middle. The sibyl would sit where she could hear all the voices, and if you visited her, you'd come through the antechamber to see her enthroned under all these lamps." She waved her light at the alcoves. "It's basically just a throne room for her. I mean, not a literal throne because she's not royalty, but it would have the same effect. The staging of it gives her authority so you believe what she says, that she speaks for the gods and tells the future."

Ash looked at her intently, his eyes narrowing as he studied her face. "You don't think she spoke to the gods, just that she had a terrific stage manager?"

"Well, yeah. Obviously," M said. "Let's look for your hidden artifact."

"Right." Ash immediately turned away and began searching the floor.

M shone her flashlight on the walls, studying the alcoves. If she were hiding something here, she'd put it up high, so you'd need a ladder to find it. Unfortunately, she didn't have a ladder. And she didn't know quite what she was looking for, either. A statue? A piece of rock?

"It would take two years to properly excavate this room. Do you have anything to go on?" she asked. "How big is the statue? How big are the pieces? What's it made of, exactly?"

"I don't know." Ash's voice was so quiet it was hard to hear him over the roar.

"Well, would your cult—"

"Stop calling it a cult!" he snapped. "I know you're using the term in the pejorative sense, not the scholarly one."

"Oh *fine*." She smirked. "Would *the Eye* have hidden it well? Like, under the floor? Disguised as part of the original room? This room is far older than the map, so they were hiding the piece in a place that was already ancient and abandoned. Would they bother trying to hide it well even though it's already in a secret underground cave?"

He shook his head in disgust. "You seem determined not to understand. This artifact, if restored, will bring chaos, destruction, and *death* to us all. Do you really think they would hide such a thing in a half-hearted manner?"

M sighed. "Nope. Fanatics don't do anything half-assed, I guess." She turned away before he could respond. How were they ever supposed to find something like this? She hadn't properly considered all the logistics of this ridiculous expedition. She'd assumed she could get her father's location out of Ash more quickly.

"My dad would have a better idea how to search," she said a few minutes later. "Why don't you get the Eye to spring him and have him help find the pieces?"

"That's not our deal," Ash snapped.

"Our deal is backwards is what I'm saying," she replied. "Rescuing him after we find the pieces makes no sense."

"It was your idea."

"Well, I'm sorry, I was busy being in shock that my dead father was alive. I didn't think it through," she said.

"Look, I've gone over every inch of this floor. Why do we think it's in here and not out in the antechamber?" Ash asked.

"Because the glyphs all lead to the sibyl, and this is the sibyl's cave." M's flashlight danced over the alcoves high in the wall. She couldn't shake the feeling that she needed to be higher up. "Let me stand on your shoulders."

"What? No."

"Wouldn't you hide something where people couldn't reach it?"

Ash hesitated, and she knew she had him. "Pile our packs and stand on top of them. Then I'll climb on you," she said.

"That doesn't sound stable," he grumbled, but he did it. Once he'd found his balance on top of the packs, he reached out a hand.

"No, you just stay still," she said. "Bend your knees."

Ash snorted, but she thought there was a laugh in there. He shook his head and bent his knees, leaning his hands on his thighs.

"Don't move," she said. She took a small hop, and half-vaulted, half-climbed from his legs to his shoulders. She steadied herself against the wall as he tried to adjust to the weight. "Got it?" she asked.

"Got it." He slowly stood all the way up. "You do this often?"

"I'm just used to climbing. Though usually I'm climbing inanimate objects." M scanned the wall in front of her. One alcove was at her waist, so she could see down into it. Nothing there. The alcove above it was at eye level, so she could see up. Nothing. "We're going to have to do this again at the next row."

"Lovely," he said sarcastically.

As she turned to jump down, the beam of her head lamp bounced off something in the alcove above. "Wait," she said, turning slowly back. With the light straight on, the alcove looked empty. But when she held it sideways, the light caused a series of tiny shadows to appear along the lip of the alcove, running vertically up one side. "Can you stand up higher?"

"No."

"Tiptoes?"

"No."

"Okay, hang on." M lifted herself onto her toes, working to stay balanced on his shoulders. It didn't give her much, just an inch or so. But it was enough for her to reach one hand up into the alcove. There were carvings along the lip. She ran her fingers over them, feeling the sharp angles and rounded ones. Lines and dots. *Glyphs.*

"Did you find something?" Ash asked.

"Maybe." M slid her cell from her pocket, trying not to move too much.

"I can't stay like this for much longer," Ash said.

"Just a few more seconds." She positioned the cell as well as she could and snapped a few photos.

"The packs are starting to shift."

M glanced at the pictures. Glyphs. One for *river*. One for *temple*. And a phonogram for *Sequana*.

With a yell, Ash collapsed. M managed to hang on to her phone as she tumbled off his shoulders. She fell backward so there wasn't a lot she could do except tuck into a ball as much as possible. She expected to hit the hard rock, but instead landed on Ash. He caught her head in his hands and they lay still for a second, shocked.

"You okay?" M asked.

"The packs moved, but luckily I fell right on top of them," he replied. "You?"

"Fine. Thanks for catching me." M stood up, slipping her cell into her jeans pocket. She drew in a shaky breath, regretting leaving his solid warmth so soon. "Sorry. I guess that was a bad idea."

Ash stayed seated, rubbing his neck. Nobody spoke. M's mind was racing. *Sequana.* Sequana was the Gallo-Roman river goddess of the Seine. Along with *river* and *temple,* and a few other glyphs she hadn't had time to translate. It was the same kind of structure used on her father's map, the language of the Horus priests. A phonogram to denote the area, and glyphs to describe the exact place.

It's a location marker, M thought, stunned. *A signpost!*

If she could figure out what these glyphs referred to, she would find the location of one of the pieces of the Set artifact.

"It's not here, is it?" Ash asked finally.

"No," she replied. "But I know where to find it."

CHAPTER 6

M: Mike, I need you.

MIKE: Middle of the night.

M: Sorry. I don't even know what day it is.
I'm in Italy. Been caving for more than 20
hours.

MIKE: WTF?

M: My dad is alive.

MIKE: WTF?????

MIKE: What? How?

M: A guy named Ashwin Sood brought
me a note from Dad. It's in the Horus
language. Says I should trust Ash and give
him the map.

MIKE: The map map?

M: Yeah. Ash says Dad's being held prisoner by a cult. They want to use the map to find the pieces of a Set statue. If they put the pieces together, Set will reincarnate.

MIKE: Sorry what?

M: And Ash has his own cult that wants to stop them.

MIKE: Sweetie, this sounds crazy.

M: I know. But it's Dad's writing. It's the Horus language. And Ash talked to Dad, I can tell. No time to explain. I need help. We came to Baiae. The piece isn't here but it used to be.

MIKE: The sibyl cave?

M: Yes. And there were hidden glyphs. In the Horus language.

MIKE: Horus language in a Greco-Roman ruin? Bizarre.

M: See? The map leads to these pieces of the Set artifact, we just didn't know it. Horus glyphs in Italy proves it. I need to translate these new glyphs, fast. If I find the pieces I can trade them for my dad.

MIKE: M, call the police. Call them now.

M: But they'll kill Dad! I don't even know what country he's in.

MIKE: That guy must know where your dad is.

M: He won't say unless I give him the map.

MIKE: Seriously, call the police.

M: You want to help me or not?

MIKE: Fine. Go on.

M: The map led to a piece of the statue that was in the cave. But it's not there anymore. Whoever moved it left glyphs to say where they moved it next.

MIKE: Why would they steal a hidden thing and then write where they were bringing it?

M: Sorry! Forgot: Ash's cult protects the pieces. If one piece is threatened, they move them all and make a new map.

MIKE: Are you with Ash now?

M: Yes. He's paying for all this.

MIKE: M, please, this isn't safe.

"Who are you texting?" Ash's voice jolted M out of her conversation. The Italian countryside flew by as he drove. M angled the phone away from him. She'd have to wipe her texts later.

"Mike," she said.

"Who's Mike? What are you telling him?" Ash demanded.

"Whatever I damn well please," she snapped.

"What if your guardians mirrored your phone?" Ash said. "What if they read what you're saying?"

"Shouldn't you be more worried they're tracking my cell?" M asked.

He thumped his hands on the steering wheel in frustration. "Well, now I am!"

"Relax, I have my own phone, my own provider, my own everything," she said, trying not to laugh. "Besides, I'd like to see Bob and Liza try mirroring my phone. They can't even use Netflix without help."

"Well, perhaps you can find us plane tickets instead of texting your boyfriend," Ash said, an edge in his voice.

M turned back to her phone. She pulled up the photos of the carvings. They were grainy and dark, the glyphs hard to make out. Hopefully Mike could work some imaging magic and clarify them. She sent them all.

> **M:** I need to figure out this location by the time we get to Paris. I haven't told Ash about them. He still thinks there's a decryption key.

> **MIKE:** Where's the map?

> **M:** Same place as always.

> **MIKE:** I don't like you traveling with this guy.

M: Well, deal with it. So the map was made around 900 C.E. It led us to Baiae. Some time after, Ash's cult came and moved the piece. They left a note for later Horus followers saying where they moved it. According to Ash, every one of the pieces should've been moved at the same time. He said they should've made a new map, too. I guess that one is still lost.

MIKE: THEY'RE USING AN OUTDATED MAP?!

M: Exactly! Dad's map will only lead to old hiding spots. That's why they haven't found anything. But theoretically, all the places should have a backup signpost in case the map gets lost. I hope, anyway.

MIKE: And you want Ash to keep thinking there's a code only you can crack.

M: Yup. I need to keep him with me until I can figure out where Dad is.

MIKE: These pics are too dark.

M: There's a glyph for Sequana. She's the goddess of the Seine, so I told Ash we have to go to Paris. I also saw temple and river.

MIKE: There's another one. Goddess, I think. The structure is odd.

M: There was a circle. Or some glyphs
carved in a curved line.

MIKE: One more glyph I can't make out.

M: Can you work on it? I have to get plane
tix. Will text when we get to Paris. Have
good news for me.

MIKE: No pressure, huh?

M: Sorry. Wipe this convo. Love you.

MIKE: Be safe.

Memphis had taken her backpack into the shower room with
her. Of course she had. Ash ran his hand through his wet hair
and let out a groan. He'd gotten them first-class lounge access so they could clean up before their flight to France—
which would be shorter than the wait to board the flight. A
four-hour wait for a two-hour flight? They should have just
driven to Paris. He'd been hoping the layover would allow
him to search her belongings, that their adventure in the
caves would have exhausted her to the point of carelessness.
Or at least would have convinced her to trust him enough to
leave her bag with him.

He'd been stupid.

The girl was never going to be careless about the map. Her
father's life depended on it. Ash was kidding himself thinking he could outsmart her.

But he wasn't about to let her outsmart him, either. She
was lying about something. There had been nothing in the

cave, he was sure of it. And if the piece wasn't there, why had they gone there at all? Or had she actually found it, and somehow managed to hide it from him? Maybe she was holding on to her pack because the piece was in there now.

She would have to sleep eventually. Until then, he simply had to go along with her. Ash pulled out his cell. Philip would want an update.

But he stared at the blank text box. How was he supposed to explain? "I disobeyed your orders, followed the girl's plan, went exploring an ancient sibyl's cave, found nothing, and am now preparing to follow the girl yet again."

"I've lost my bloody mind," he muttered. Philip would be furious if he got an update like that, and Philip was the master of holding their god's stillness in his heart. One thing was certain. Philip must not learn where he was. The Eye would show up in force to take the map from Memphis. They would take her entirely, in fact, lock her away forever if need be. Or worse.

Ash couldn't let that happen. The girl was infuriating—amazing, but infuriating. He couldn't help but be impressed by her fearlessness. Her stubbornness, too. She was trying to save her father. It was not as important as saving the world, but it was noble. After all, she didn't believe she was putting them all in danger. She thought they were all insane.

You could prove it to her, a voice whispered in his head. But it was forbidden. He was already disobeying orders as it was. Slowly, he put his cell back in his pocket. He'd update Philip later, once he learned why Memphis was bringing them to France. After they had the piece of Set in their possession, if that was really her plan. It was a matter of hours, a day at most. Philip could wait.

Ash felt a wave of self-hatred. He'd never lied to Philip before. Never disobeyed. What was he doing?

I want to find the pieces of Set. The thought snuck in before he could stop it. *I've always wanted to.*

But that wasn't what Philip wanted. A bead of sweat formed on Ash's forehead. He took a deep breath, trying to force his thoughts in order. It was too dangerous to go after the pieces, Philip had said so. And Philip was his mentor, his constant, the one person who had always been there for him. He had never betrayed Philip and didn't intend to start now.

His mother's face burst into his mind. Seething and filled with hatred. Was it a memory, or just him imagining her reaction when she discovered his betrayal?

"No," he whispered. He must not think of her and her bitterness. The revulsion in her eyes when she looked at him. He had to be calm, like still water. He closed his eyes and tried to quiet his mind.

No matter what I do, the voice in his head whispered, *I will be betraying a god to whom I owe loyalty.*

"We need a room for the night," Ash said in surprisingly good French. They were at a five-star hotel on the outskirts of Paris. M got the feeling he never did anything on the cheap.

The desk clerk tapped away at her computer. M yawned. "Two rooms," she corrected. She still needed to translate the signpost glyphs tonight and couldn't let Ash know.

"One room," he repeated.

The desk clerk raised her eyebrows and waited.

"I'm not sharing," M told Ash, speaking English.

"And I'm not letting you out of my sight," he replied. "You won't tell me what you found in Baiae. You won't tell me what we're looking for in Paris. Or where we're looking. For all I know, you're using me as your private travel service and now you're going to ditch me and try to go it on your own."

"I don't know where my dad is, remember? Want to tell me that, and I'll tell you where we're going next?" M asked.

"Did you find the piece in Baiae?" he demanded. "Are you planning to call your guardians to make a deal?"

M blinked at him in surprise. She'd been so busy trying to hide the truth that it hadn't occurred to her he might suspect something else entirely. "What? No."

"We're in this together, remember? One room," he said.

Damn, she thought. No argument came to mind. She was so tired she couldn't think straight. When was the last time she'd slept?

The clerk was still waiting.

"One room," M told her in French. "And can you have a pot of coffee sent up?"

"You should really sleep," Ash said as they took the small elevator up to the top floor. "You must be exhausted."

"I closed my eyes on the plane," she said. Not that she'd slept. She knew the instant she was out he would grab her backpack and start looking for the map. He wouldn't find it, but that in itself might prove she was lying. He was right, though, she was exhausted. She barely knew what day it was, to say nothing of the emotional fatigue.

Ash was watching her, his expression thoughtful. M forced a sarcastic smile. "Is there something on my face?"

He rolled his eyes, exasperated—which seemed to be his typical emotion when it came to her. That suited M fine. If he underestimated her, he wouldn't be as careful. "You can have the bed. If you're planning more spelunking, I'm not going until you've slept. The last thing I need is you collapsing from exhaustion fifty feet underground." He unlocked the door and stepped back, letting her into the room first.

M headed straight for the bathroom. "I'm gonna be a while," she called. Her cell was in her hand the second the door closed. Mike had sent the cleaned-up photos, with a detailed note describing how the fixes were done. M skipped over it, opening the first image, and stared.

There was a phonogram for *Sequana* and glyphs for *river* and *goddess*. Then three glyphs for *temple*—one on top of the other. The glyph for *crown* was carved beside the second temple glyph. Then, under the temple glyphs, the *Sequana-river-goddess* glyphs repeated. M frowned, zooming in. On closer inspection, this set of glyphs and the first set were the curved line she'd seen. The glyphs themselves were carved on a curve, almost like they were circling the *crown* and *temple* glyphs.

M: The glyph positioning is unusual.

MIKE: Hi, Mike! Trip was fine, strange guy I'm traveling with didn't kill me.

M: Well, obvs.

M: Glyphs that indicate the Seine are sort of wrapped around the others.

MIKE: My theory is it's an island. The glyphs for Seine wrap around the other ones like a river flows around an island.

M: So the temple we're looking for is on an island? And it's a royal temple (crown)? Or is it a castle? A royal residence? The house of a king who was worshipped? Unclear.

MIKE: There are def islands. But a temple in the Seine? Any Roman ruins up there?

M: Doesn't have to be a pagan temple. It could mean any place of worship. Synagogue. Church.

MIKE: Cathedral.

M: Notre Dame!

M sat back against the cool tiled wall. *It couldn't be that easy, could it? Or that obvious?* She stared at the photo. The Seine wrapped around three glyphs for *temple* and one for *crown.* Maybe she should be looking for a church called Holy Trinity or something like that. One on an island in the river. One where a king or queen had been buried, or coronated, or something.

MIKE: Too easy?

M: I think so.

MIKE: I dunno. Checking something.

M closed her eyes, waiting. She could picture Mike at the computer, fingers flying over the keyboard. She'd never met a better researcher. Thank god she didn't have to do all the translation work herself—just being able to share the burden made everything seem bearable. She'd almost fallen asleep when the cell buzzed again.

MIKE: Yes! Notre Dame was built on the ruins of another cathedral. Saint-Étienne.

M: Étienne. Stephen.

MIKE: Yes, St. Stephen's.

M: Holy snakes! Stephen, from the Greek Stephanos, which means crown!

MIKE: Yup.

M: Notre Dame on top of St. Stephen's, like one temple glyph on top of the other. Wait. Crap. There are three temple glyphs, not two.

MIKE: No, it's OK. St. Stephen's was built on top of a Roman temple dedicated to Jupiter. Three "temples."

M: Cool. So I get under Notre Dame and search St. Stephen's. Simple.

MIKE: But there's no record of the church still being there. They demolished it to build Notre Dame.

M: Details.

MIKE: It's not details! How do you plan to get under the foundation of the most famous cathedral in the world?

M: I don't know yet.

MIKE: M! Don't be an idiot.

M: Stop worrying. This is why you stay home and I'm the field person.

MIKE: It is not why I stay home.

M: Fight later, help now. How big was St. Stephen's?

MIKE: Pretty big. A basilica with five naves.

M: There must still be some of it left under there.

"Memphis! *Please* finish up!" Ash banged on the door, desperation in his voice. It sounded like she had blocked out his calls a few times already. If the poor guy needed the bathroom . . .

"Coming," she said, quickly erasing her texts. Mike was used to her not saying goodbye. She opened the door and found herself face to face with a visibly angry Ash.

"You've been in there for an hour," he snapped.

"Sorry," she lied. "You can use it now. I'm going to bed." Suddenly a wave of weariness overtook M. Her eyelids felt heavy, and she wondered if she'd be able to make it to the bed without collapsing. M had to make sure her bag was safe from Ash.

"Oh *now* you're tired?" Ash said. "What have you been doing in there?"

M raised her eyebrows. "In the *bathroom*?"

"I'm not an idiot," he growled.

"Fine. I was talking to Mike," she said, yawning.

He sighed. "Where are we going tomorrow? Do I need to reserve a car or skydiving gear or anything else?"

"Let's talk about it in the morning." There were two of him floating in front of her, and her voice seemed to echo in her head. "I really need to sleep."

Ash's expression was skeptical. "I'm sleeping on the floor in front of the door," he told her. "Just to make sure you don't decide to go off to this secret place without me."

I would absolutely do that, M thought, as she looped her arm through her backpack strap and fell heavily onto the bed. *If I had the slightest idea how to get there.*

CHAPTER 7

Memphis was on her fourth cup of coffee. He couldn't fathom how she could drink so much of the stuff. It didn't appear to be helping, either—she showed no signs of moving any time soon.

"We've been sitting here for an hour," he said.

"It's a café in Paris. They don't care if we stay all day." She gazed out over the square where they sat and took another sip. Ash glanced around. She was clearly hiding something.

"We're wasting time. Let's get going," he said.

She shifted in her seat, nervous.

Ash studied her. He had yet to see her nervous. Something was definitely wrong. Should he summon the god within? Or would that be an overreaction? He stood abruptly. "Memphis. Now."

"Ugh, fine," she replied. But she didn't get up. She took another sip. "I can't figure out how to get where we need to go. I've been wracking my brain all morning and . . . nothing."

Ash realized he was still standing there awkwardly. He sat back down.

"Your piece is in a medieval basilica," she told him. "*Underneath* Notre Dame. The current cathedral was built on top of the old one. Well, the old one was demolished first, supposedly, but given that all the—" She stopped.

"All the what?" he asked.

"It was called St. Stephen's, the old cathedral," she said. "That's where your piece is."

He was certain she'd been about to say something else. "You said it was at Baiae, too."

"Are you going to question me or are you going to help?"

Ash sighed. "What exactly is the problem?" he asked. "That we are searching for a destroyed church?"

"Not necessarily. Île de la Cité," she said, leaning forward. "That's the island Notre Dame is built on."

He nodded.

"Well, Paris has been occupied for a long time, since well before it was called Paris," she went on. "The city we see now was built on top of the previous settlements. So Notre Dame is built on top of St. Stephen's, and St. Stephen's was built on top of the pagan temple that came before. Archeologists can usually find evidence of the earlier buildings below the current ones."

The corners of Ash's mouth began to tug upward. Memphis's eyes took on a special spark when she talked about archeology, her sarcastic facade disappearing entirely when she let her inner scholar show. "Often you'll find that materials from the older structures were reused to build the newer ones—stones, columns, whatever they could use," she continued.

A chill crept through his body. "You mean the piece of Set may have been disturbed by the construction? That it could be inside a random piece of Notre Dame? Or, worse, lost entirely?"

Memphis chewed on her lip. "It's possible . . . but I have reason to believe it's hidden in the actual church, St. Stephen's.

That the ruins are there, below Notre Dame and above the pagan temple."

"Reason to believe?" She was keeping something from him. "Even though it was destroyed?"

"Sometimes the history books are wrong." She shrugged. "Usually they're wrong."

"So. A ruin under the cathedral."

"Yes. But that's the problem!" She dropped her head into her hands. "We can't exactly take a jackhammer to the floor of Notre Dame. I've been trying figure out how we can sneak down to the basement and search for lower levels. There must be a way, but it would take a lot of research to figure out the access point."

"Don't worry about it," Ash said.

"We don't have unlimited time," she argued. "My father—"

"No, I mean don't worry. I'll handle it," he said, pulling out his cell. He hadn't spoken to Baptiste in five years, not since *before*. But Baptiste would help. Baptiste would do anything if the price was right.

Memphis was watching him curiously. "You'll handle it how?"

"You'll see," he said. Let her see how not knowing felt for a change.

Annoyance crept over her face, but then she laughed. Ash ran his eyes over her, from her thick dark hair, to her faded black T-shirt, and down her beat-up jeans.

"But first," he said. "You need new clothes."

"I already had jeans," M complained.

"They were the wrong kind," Ash said, leading her down a cobblestone street.

M peered down at her new jeans in the dark. They were tight and artfully distressed and had cost about as much as the beater car she and Dad had bought in Cambodia when she was twelve. The leather jacket Ash had picked out for her was obscenely priced, and the sleek leather backpack almost as expensive. But it was his money to waste. Besides, the jacket was gorgeous, the leather unimaginably soft. She hadn't told Ash, though.

"At least I got to keep my shirt," she mumbled. The guy at the last boutique had complimented her on it. She'd gotten it at a thrift shop in Brooklyn for two dollars. When she told the shop boy, he pronounced it to be flawless. "Hey, can we stop for coffee?"

"You've had enough coffee to last you a week," Ash replied.

M yawned. She'd taken a nap in the afternoon, but it had only served to highlight how tired she still was. Now it was 1 a.m., and they were finally meeting Ash's friend. She'd stopped asking why they had to meet so late.

"Here," he said, abruptly turning into a butcher shop. M was astonished it was open so late. Or sort of open. The lights were off, but the door was unlocked. Inside, a tall, thin black man stood checking his phone.

"You're late," he said in French, not looking up.

"I am not," Ash replied, unperturbed.

The guy grinned, putting his cell away. "*Years* late," he said. He hugged Ash and kissed him on both cheeks. "And your hair looked better long."

"Nice to see you, too," Ash joked. He ushered M forward, a hand on her back. "Memphis, this is Baptiste."

M was so thrown by the sudden change in Ash's behavior that all she could manage was a weak smile.

Baptiste regarded her suspiciously. "American?"

"Half," she answered. "My mom was from Malaysia."

"Mmm. What kind of a name is Memphis?"

"It was her father's favorite ancient Egyptian city," Ash told him.

Again, M stared at him in surprise. Had Dad told him that? "Everyone at home thinks I'm named after the American city, though," she added.

Baptiste kept looking at her. M held his gaze. He had three earrings in his left ear, a stud in his right ear, and a tattoo of a snake on his neck. She figured he was about thirty.

"You can call me M," she said.

"Your accent is good," he announced. "I'll take you." He winked at Ash. "She speaks better French than you, my friend."

"You say that like it's a compliment," Ash retorted.

M laughed. Where had this wiseass version of Ash come from? "How do you two know each other?"

"Ah, sweet M, it is a long and sordid tale." Baptiste gestured them toward the back of the shop. "Let's go down first. Have you been to the catacombs before?"

"I haven't," she said, shooting a look at Ash. At least now she knew his plan.

"I love a virgin. Quietly now," Baptiste added, opening the back door into an alley. "The police sometimes watch here. You two wait." He slipped outside, vanishing into the darkness.

"How are the catacombs supposed to help?" M demanded, switching back to English. "Notre Dame is on an island. We're on the Left Bank. Even if we're underground, there's still a river between us."

"Just trust me," Ash said.

M raised her eyebrows. *Trust* him?

Ash raised his eyebrows back, mimicking her incredulous look.

M snorted. "What's with you tonight? You're almost . . . fun or something."

He shrugged. "I like Paris."

"Come, children!" Baptiste called. "Quick! Quick!"

Ash grabbed her hand and pulled her out the door and

across the alleyway to where Baptiste was standing above an open manhole. Ash swung himself down into the hole with no hesitation. M followed, the old iron rungs cold against her hands as she descended. Above her, Baptiste climbed in and pulled the cover back over them.

"That manhole cover doesn't seem as heavy as I would expect," she said.

"I had it specially made," Baptiste replied, laughing. "It is a cat and mouse game, always. The police try to keep us from exploring, and we find new ways down."

"Bottom!" Ash called from below.

M felt his hand on her leg a moment later, so she let go of the rungs, dropping the last couple of feet. Ash held his cell up, flashlight app on, illuminating a musty access tunnel filled with cables strapped to the walls. It looked like an electrical crawl space and smelled like rat dung.

"I assumed the Paris catacombs would be a little more exciting and creepy," M commented.

Baptiste jumped down next to her. "The tunnels beneath the city are vast and confusing. There are different layers, different depths. Some were for burials, some were for travel, some for storage, others for hiding, others still for worship. Even some for fixing the lights."

He pulled out a flashlight and headed off down the tunnel.

"Baptiste knows the catacombs better than anyone. He's a type of tour guide," Ash explained, as they took off after him.

"And you know him how?" she asked again.

Ash hesitated. "We used to do . . . business . . . together in a different life," Baptiste called back.

M glanced at Ash. He was wearing a new jacket too, though he'd kept his old jeans. She figured they must be the "right" kind. Otherwise he looked the same as always, yet there was something different about him tonight. A strange expression in his hazel eyes.

"Here we are. Perhaps this will be exciting enough for you, hmm?" Baptiste waved them up to where the tunnel ended in a blank concrete wall. "But first, we should prepare. I have Molly and some hash. Ashwin? Molly for you, yes?" He pulled a small plastic baggie from his pocket.

"No," Ash said. His tone made it clear that there would be no further discussion.

Lips pursed, Baptiste turned to M and held out the baggie.

"None for me, either. Thanks," she said.

Baptiste shrugged, popped a pill into his mouth, and shoved the drugs back in his pocket. He pointed up. There was a small hole blasted through the wall where it met the ceiling.

Without a word Ash jumped up, grabbed the edge, and pulled himself through, vanishing into the darkness on the other side. M turned to Baptiste. He smiled knowingly at her. "I have never seen my friend Ashwin turn down any type of enhancement. He has changed."

There was a question in his words. "I haven't known him that long," she replied.

Baptiste smiled and laced his fingers together, forming a stirrup for M's foot, to boost her up. "Thanks," she said. She pulled herself through the hole, not sure what to expect on the other side.

"Watch your head," Ash told her as she climbed out into a small, round room. "The ceiling is low." Ash hunched over, and when Baptiste came through, he had to crouch. He led them quickly out through an arched opening that led to a much larger hall.

Skulls. Skulls lining the walls, stacked on top of one another from floor to roof. Most had teeth, but others were toothless, mouths filled with candles, flickering and other-worldly.

"Don't be alarmed," Baptiste said. "They've been dead a long time."

"Bones don't scare me. I've been hanging out in graves since I was a toddler," M replied.

"Have you?" He seemed thrilled. "Then you are the perfect girl for Ashwin!"

M glanced at Ash, but if he was bothered by Baptiste thinking they were together, he didn't show it. He just laughed. "It's not the skulls I like in the catacombs, it's the art," he said. "Show us something new, Ba. I haven't been here in years."

"Come! I will take you to the garden," Baptiste said. He headed down the hall of skulls, veering left between two tall piles of bones. They were tightly stacked, mimicking two columns on either side of the entryway.

Inside someone had placed black lights operating off a generator. The eerie blue glow filled the classroom-sized space. A narrow path snaked through its center, like a path through a garden, just as Baptiste had said. Skulls and other bones had been painted different florescent colors and arranged into flower shapes on the floor. They glowed in the black light. Daisies made of bones arranged around a central skull—or a circle of central skulls for the bigger flowers. Tall bushes made of bone piles, with painted skulls scattered throughout as flowers. One long vine of long, thin bones, laid end to end, trailed through the whole room and up onto the walls, where the bones had been attached with mortar.

M stood still, staring. It was beautiful, and horrible, and strange. A few others walked around, snapping photos or examining the bone flowers. M wasn't sure where they had come from. Ash had gone ahead and now leaned against a wall at the other end of the pathway, gazing at the room. His expression was intense, but not the intensity M was used to seeing—the tense, worried, vaguely annoyed look he wore whenever they argued. This intensity was something different, almost like he was praying.

"He is an artist, you know," Baptiste murmured in her ear, "or at least he has the heart of one. His troubles, I think, kept him from following his passion."

"I thought he was into archeology," she said, surprised.

Baptiste shrugged. "He came to Paris for art school. I don't think he ever got there."

A loud shrieking sound split the air, making her jump. "Is that a guitar?" M asked. It seemed so incongruous down here.

"Yes!" Baptiste's face lit up. "I'll show you." He practically danced along the garden path toward Ash. The pill he took was obviously starting to kick in. "Come, Ashwin. I want to dance," he sang, grabbing Ash's arm as he passed.

They ducked through an archway, and M was taken aback to see that they were in a subway station—one with a modern tunnel the Metro must still pass through, given that the signal lights were on. But it was abandoned, the platform dark, the walls covered in graffiti. Baptiste led them down some side stairs to the tracks, quickly ushering them through a busted metal door. M found herself on another set of stairs, this one much older, leading down into the catacombs below.

"I told you, new friend, many layers," Baptiste said, snaking his way through people lounging on the stairs, a cigarette sparking in the dark. The music was louder here. M heard a murmur of voices, peals of laughter rising above the throbbing bass.

A huge cavern opened up before them, giant stone arches holding the roof high above wall-to-wall shelves originally meant to hold corpses in repose. Now they held nothing but candles, thousands of candles. In one corner a DJ had set up a booth running off a generator.

"Children of the dark!" Baptiste bellowed, his voice echoing. He was greeted with cheers and laughs as he disappeared into the crowd.

"There are at least hundred people here," M said.

Ash nodded, his body moving to the beat. "Usually there are more," he said. "This must be a new DJ."

M cocked her head to the side. "That might be the weirdest thing I've ever heard you say. Because it's the most normal."

He cocked an eyebrow, one side of his mouth tilting up in a lopsided grin. "I can pretend to be normal," he said.

"Drink, my little M." Baptiste appeared again, shoving a flask into M's hands. "You cannot be sober for your first experience in the catacombs." His words were playful, but the look in his eyes suggested something else.

Ash caught her eye and nodded meaningfully.

There didn't seem to be much choice, so she took a long swig. Whiskey, with a little something extra, burned her throat. She drank again, then handed the flask to Ash. He gave it back to Baptiste without drinking.

Baptiste made a face, but didn't argue. He danced away into the crowd again.

"Why did I have to drink but not you?" M complained.

"Baptiste has to trust you or he won't take us where we need to go," Ash said. "He already trusts me."

"What are you even talking about? The catacombs are great, but they're not under Notre Dame. They won't get us across the river and into the cathedral." M blew out a frustrated breath. This was a waste of time.

"They will, if Baptiste shows us where," Ash told her. He leaned close so he could talk quietly. "Rumor is, there's a tunnel below the riverbed, one that leads to a Roman ruin. Most people think it's an urban legend. After all, why would there be Roman ruins in France?"

M's heartbeat quickened. "The pagan temple that St. Stephen's was built on."

He nodded. "If anyone knows the truth, it's Baptiste. Most of us thought he was the one who started the story, just to get people to pay him for tours."

"Most of *us*?" M repeated.

"Baptiste said he'd show us the path. But he's mercurial. He'll only do it if he thinks it's fun. So if he wants you to drink, you drink. And if he wants us to dance, we dance." He held out his hand.

"Are you kidding me?" M asked.

Ash shrugged and turned away, melting into the mob of people swaying on the floor. M looked around. The candlelight gave everything an orange glow, but despite the many flames, the room remained dim. She smiled. The societies she'd studied with her father lived in candlelight. She'd never been able to experience it herself. If she closed her eyes and listened to the voices, breathed in the smoke, she could imagine she was in a banquet hall in ancient Greece, or a crowded public square in ancient Egypt. Except for the music. She began to sway to the hypnotic house beat.

Hands grabbed her hips. M opened her eyes, startled. A guy with a buzz cut and a complicated beard was grinding against her, dancing. She elbowed him in the gut.

"What the hell?" he gasped.

"I'm—"

"She's not interested," Ash interrupted, stepping in between them. He took her elbow and towed her into the throng of partiers. Keeping his arm around her waist, he went back to dancing, moving her with him.

"Sorry," M said. "I seem to have a habit of beating up people who touch me when I'm not expecting it."

"And you're drunk."

"Maybe a little." She closed her eyes again, and the floor

went liquid beneath her feet. She leaned back, stretching her arms high. Ash's hands slowly shifted to her lower back, supporting her. Her body hummed. She wrapped her arms around his shoulders, feeling as though her body had gone liquid too. Hers and his. Melding. Pulsing with the music. "I can still take you, though, so don't get any ideas," she mumbled, lips brushing against his neck as she spoke.

Ash chuckled. "You wish."

He let go of her and spun away. M stumbled a little, feeling as if he had taken part of her body with him. She opened her eyes and drew a few deep breaths, attempting to clear her head. There'd definitely been more than alcohol in that flask.

Her gaze found Ash. He looked like the music come to life—every movement fluid. She found herself wishing she was still wrapped around him, one with the music and with him.

It was hard to believe the posh Brit, the crazy cultist, the always-annoyed travel companion of the past few days was the same guy. Ash's face relaxed into a smile, the most genuine one she'd seen on him.

He noticed her staring and gave her an exaggerated wink, making her laugh in a heady, hazy sort of way. Focus. She needed to focus. And not on hazel eyes and unexpected smiles and the feel of his body against hers. She was supposed to be finding her way to Notre Dame, finding a valuable artifact, or at the very least tricking Ash into telling her where Dad was. But now he was fine and she was impaired.

Baptiste materialized at her side. "Fun, yes?"

"Yes," she breathed, knowing it was what he wanted to hear. And it was, but it was also overwhelming. She swallowed, trying to clear her confusion. She had to shake this off. "I've been all over the world," she went on. "Drop me in some tiny village in Indonesia and I'm fine. But this . . . ."

"You traveled with your parents? They did not bring you

to parties in boneyards?" Baptiste took a swig from the flask and offered it to her.

"No, she needs water." Ash was next to them now, holding out a bottle of water. "M? Drink."

She took the bottle and drank the whole thing, shooting him a grateful smile. Wordlessly, he handed her a granola bar from his pack. She ate it quickly.

Baptiste looked out over the swaying crowd. "It is becoming tiresome," he decided. "Let's go."

He strode off toward the back of the room, cutting his way through the dancers without waiting. "Are you okay?" Ash asked her.

"I will be." But she couldn't move. The room was slowly spinning around her, all the dancing bodies spinning with it.

Ash took her hand and pulled. "We need to follow him."

"He was right," M said, hanging on to Ash's strong fingers like a lifeline. "It's a completely different experience without parents."

"What?" Ash sounded amused.

"Everything. Traveling. Boneyards. Everything." M laughed, realizing how dumb she sounded. "I just mean . . . parents keep you safe."

Ash didn't look at her. "Some parents do." His jaw was clenched again, more like his usual self than the Ash of tonight.

"Wait. What do you mean?" She pulled him to a stop, hand still clasped in his. She stared searchingly into his eyes.

He stared back. "I—" he began.

"This way, little ones," Baptiste interrupted. He stood near a grave alcove close to the floor. "We crawl through here and find our way to a different level, yes? A very different level."

CHAPTER 8

"Almost there," Baptiste said. He sounded tired. M figured he must be coming down from the Molly. Thankfully, she was coming down too, from whatever had been in that drink. They'd been tromping around the catacombs for what felt like hours. At first, it had been fun to follow him through more of the twists and turns of the tunnels, although as they moved farther from the party it felt strange to be so alone among all the bones. Once in a while they'd come across a few explorers or somebody painting graffiti on a wall, but that was it.

In one small room with exaggerated arches carved into all four walls, Baptiste had stopped short and pointed. A painting of Ash was in the center of one arch. It was a good likeness, instantly recognizable as him, though with longer hair. One of his eyes had been replaced with the symbol for the Eye of Horus. "Remember him?" Baptiste had asked.

M had kept her flashlight beam on the painting, but she could still see Ash's confusion. He physically recoiled from the image. "I didn't know we were near this room," he had whispered.

Baptiste had glanced at M. "A mutual friend of ours did this portrait. It was shortly before Ashwin left us."

"What happened to the friend?" M had asked Ash. But he had turned away, the blank expression she'd seen him wear when he got especially stressed taking over his face.

"He is still in prison, I believe." Baptiste had shrugged. "This is where we descend." He had led them to a spiral staircase hidden in the corner, and as they continued their journey, none of them had spoken of the painting—or the friend—again.

The rest of the way they were alone, no other explorers to be seen. Soon enough, even the graffiti disappeared. The passageways were no longer well made, but rather a criss-crossing series of access tunnels for pipes and rough-hewn holes bored through the rock, leading to other access tunnels, and sometimes sewage tunnels.

"Did you blast these holes yourself?" M asked Baptiste as they crawled through one.

"No. But my old friend said he knew who did. The man who taught me to navigate this labyrinth," he replied. "I don't know if I believe him. He was a bit touched in the head."

"Well, somebody made them," M said, shining her light on the walls. "I wonder why."

"People use the tunnels for crime. Drug deals, opium dens the police can't find, getaway routes," Ash said from behind her. "They connect the passages for their own pur- poses."

"And sometimes they do it and change the shape of this maze," Baptiste added. "I don't like when they throw off my memory. I haven't come this way in a long time."

After a few hours, M had begun to doubt he really knew a way under the river.

But now they stood in front of a crack in the wall of a low-ceilinged tunnel that was filled with knee-high water. "Through here." Baptiste waved vaguely at the fissure. "It drops down into the foundation of the Pont au Double, then there is a passageway beneath the riverbed. My old friend told me it was dug to allow them to pull construction supplies through when building the bridge. Who knows?"

Ash eyed the crack warily. "Have you been through it?"

"Once. I was tripping." Baptiste chuckled. "There were statues on the other side. Columns. Or pieces of them, at least."

M wasn't thrilled at the idea of crawling underneath a river. Who knew whether this fabled tunnel was still intact? Still, they'd come this far. "Let's get it over with," she said.

"Good luck, children." Baptiste turned away.

"You're not coming?" Ash looked as appalled as M felt.

"It is late, I am tired." Baptiste patted Ash's cheek. "Do not stay away so long this time." He headed off the way they'd come. "And do not lead others here! It is my secret!" he called over his shoulder.

Watching his flashlight beam grow smaller in the distance, M realized with a sick feeling that she wouldn't even be able to lead anyone else here because she hadn't been noting the turns they'd taken. She usually kept track of her route without even trying, but between the whiskey, the strange vibe coming from Ash, and the uncomfortable feeling of being out of her element, she hadn't been paying attention. Would they be able to find their way out without Baptiste?

"Do you know how to get back to the surface?" she asked Ash. She couldn't tell how well he really knew the catacombs. He'd clearly spent a lot of time here back in the day.

"No. But I'm sure I can find a way," he said.

She was amazed to realize she believed him. Ever since they'd left Boston, she had been relying on only herself. Well, and Mike. But Mike wasn't here. Ash was. And he'd been the one handling everything tonight. He could handle this, too.

"It will be fine. So what if it's an unmarked tunnel rumors say will take us underneath an entire river?" she joked.

"Not just rumor. Baptiste says it." Ash's lips twitched in a smile. "And he's *extremely* trustworthy."

"You can't even say that without laughing," she pointed out.

They both turned to the crack in the wall. It didn't look like a tunnel. It looked like a broken wall.

"I'll go first," Ash said. He had to turn sideways to squeeze through the fissure, and M had a flash of Baiae. Would they have to deal with another long, nearly impassable tunnel now? But in a matter of seconds, Ash called, "I'm through. It's okay!"

M shimmied through the crack into an old stone tunnel. The roof was low, making her crouch, but otherwise it was a much better situation than the access tunnel they'd just come from. This space was five feet wide, with a smooth floor and dry walls. They were able to walk quickly. She tried not to think of the weight of the water above, pressing down on this subterranean passage.

"You didn't tell me you lived in Paris," she said.

"It was a long time ago." Ash sighed. "Another life."

"A life where you were an art student?" she asked.

"No. What? Did Baptiste say that?" He shook his head. "I wasn't any kind of student. I was an out-of-control kid."

"I thought you lived in England."

"I did," he said. "Until I didn't."

"Nice," she replied. "Very cryptic."

"I hope we're almost there. I'm getting worried about battery power," he said, frowning at the flashlight beam.

M let the subject change slide. Curious as she was, she wasn't here to get to know him.

"We're going up," Ash said. "There's a breeze."

M nodded. "I feel it." She moved ahead of him, peering into the darker blackness ahead. "There's a bigger room there." She hurried forward, forgetting the strange effect of the catacombs, and the worry of tunneling under the river. Her flashlight beam caught on a ridged edge of whitish stone. It was a carved bit of marble—fluted, like a column.

"It's just like Baptiste said! This is a broken column." She crouched next to it. "It's only a small chunk, but it's clear. And look!" She ran her hand over a lip of stone jutting out from below the column. "There was a step here." M turned and studied the ground behind them. "I wonder if the river was used as a sacred place? There *could* have been a well dug here—" She pointed to a tiny curve in the rock floor. "The temple would've been built above the river and they would've walked down here to use the water in rituals."

"So it's the Roman temple?" Ash played his flashlight over the floor, a jumble of rock shards and dirt. M heard the doubt in his voice. To her, it was a treasure trove. She saw pottery and statuary instead of shards. The dirt was simply evidence of the years this place had lain hidden, waiting for discovery and excavation. But there was no time to study it.

"Yes. I can't say temple for sure, of course. It's not an early Christian basilica, though."

"And that's what we need." Ash pulled off his jacket and wiped his brow. He looked tired. "How do we get there from here? Ruins on top of ruins, all underneath Notre Dame. How does that work?"

"Well . . ." She took in the debris filling the room. "Usually all this would be flattened and broken, just sort of piled under the newer building. But this is an actual room with intact walls. Mostly."

"Which means?"

"That it must've been used for something after the newer church was built. Storage or something. It wasn't filled in. It's essentially a room within the foundations of Notre Dame."

"But where is St. Stephen's?" he asked, frustration creeping into his voice.

"Above us, somewhere." M rubbed her neck. "Maybe. There's no reason to think the three buildings are neatly stacked. This ruin might be two hundred yards away from the ruin of St. Stephen's. It could even be higher than St. Stephen's—just because they were built on the same site doesn't mean they're literally on top of one another."

Ash groaned. "Then what are we even doing here?"

"You tell me," she said. "You *could* just help me rescue my dad instead. Then I'd give you the original map and we wouldn't have to do any of this."

"Or *you* could try to understand what's at stake, and give me the map to make sure the world doesn't end."

"Listen to yourself!" M cried. "This is my father's life we're talking about! I'm not going to hand over my only chance to save him because you believe in some doomsday cult nonsense."

The beating of wings filled her ears, and M felt something soft brush by her. Ash ducked, covering his head. "Oh, calm down, it's just a bat," she told him.

A bizarre sound filled the air—birdsong.

"Since when do bats sing?" Ash asked.

"They don't." She listened. "A wren. What's it doing down here?"

The little brown bird flew past again, swooping close to their heads.

"There must be an entrance somewhere. But now it's trapped, poor thing," M said. "It must be terrified."

"It keeps looping back to us . . ."

"Like it wants us to follow it . . ." She was mostly joking, though the little bird *did* keep circling them.

Ash chuckled. "You know you sound crazy, right?"

"This from someone in an ancient cult?" She shined her light around the room. "It's as good an idea as any. The bird got in here somehow. Maybe it knows a way back up to another level. If I can find a place to get my bearings, I'll have a general idea where to look for St. Stephen's."

"I thought you didn't know where it was."

"I know where it was located on the island. Roughly." Mike had sent her a description found in a letter from a Roman general.

"Can't you figure it out based on the bridge? Baptiste said the tunnel we came through runs parallel to the Pont au Double," Ash said as they climbed over the rubble, following the wren as it swooped and sang.

"I've been trying. But it's hard to tell for sure underground. My best guess it to head northeast."

The bird whooshed by her head again, circling back in the same direction—northeast. M couldn't bring herself to say it.

Ash pointed reluctantly. "As far as I can tell, that's exactly where it wants us to go."

"Yeah. Well. Just a coincidence."

When they'd finally climbed over most of the rubble, they found a crumbling wall with a heap of rock hiding it from view. The little wren perched on the ledge, tweeting at them.

"We can fit through if we dig out the opening a bit," Ash said. He picked up a curved piece of pottery that had once been an amphora. M grabbed it before he could throw it and break it.

"This is valuable," she hissed. If she ever did save Dad, she definitely had to bring him here.

"It will be slow going if we examine every piece," Ash pointed out.

"Let's just try to move things carefully," she said, placing the amphora to the side.

Ash sighed heavily, but he did as she asked. The bird sat up above, no longer singing, as if it were waiting for them to finish.

"You know, there's a wren in one of the legends about St. Stephen," M said as they worked. "Because St. Stephen was a martyr, his remains were considered holy, and they were moved around a lot through the Middle Ages. Stories about him spread all through Europe. One says that, when his enemies were hunting him, he hid inside a bush, and a wren sat on one of the branches, singing. It led them right to him."

"What happened then?" Ash asked.

M shrugged. "They stoned him to death. So now people hunt wrens—"

"—on St. Stephen's Day!" Ash cut in. "In Ireland. They don't hunt *real* wrens, of course—"

"They used to," M said.

"But there are songs and games involving a stuffed wren." Ash moved another slab of stone. "I never really thought about why they did that."

"History explains everything," she said. "The wrens have to pay for betraying St. Stephen."

Ash stood still, gazing at the little bird.

"What?" M asked.

"It's a meaningful bird. I think it's a messenger. We are on the right track." He resumed digging at a renewed pace.

"You're kidding, right? A messenger from who?" When he didn't answer, she continued. "From Horus?"

"It's strange that someone who knows so much about religion has such little belief," Ash commented.

"I don't believe in magic, if that's what you mean. An ancient Egyptian god sending a bird to guide us to a statue of his enemy, in the twenty-first century? Come on."

"Your father is an open-minded man."

"And my mother was a scientist. My parents taught me to think logically. Magic—or miracles, if you want to talk religion—isn't logical," M argued. "I can name twenty so-called miracles that all have scientific explanations."

"We'll see," he said.

By the time they cleared a big enough space to crawl through, M felt her eyelids growing heavy. Even the wren seemed to have fallen asleep. They'd gone down into the catacombs more than twelve hours ago.

"Maybe we should nap before the next step," she suggested.

"Could you really sleep down here?" Ash sounded appalled.

M thought of the huts she'd slept in as a child with her mother, and the rocky campsites at her dad's digs. "I can sleep pretty much anywhere. Eat, too." She pulled a packet of jerky out of her jacket pocket and tore it open, offering it to Ash.

Ash ripped off a piece with his teeth. "Let's keep going." He stuck his head through the broken wall. "Oh good. Another chamber."

"Let me see." M shoved past him, climbing into the new space. She took a quick look around. The walls were smooth plaster rather than rough stone, and the floor was covered with dirt and dust, but no rubble. "It's a crypt," she said. "Or was. There are inscriptions on the wall." She pointed her light at the faint lines. "The paint has chipped in most places. I can't make out the words."

"Is it more of the pagan temple?" Ash had climbed in behind her.

"No. It's constructed differently. The last space was neglected, filled with waste. This room was tended, cared for. Revered. If I had to guess, I'd say this was a sacristy, or the crypt of an important person, a noble or a rich patron . . ." Her voice trailed off as her eyes found the wren. It had alighted on a triangular structure of stones in the middle of the room, like a cairn. M followed the bird over. Lifting the top rock, she peered inside. ". . . Or a saint."

"What?" Ash rushed to her side. "That's a skull."

"But see how it's placed? What do you see when you look into the cairn? The crown of the skull. *Stephanos*. Crown." A thrill ran through her body. This was what the glyphs had meant!

"So that's St. Stephen's skull? His remains are here?" Ash asked.

"Maybe," M said. "They were lost. And this church was dedicated to him."

"And the wren led us directly to them," he pointed out.

M ignored him. "A crown in a temple," she whispered, picturing the carving from Baiae. She reached into the cairn, lifted the skull, and stared at the dense, black rock below it.

Two long, thin arms ending in what were unmistakably the feet of an animal, perhaps a dog, or a jackal.

Like the feet of the god Set.

CHAPTER 9

"It's a piece of the statue," Memphis gasped, stunned.

Ash nodded, too choked up to speak. The very thing Philip had told him so much about was before him, the object of lore passed down through a hundred generations of Horus devotees, the artifact his parents had spoken of in hushed tones.

It shone like obsidian in the flashlight beam. The entire piece was small enough to fit in the palm of his hand. He gaped at it, forcing himself to remember the destructive power contained within that tiny bit of rock.

"These could be the arms of a Set animal." Her voice had regained its composure. She always seemed the most at ease when talking about archeology. "Set was often depicted as a strange creature, possibly canine, but with an oddly shaped head that led most experts to believe it was a fictional beast, or a composite of different animals. Or originally based on some creature that's now extinct."

It's a composite, Ash thought. *Proof of Set's ability to disfigure nature itself.* But he couldn't manage to find his voice. Hugh used to draw the statue when they were children, what he imagined it would look like. Obsessively. Over and over.

Hugh was a fervent believer, more so than Ash. He would envy this.

Memphis continued talking. None of what she said was new to him. He'd known all of it since he was a toddler. "Frequently he was shown with a human body and oddly shaped head." She carefully lifted the piece from its place. "It's really the head that would definitively tell us this was Set—"

"It's Set," he croaked, swallowing the lump in his throat.

"Then it's a Set animal," Memphis went on. "The arms aren't human."

"I can't believe it's really here." He reached out to touch it, his hand trembling.

Memphis jerked away, shooting him a look of such venom that he stepped back. He understood instantly. She didn't trust him anywhere near it. He could hardly blame her—every member of the Eye would tell him to grab the piece and run. He wasn't exactly sure why he hadn't done that already.

She turned her back, blocking his view of where she put the Set piece in her pack. He took a deep breath, unexpectedly relieved it was out of sight. Just one look had seemed to squeeze the air out of his lungs. Deep inside, he felt Horus stirring, as if the black piece had awakened his god.

The little wren suddenly took flight, zipping up and out of the crypt so quickly he didn't see which way it had gone. He cleared his throat. "I guess its job was done," he joked, trying to break the tension.

Memphis made a noncommittal noise. She aimed her light around the room. "St. Stephen's skull would be kept in a sacred space. This chamber would've been treated as the holy of holies, which means they would have protected it. That might be why it wasn't destroyed when they built Notre Dame. The chamber might be hidden somehow."

Ash steadied himself on the stone altar—what had she called it? A cairn? The piece of Set was still forefront in his mind, and he couldn't shake it.

"It's a strange room. Why build a cairn inside? That's very unusual. The remains of a saint should be in a reliquary." Memphis paced as she spoke. Ash focused on achieving stillness. He couldn't let the statue throw him like this.

"But it's only the skull. The top, actually, the crown. Which means your little group did it on purpose! *Crown* is the clue, and they put it under a crown. But what did they do with the rest of him?" She turned to him as if he knew the answer.

"I have no idea. I'm sorry." He held up his hands, helpless. "We have lost much of our lore."

Memphis spun away, pacing again. "It just doesn't make sense. The original reliquary would have been taken from here before the old church was destroyed. So did they take his crown and bury it here? Or did they use someone else's skull to represent the crown? The clue for St. Stephen could have been separate from the actual crown part, I guess . . ."

"What clue?" he asked. She wasn't making sense. Or was it simply his own confusion? His pulse still raced from seeing Set.

"Oh, I know!" she continued. "The Eye hid it here after Notre Dame was built! How could I forget that? That's how they knew to put three glyphs for temple!"

She was definitely not making sense.

"Anyway, it doesn't matter. He's a saint, and it's his skull. So you give him a proper burial, which means you build a cairn over him."

You do that over the body of the god Set, as well, Ash thought.

"But the room was holy, a part of St. Stephen's, and clearly wasn't disturbed by the construction of Notre Dame. Which means it's disguised, hidden. In some ancient churches and temples, they would hide the holiest of holies in the floor. That way, if they were attacked, the important things would be safe." She was getting more and more agitated, talking faster as she did. How could he practice stillness when she was such a whirling dervish?

"So we're underground!" she cried.

"We've been underground for the better part of a day now," he pointed out wryly.

"No." She frowned at him as if he were an idiot. "I mean we're under the floor. Or something. So there's a way up." She turned her light on the ceiling, suddenly still. Inch by inch she moved the beam of light, studying every bit of stone in painstaking detail.

"What are we looking for?"

"I don't know."

He groaned. She really was the most impossible person.

"Oh, be quiet," she snapped. "I'll know it when I see it."

Ash found himself staring at the ceiling with her, though he had no idea why. It was dark rock, just like the floor, nothing special. Strange to think another member of the Eye had been in this very room, with that small black piece in his hands, hiding it forever. It should have been forever anyway.

"There! I knew it." Memphis grabbed his arm and shook it excitedly. "See?"

Her light illuminated a patch of rock that looked exactly like the rest of the ceiling. "No," he said.

"The chink? That rounded depression? See? It's too perfect to be natural. Boost me up." Without waiting, she began to climb onto him. Ash recovered quickly, grabbing her foot before she fell. He lifted her to the ceiling. She pressed one hand against it to steady herself, then fit her other thumb into a small dent in the rock, and pushed.

A sharp pinging filled the room, like a latch had been sprung. Then, slowly, the rock above Memphis slid away with a loud grinding noise. Cool air hit his skin, and he saw lights twinkling above.

"What is that?" he gasped.

"Notre Dame," she said. She pushed off from his hand and pulled herself up and through the hole, disappearing before he could stop her. A sudden panic filled him. Was she going to run off with the piece of Set? Ash leaped into the air and caught the edge of the door, swinging up and scrambling through so fast that he scraped his side against the rock.

Memphis stood waiting, the cathedral of Notre Dame soaring against the darkening sky behind her. Ash blinked in surprise. They were in a small courtyard about fifty yards from the church. He turned to look at the trapdoor he'd come through. From this side, it was nothing more than a large paving stone. He moved closer to Memphis, not wanting her—or the artifact—out of reach.

"Ash . . ." Memphis whispered, her voice odd.

He couldn't answer. A sudden, deep pulsing noise had hit him almost like a physical punch.

"It's the piece," she said, eyes wide. "It's *throbbing*."

"Did you just come from underground?" a voice asked.

Ash glanced over at two boys sitting on a nearby park bench.

"Ash. A little help?" Memphis said, nodding toward the trapdoor. He bent to grab one side of the stone while she took the other, and they slid it back over the hole. Then she turned to the kids and nonchalantly asked what time it was.

"Seven at night," one boy replied.

Memphis glanced at Ash and raised her eyebrows. "Wow. That took a long time."

"What's down there?" the other boy asked, frowning at the ground.

"A medieval crypt on top of an ancient temple next to a tunnel under the river," Memphis told him. She slung her pack over her shoulder and took off, leaving Ash and the boys behind.

"She's joking," Ash said.

"Obviously." The first boy rolled his eyes.

Ash jogged after Memphis, catching up to her near the Pont au Double. "I'm much happier walking over it than under it," she said, turning onto the bridge.

"Me too." They strolled in silence for a couple of minutes, just like any other tourists. In the middle of the old bridge, she suddenly stopped.

"Why is it making that sound?"

"I don't know," he replied. "I think it's quieter now."

"No. We're just more used to it. I can still feel it. It's almost . . . vibrating." She wrapped her arms around herself. "Is it magnetic?"

"I don't know," he said again. He didn't bother reminding her that it was part of an ancient and powerful god. "I can't believe we really found it."

"I told you we would." She leaned against the iron railing and tipped her head back, stretching her neck.

She had, but he hadn't truly believed her. It was too mythical, too impossible. As much as he'd always known the Set artifact was out there, hidden, he'd also known it hadn't been seen in centuries. He'd gone along with her, out of hope, but he'd assumed she was leading him in circles, buying time until she figured out her father's location.

"You did. I'm impressed." His arm brushed hers as he leaned next to her. "How did you know where to go? St. Stephen's wasn't on the map. Was it?"

"Nope." She grinned broadly. "It takes more than the map to find the pieces. That thing is useless without me. Only I can figure out where the pieces are. So you can take the map if you want, it's right here." She fingered the small glass pendant around her neck.

He grimaced, shifting away from her. The map had never been in her bag. He'd been outrageously stupid. She would never put it someplace so obvious!

"You'll have to stick with me if you want them," she added, pushing away from the railing. She headed off along the bridge without a backward glance.

With a sigh, Ash pulled out his phone. He couldn't keep all this from Philip.

> **ASH:** We found a piece. The girl has it. It's giving off some sort of low-pitched sound.

> **PHILIP:** I told you to get the map, not the pieces.

> **ASH:** I found it, just not in time.

> **PHILIP:** Well, now you can take it by force.

> **ASH:** The map doesn't lead to the rest. She gets info from the map sites, but I don't know how. If I take it, she'll go to Set and offer her services in return for her father's life.

> **PHILIP:** Then bring in the girl as well.

> **ASH:** To do what? We can't hold her forever. And she won't cooperate unless her father is safe.

> **PHILIP:** Protecting the pieces is our primary concern. We are all in danger with the piece out there. It must be hidden

immediately and the map destroyed. Will decide how to handle the girl later.

ASH: Or we bring them all in to be rehidden.

PHILP: Finding multiple pieces increases the danger. We cannot allow them to be rejoined. Bring me the piece you have. IMMEDIATELY.

ASH: She won't let me near it.

PHILIP: Then overpower her.

Ash shoved the cell in his pocket. He wasn't going to overpower Memphis. If he used force against her, she would never trust him enough to help him find the other pieces. Then the pieces would still be in danger. If the cult of Set ever got the idea to bring her father to one of the sites, he would be able to find the same information she had.

Or do you just want to find the rest of the pieces? a voice in his head whispered.

It didn't matter. He knew what he was going to do.

By the time he caught up with Memphis, she was halfway back to their hotel. "Where are we going next?"

She grinned. "Norway."

M: Mike, help me figure out the Norway site.

MIKE: Where are you? I looked into that Ashwin guy. He has a record.

M: I'm fine. We found a piece!!!!!!!

MIKE: Shut up.

M: In St. Stephen's. We went thru catacombs. There's a ton of work to be done there, BTW. Pottery from old pagan temple. Possible remains of actual St. Stephen.

MIKE: Too many questions for a text . . .

M: Sorry. Next time I see you!

M: Anyway, the piece!!! It's an animal. I have the arms. Can't tell what it's made of. Looks like obsidian but it's not.

MIKE: So these cultists are right?

M: Right that it exists, anyway. Ash looked like Gollum staring at the Ring.

MIKE: Do you think he would use violence to get it? Please let me call the police, sweetie.

M: No! Ash is totally fine. And I can handle myself! Anyway, we're going after another piece. I'm most confident in the Norway translation b/c Dad helped us with that one.

MIKE: But you're looking for another signpost.

M: Right. Assuming they moved all
the pieces last time. Ash said that's the
Eye's MO.

MIKE: What's the Eye?

M: Horus cult.

MIKE: I really don't like this.

M: Focus. We had a phonogram for
Norway and glyphs for old woman, young
woman, tomb, and ship. Wasn't there
another one?

MIKE: Tree.

M: Tree! Dad thought it was that burial
boat. Viking ship. Where was that?

MIKE: Oseberg farm near Tønsberg.
Sending map.

M: Thanks. What about the tree? We said
a large sacred tree, but left it at that. I need
to find the tree.

MIKE: Our map is more than 1,100 years
old. Whatever tree it refers to would likely
be dead and gone.

M: Can you research? Getting on a plane
from Paris. Ash coming back from ticket
counter, must erase convo.

MIKE: I hate this.

MIKE: M?

MIKE: M?

MIKE: I really hate this.

CHAPTER 10

"A tree?" Ash sounded skeptical. "I thought you said there was a Viking ship."

"That was in Tønsberg, which is where I originally expected to go," M said as they hiked. "But Mike texted me about this old oak, and it makes more sense. With the code." Dad had thought the tree glyph referred to some kind of Viking ritual. But they'd never gotten around to researching it before he died. *Was taken,* she corrected herself. "Mike says the tree we're looking for is more than a thousand years old. It's supposed to have been sacred back then. Norse gods were worshipped outside, in nature, not in buildings. It should be close."

"I don't see the Eye hiding a piece of Set in a tree," Ash argued. "Trees die. They fall. They're chopped down. It's not a safe hiding place."

"You're forgetting we're in Norway, and it was a long time ago. Oaks were considered sacred to Thor, immune to lightning strikes," M told him. "It probably seemed much safer to your crazy cultmates back then than you think."

"You do realize you're talking about my religion," he commented. His voice was strained.

She opened her mouth, then closed it. "Sorry. You're right."

His astonished expression didn't escape her.

"I don't question anyone's religious beliefs," she said. "And I don't question the ancient Egyptian belief in Horus, or Set. So I shouldn't be dismissive of you still believing it even though it sounds bananapants to me."

"I appreciate that," he said drily.

"I'd be nicer if you'd help me find my father," she added. "I mean, that does color my behavior a little. Just saying."

He didn't answer.

"Anyway, we don't know if the old tree is the actual hiding spot," she went on after a minute. "If it's a sacred tree there may be a bog nearby. Bogs were used for sacrifices—human and animal. Or there could be a rune stone. Or it could be buried beneath the tree. Or nearby if there are meaningful plants around."

Ash stopped walking. "I think that's your tree."

The tree was enormous, as if several trunks had grown together. Up and down the bark were blackened lines—old injuries from lightning. Yet the tree itself still stood, healthy and defiant.

M went to it, running her hand across a fresh wound, only a thin layer of woody bark grown over it. "My father always said myths begin in truth. This thing has weathered a lot of storms."

"Perhaps it is protected by a god after all," Ash murmured.

She forced herself not to roll her eyes. He seemed to think they were being helped by Horus every step of the way. "Or else it's just really adaptable," she said.

Ash had circled around to the other side. "Are we looking for a bog?"

"You do that. I'm going to climb," she replied. She needed to find a signpost. And the Eye couldn't very well leave a signpost inside a bog—which left a rune stone or the tree.

Before she started up, she took a moment to make sure her pack was securely fastened. She had the piece wrapped in her underwear inside. Ash was too proper to go rummaging through her panties.

She frowned. The low thrumming the piece was emitting had stopped. She'd gotten so used to it, she hadn't noticed. She twisted around and urgently felt the pack. It was still there.

Reassured, M found a foothold on a knot in the trunk and pulled herself up to the lowest branch. She had no idea when the Eye had last moved the pieces, but it had to be after Notre Dame was built back in the eleven hundreds and long enough ago for the locations to have become lost to the Horus cult. The tree had had a lot of growing time since then. The sign would be near the top.

"I still don't see how it could be up a tree," Ash called from below. He was following her up. Not good. The less he knew about how she found his precious statue pieces, the more valuable she was to him. And the more valuable she was to the Set worshippers holding her father. As long as she, and only she, could find the statue, she had a bargaining chip.

"I told you it could be buried at the base," she replied. "Climb down and look—maybe there's a marker of some sort." Ash grumbled, but to her relief, he shimmied back down the tree. She put him out of her mind and focused on climbing.

Another branch, a handhold or foothold on the massive trunk, another branch. She lost all sense of time, looking only at the tree, its knots and bumps, its spring-green leaves and occasional squirrels. She didn't notice the rain until a huge droplet landed on her hand. A quick glance down revealed that the base of the trunk was lost in shadow, and its top was just as murky. The sky had gone dark all around her.

"Memphis!" Ash's voice sounded distant, as if he were yelling through a thick cloth. "Come down!"

An ominous rumble rolled through her, long and low. Thunder.

M bit her lip and squinted through the leaves. Up the tallest tree around was not a good place to be in a thunderstorm. A fork of lightning split the blackened sky. She gulped.

But she was already much closer to the top than the bottom. And who knew how long the storm would last? It could be over in two minutes.

"Memphis!" Ash's voice was a mix of anger and worry. She knew she was being an idiot for staying in the tree—it obviously got hit by lightning all the time. There wasn't a whole lot of choice, now, though. She couldn't just jump down, she had to climb, and that would take a while. She'd be in danger the whole time. So why not climb *up* instead? She reached for the branch above her and pulled herself onto it. The limbs were thinner here, and this one swayed under her weight. The wind had picked up, whipping her hair into her eyes.

"Get down here!" Ash was even harder to hear now. The rain and wind roared in her ears. The thunder came again, a sharp, loud crack.

M searched for another handhold. Just a few boughs to go. She needed to start looking for a signpost. She'd been so preoccupied by the storm she had stopped paying attention.

Her right foot slipped on the slick bark and she fell backward.

Far below, she heard Ash cry out.

M hooked a branch with her legs, jerking herself to a stop so abruptly that she spun around like she was on the uneven bars. On the way back up, she grabbed on to the next limb and held on. She sat on the branch to catch her breath. Another flash of lightning illuminated Ash coming after her.

"Are you okay?"

"Yeah. Get out of the tree!" she yelled.

"Come down! This is dangerous!" His expression was obscured by the darkness, but it couldn't hide the terror in his voice.

"I know, so stop!" She resumed her climb, moving quickly as though to outrun the storm. The next flash of lightning arced from the sky, illuminating everything in an eerie blue light, and a peal of thunder followed immediately. The storm was right on top of them. This was a terrible idea.

Just as she decided it was time to bail, another fork of lightning hit right at the tip of the oak, sparking and sizzling. A strange electrical smell filled the air, and the branch above M's head snapped clean off the tree. She only had time to flatten herself against the trunk and hope not to get hit. As the smoking wood fell past her, she spotted something glowing in the space left behind. Thin lines on the tree trunk . . . going against the grain. Or else her eyes, dazzled by lightning, were playing tricks on her.

"Memphis! Are you all right?" Ash's voice sounded closer now. The lunatic wasn't still coming up after her, was he?

"Fine!" She was already climbing, her gaze fixed on the spot where the strange lines had been. "I'm coming down. You get down first!"

She hauled herself onto the closest tree limb, studying the rough bark just above the missing branch. There *was* something there, thin strokes of silver, too delicate to make out in the gloom.

Lightning flashed again, a sheet of brilliant blue that turned the entire tree into a blacklit funhouse. The silver lines blazed out, glowing incandescently in the illumination.

"Holy snakes!" M fumbled for her cell, snapping photos without even aiming, hoping to get a shot before the lightning ended. She was too late.

But the delicate silver lines were still aglow, as if the lightning had activated them somehow. Eyes wide, she raised her phone again, taking as many pictures as she could before they faded.

When Ash pulled himself up onto the branch next to her, they were gone, invisible again in the gloom of the storm. "I told you to go down," she said.

"And I told *you* to go down," he retorted. "What's going on?"

"The lightning struck a branch off and I was holding on so I didn't get knocked off by it," she lied. "Let's go before it hits again."

The thunder rumbled threateningly. Ash didn't move.

"Fine, jeez. I'm going." M lowered herself onto the tree limb below. "Stay close. It's dangerous up here."

"No kidding," he said sarcastically. "Why do you think I've been yelling at you?"

"I'm a better climber than you are. It's worse for you to be up here." He was following her now, moving away from the silver before it lit up again.

"You are not!" Ash shot back.

"Of course I am," she said. "I grew up climbing and digging and doing martial arts. You grew up rich and went to art school."

"I told you I never went to art school," he grumbled, sliding a bit on the branches as they moved lower.

"Baptiste did. You told me you went to university for archeology. Which is true?" she asked.

"You told me I studied archeology. I just didn't correct you," he pointed out. "For all you know, I've been climbing and digging and all that too."

She jumped the last few feet to the ground. He jumped a moment later and slipped on the mud below, falling on his butt. M laughed. "I can see for myself that's not true."

"Look," he said. "The sky."

She glanced up and saw nothing but blue. No clouds, no rain. No storm. "What the hell?"

"The storm ended as soon as we left the tree. And it started when you began to climb." Ash stood and brushed himself off.

"We just didn't notice it moving past, that's all," M replied. "It blew in fast and blew out fast."

"Or else the god of thunder didn't want us in his tree," Ash said.

"Doesn't matter. We're done here," M told him. "I know where to find the next piece."

M: It's Elder Futhark.

MIKE: Not my best language.

M: I'm pretty good at it. Dad wanted me to learn something he didn't know. But I'm not getting the location.

MIKE: The top two are for the goddess Ostara. I know that.

M: Yes. Then runes for cattle and mother. But they're all in the circle together. The only rune outside the circle is temple.

MIKE: Is it like the clue for the Seine? The curved line depicted the river.

M: Don't think so. Those were glyphs written on a curve. This is just a circle around 4 runes. On the map, circles were used to denote a single idea made of several glyphs.

MIKE: Right. But none of the map was in Elder Futhark. How do we know this is related?

M: Look at the phonogram at the bottom.

MIKE: Nile.

M: An Egyptian marker in a hiding spot referenced on a map made by the cult of Horus. Prob not a coincidence.

MIKE: But this is a different language. Makes no sense.

M: I think it's the same language written in a different alphabet. Like using English words but writing them in Cyrillic. The pieces are moved at the same time, so it's different people moving the pieces in each place.

MIKE: So you think local ppl moved them and left the signposts.

M: Explains why the runes are different.

MIKE: Did Ash see these?

M: No. He thinks I'm looking at nude pics you sent.

MIKE: EXCUSE ME?

M: Kidding. Maybe. He just knows I have pics, am texting with you, and not letting him see.

MIKE: None of this is okay with me.

M: He does the same thing—secret texting. Thinks I don't notice.

MIKE: Repeat, none of this is okay with me.

M: Focus. Ostara is in the circle with mother and cattle. So if it's a single idea made of different glyphs . . . it makes no sense. Ostara is a maiden goddess, not a mother. Her sacred symbols are a hen and eggs, not cattle.

MIKE: OK. Thinking.

M: Does she have another incarnation? An obscure mother form we don't know?

MIKE: Lemme ask my friend at U of Iceland.

M: Jafet? I thought he moved to Chicago?

MIKE: No, Rafney. You don't know her.

M: I know everyone you know.

MIKE: Not anymore. Jealous?

M: Yes.

MIKE: ☺

M sighed and stretched, then lay back on the bed. Ash had gotten a room with two this time, an improvement. She cradled her pack against her. The piece was back to producing the low tone that was as much vibration as sound. She liked the constant reminder it was there, that she was making progress.

"Are you done?" he asked from his bed. "Can we turn off the lights?"

"You can. I'm waiting for Mike," she replied. She made sure her cell was still angled away from him as she deleted her last conversation.

Ash groaned. "You've been texting for an hour. Why don't you just call and talk for five minutes instead? Then we could get some sleep."

"Mike's not allowed to get calls," she said.

"But he's allowed to text?"

She shrugged. "Go to sleep if you want."

"The light from your phone keeps me up," he grumbled. "I'm not used to sharing a room."

"I'd be totally happy to have my own room if you prefer," M said sweetly. "Just give me your credit card and I'll go down to the desk and ask."

"Not bloody likely," he said, clicking off the light. "Just . . . I don't know. Hide under the blanket or something." He put the pillow over his head, and M snorted. Light sleepers had no place being on a treasure hunt. Dad always said that was the difference between people who taught archeology and those who preferred fieldwork—professors were light sleepers.

MIKE: Heard back. Ostara is always a maiden. No cattle.

M: Damn.

MIKE: But I was thinking about the rune problem. If you were using a Nordic alphabet but an Egyptian language, you wouldn't always have the right runes to use.

M: Right. Probably why they use several together for one idea. That's how the Horus language works even on the map— the circled words are different than what the individual ones mean.

MIKE: And far fewer people were able to write in the past—their ability was limited. So if you're a medieval Horus devotee in Norway and you're writing a fast signpost for later followers, you don't necessarily have the ability to write the hieroglyph for the specific goddess you mean.

M: So you use the goddess you're familiar with and add other runes to describe her!

MIKE: YUUUUUUP!

M: You're a genius. OK, Ostara is goddess who represents renewal/spring/rebirth.

MIKE: Like Proserpina or Inanna. Who else?

M: Brigit. Freya. Hare Ke. Lada. Olwin. Sita.

MIKE: But the rune for mother. Could be we want a mother goddess. One who also represents spring or rebirth?

M: There are a lot of those. Haumea. Ala. Lakshmi. Plus several in the Asian mythologies. And Hera.

MIKE: And Isis.

M: MOTHER OF HORUS!!

MIKE: Depicted as a woman with the horns of a cow! CATTLE!

M sat back against the headboard, stunned. It was so obvious, so absolutely perfect. Mother, cattle, Nile, temple . . .
"Isis temple in the Nile," she breathed. "Philae."
Her phone lit up with another message.

MIKE: Philae.

M: It has to be.

MIKE: But M, it was moved.

M: I know. Relocated in the 1970s to
Agilkia Island. They reconstructed it stone
by stone.

MIKE: If there was a hidden statue,
wouldn't they have found it?

M: It's small. Maybe it was inside
something.

MIKE: How likely is that? They moved the
temple because it was submerged after
they built the dam. Your Set piece probably
washed away in the water.

MIKE: M? Still there?

M: Yeah. I guess I'll just have to see.

MIKE: Keep me in the loop, understand?
I don't trust this Ash guy.

M: I'll ping you from Egypt. Night.

MIKE: Night. Love you.

M sighed. What would happen if they went to Philae and
the piece was no longer there? Ash wouldn't think she had
anything of value to offer. Saving her father would become
even more of an impossibility. The now-familiar panic rose
in her chest, and she tried to shove it down.

"What's wrong?" Ash's voice asked in the darkness.

The panic was still there, and she worried that if she

opened her mouth to answer, a sob would come out. M screwed her eyes shut and willed herself to calm down.

"Had a fight with the boyfriend, hmm?" he asked.

"Screw you!" she snapped before she could stop herself. "I'm worried about my father. I'm *terrified* about my father. You tell me he's alive like it barely even matters, like it's not supposed to rock my whole world, and you expect me to not be a little upset from time to time? You care more about a freaking piece of rock than you do about my dad's safety. You could tell me where he is right now, you could save him by just telling me so I could call the police, but you won't. Meanwhile, those fanatics could be torturing him this very second, or they could've killed him and we wouldn't even know—"

"Hey." Ash sat up in his bed. "It's okay. They won't hurt him, not unless they think they have to. They're going to do everything they can to find the pieces of Set, and your father is smart enough to take a long time with his translations."

"You said if they thought he was useless . . ."

"If they threaten him, he'll tell them about the map using a code. He'll tell them he needs to find the key, and he'll send them on a wild goose chase looking for it. He'll tell them it took five years to translate part of the map the first time and that he needs that much time to retranslate it with the code. He's smart."

Her pounding heartbeat slowed a bit. "But they'll run out of patience eventually."

"Yes," he conceded.

She turned so she was facing him. "Please, Ash, just tell me where he is."

"Give me the map, and the piece of Set, and I will."

M sighed. They weren't getting anywhere. For a long while neither of them spoke.

"You're like him that way," Ash finally said. "You don't

stop. You don't hesitate. You just keep thinking of different ways to solve your problems. You make it up as you go."

She smiled. "He who hesitates is lost." It was Dad's favorite saying because it had been Mom's favorite. Although Mom had said *she* who hesitates is lost.

"It's fairly annoying, especially when trying to get either one of you to do something you don't want to do." Ash chuckled. "I mean, do you *ever* think you're wrong?"

"Um . . ." She felt her cheeks heat up. "No." They both laughed. "That sounds so obnoxious! I don't mean I think I'm infallible or anything," M went on.

"Your father told me every moment in life is an opportunity to learn. That there's no point in dwelling on what went wrong because it wasn't really wrong—"

"It was just not what you expected," she interrupted.

"Exactly. It was really quite remarkable, how calm and cheerful he was in the face of captivity," Ash said. "Most people would have been frightened, and I imagine he was, but he was using the time to study the map and the people around him. It was impressive how much self-control he had."

"Sounds as if you liked him," she said.

"I did like him, do like him. Quite a bit. You should be happy you got that from him," Ash told her. "Not everyone is lucky with their parents."

She frowned. Hadn't he said something about parents back in Paris?

"Were you?" she asked.

"Hardly." His bitter tone shocked her. In their time together, she'd never heard him sound so raw.

"Why? What happened?" she asked, leaning toward him.

She heard him suck in a ragged breath.

"Ash?"

"Get some sleep," he rasped. "You won't tell me where

we're going tomorrow, but I imagine it will involve skydiving or rappelling down a cliff."

Way to avoid the question. They'd finally been having an honest conversation for maybe the first time ever. He obviously didn't want to talk about his parents. Fine. But he could still just keep talking to her.

She rolled over on her side. Why should she care? It wasn't like they were friends. "Good night."

CHAPTER 11

"Searching at night is maybe not the best idea," Memphis said from her seat next to him. They were on the boat to Agilkia Island.

Ash shrugged. "It's a touristy place. Too many people could see us in the middle of the day." He hadn't been to the Temple of Isis for a few years, but he could still remember the oppressive crowds. It was a sacred place, and he'd wanted quiet, space. He wanted that now. The past several days had taken a toll on his self-control—not only because of Memphis and her constant reminders about her father, but because of Set. She'd hidden the piece in her pack, but he felt it. The strange throbbing emanating from the artifact had continued. Occasionally he fancied it was calling to him.

"It can be helpful to have a lot of people. When there is a crowd, nobody's looking at individuals," Memphis said. "We could disappear in the shuffle. And there would be sunlight."

"We've been searching in the dark all along. Why change now?" he asked with a smile. "Here. We're docking." He stood, eager to be off the boat, to be in the temple, to feel the presence of Horus.

A light show was just beginning when they reached the

temple of Isis. Enormous pictures projected on the high walls, with narration that told the story of Isis and her family: her husband, Osiris, their brother, Set, and their son, Horus. The few tourists had gathered around to watch it, so Memphis drifted off to the right, melting into the shadows, heading for the outer buildings. Ash followed slowly, sudden reluctance filling him. To hide a piece of Set here, at a temple to the mother of Horus, felt wrong. Set was the eternal enemy of Isis and Horus. Would the Eye really have done that?

Memphis would say the least expected place was probably the best hiding spot.

She was out of sight already, so he walked to the nearby mammisi, the small temple depicting the birth of Horus. If he were an ancient member of the Eye, that would have been where he would go. Who knew? Perhaps they thought the power of their god would protect the artifact from being found by Set's acolytes.

Once he was inside the stone walls, he forgot about searching. It was too still, too perfect. He let himself breathe in the presence of the god.

Deep within, he felt the stirring of Horus. Ash stopped in front of a relief of Isis suckling Horus in a swamp. He let the stillness enter, meditating on how Isis had kept her son safe from Set as Horus grew to manhood. The constant throbbing from the Set artifact had vanished. M was far enough away that he couldn't feel it. He was able to sink more deeply into stillness without the piece pulling at him. He had last been at the temple with Philip, at the start of his training. Now it was as if no time had passed. The years in between melted away and young Ash stood with his god, finally understanding where his gift came from, what it meant.

Philip's voice filled his memory, teaching him the secret prayers. Ash had been in this exact spot, the words strange in his ears, their sounds new, yet familiar, as if his blood remembered them.

His lips moved in prayer now. The god was there, moving within, the electric feeling stretching from his belly all the way out to his fingertips. But something was missing, or wrong. The words were ancient, but they were in the Coptic language instead of the true tongue of the priests of Horus. And while the temple was an ancient shrine to Horus, the island wasn't Philae. The temple wasn't intact. It had been moved, tampered with. His religion was nothing more than an imitation of its true self.

Ash shook his head, trying to rid himself of these impious thoughts. It was Memphis's influence. Philip had never taught him to consider the Eye inauthentic.

The cell in his pocket buzzed. He didn't have to look to know it was Philip. His mentor had been texting more and more frequently, demanding to know Ash's whereabouts, insisting he come home with the map and piece of Set.

Reluctantly, he checked the phone.

PHILIP: Send your flight information.
We will pick you up.

ASH: I don't have the map.

PHILIP: Then bring the girl. I will discover
where she has hidden it.

ASH: She's starting to trust me. If I betray
her, she won't translate the map for us.
She won't find the pieces.

PHILIP: I've told you to stop this effort to
discover them. Your only mission is to

retrieve the map. You've created
unnecessary danger by unearthing a
piece. If you don't bring it to us
immediately I will be forced to act.

ASH: What does that mean?

PHILIP: If I don't have flight information
within the hour, I will alert our brethren in
Norway to retrieve you.

ASH: This is the wrong course of action.

PHILIP: Careful, Ashwin. You risk losing
your salvation. We cannot survive a
dissenter in the Eye.

Ash felt a wave of fear that quickly morphed into intense
anger. He shoved the phone in his pocket without answering,
then pulled it out again. As his fingers flew over the keys,
securing funds before Philip cut him off, his head buzzed.
Anger was an old emotion from his childhood, one that the
Eye frowned upon. Knowing Philip would disapprove of
his anger only made it blaze more strongly. Ash hurled the
cell to the ground.

"Guess I should've known you'd be here." Memphis appeared from the darkness. "Have you bothered searching at
all, or are you just here to worship and get in a fight with your
phone?"

"Your mockery is blasphemous, especially in the presence
of Horus," he snapped.

She flinched, stepping back.

"I'm sorry," she said softly. "I was only teasing, but I
should've been more sensitive. This is like church to you."

"Yes." He was surprised by the sincerity in her voice. Her apology drained all the anger out of him.

"To me, archeological sites are just that—sites. Interesting from a historical or anthropological perspective, but not . . ."

"Not sacred," he offered.

"Right." She bit her lip. "Do you want me to leave you alone?"

He hesitated, not sure *what* he wanted.

"I'll go watch the show," she said, and walked off.

Ash took a shaky breath. He wasn't used to this version of Memphis, the respectful one. Her father had been respectful too, even to the followers of Set. Perhaps she had simply never realized how deeply Ash's life was entwined with his god.

"And how deep is that?" he murmured. He reached out to touch a relief of the adult Horus, a man's body with the head of a falcon. It was here he had learned Horus loved him and had given him true power. He'd grown up feeling ashamed of himself, but Philip had taught him to allow the god in. You shouldn't feel shame when you were an instrument of Horus. So why did he feel such doubt now?

"I should listen to Philip," he whispered to the carving. "But the piece of Set . . . it's incredible to see such a thing with my own eyes. And Memphis will find the rest. Is it truly wrong to help her? Her father's life is at stake."

The world is at stake. Ash no longer knew if it was his own thought or that of the god speaking to his heart.

He slowly bent and picked up his phone. A message across the cracked screen said the money had been transferred to his private account. He breathed a sigh of relief. When members of the Eye discovered Ash was no longer in Norway, Philip would certainly cut him off from the Eye's funds. He'd know Ash had been lying to him. Ash had eventually admitted he and Memphis were in Norway rather than

Paris, but he'd never mentioned Egypt. Deep down he knew he had wanted to throw the Eye off track, to make sure they couldn't take Memphis by force. And now he'd stolen money. "I'm sorry if this is wrong," he told the falcon-headed god. "I should trust the Eye. But I don't feel anger from you, only stillness."

Perhaps Philip didn't know the desires of Horus. Or maybe Ash was letting his lifelong obsession with the pieces of Set cloud his judgment. It didn't matter. He had made his decision days ago. He simply hadn't admitted it to himself.

Memphis was waiting with the rest of the small crowd, gazing at the images projected on the high stone walls. The speakers were narrating the show in Spanish, which he didn't speak. Memphis nodded toward the pictures.

"It's a retelling of the Contendings of Horus and Set," she said. "I think this is what you and I started with, over coffee, right?" Her tone was light, but he remembered her face from their first conversation at the diner well. She'd been elated and then terrified at the news of her father.

"Are they getting the story right?" He'd never actually bothered to watch the tourist show.

"I doubt *you* would think so. But they've got the basics: Set killed Osiris because he wanted to rule Egypt by himself. He chopped up Osiris's body and scattered the pieces across Egypt. Then Isis, because she's the best wife ever, went and found the pieces, put them back together, and brought him back to life. She should really get more credit for that."

"Is that what it says?" he asked.

"Of course not," she said. "It just talks about how they then conceived Horus, and Osiris went to rule the underworld. Then blah, blah, blah, Horus grows up and Set challenges him for the throne, and they fight like a couple of overgrown toddlers."

"We're done being respectful, I see," he said.

"Sorry, but come on. They turn themselves into hippos—freaking *hippos*—in order to wrestle. And Isis is always messing with the contests, trying to rig them for Horus. It's like an ancient Egyptian reality show," Memphis said. "Both of them are completely juvenile. They should've just given the throne of Egypt to Isis. At least she knew how to use her power in ways that made sense."

Ash frowned. It had never occurred to him to think about Horus and Set in this manner. And he realized, she wasn't wrong.

"I'm just saying, I assume the version you learned was different."

"Well . . ." It wasn't. "It has more gravitas when you say it in the Coptic language."

Memphis burst out laughing. "Awww. You made a joke about Horus," she cried.

He shrugged. "I focused on the devastating consequences of their battles. I didn't really stop to think about how the battles themselves took place."

"Maybe they were metaphors," Memphis suggested. "The generally accepted view is that this whole story was a way of describing how Upper and Lower Egypt came together to be one kingdom."

Philip had taught him that the Contendings were literal truth. Maybe it didn't sound so ridiculous when you knew the magic in the story was real.

"Anyway, I've always liked this myth," Memphis went on, surprising him. "It's all about family loyalty."

It was impossible to miss the pointed message in her words, but he didn't know how to respond. She was fiercely loyal to her father. She loved him, completely. It was the sort of thing Ash couldn't imagine. His parents had no loyalty to him—quite the opposite. So he had none to them. The only true loyalty, the only true love, he'd ever known was to Horus. The Eye was his family. His salvation.

Sitting here with Memphis, though, it was difficult to muster the loyalty he was supposed to feel. He was lying to the Eye about his whereabouts; the Eye was hunting him.

"They stick together, even when one of them gets chopped up or turns into a hippopotamus." She shot him a look, daring him to get angry. But by now he knew she was just teasing.

Ash pulled out his flashlight. "We should be searching."

"It's not here," Memphis said, rejoining Ash.

They'd spent five hours separately searching the temple for the next piece of Set. Ash paid special attention to every hieroglyph he found that depicted Set, Horus, or Isis, making sure to check for any hint of a hiding spot. Nothing revealed itself.

"Unless they managed to get it up high," she went on, gazing up at the sixty-foot-tall walls of the first pylon. "I climbed as high as I could, but I couldn't risk anyone seeing me. I'd get thrown out for sure."

"You're certain this is the right place?" he asked doubtfully. Uncertainty flickered on her face briefly, replaced almost immediately by her usual confident look.

"Yes."

She was lying, but he didn't challenge her. A tour guide leading a small group of French tourists caught his attention. The guide was giving the history of Philae Island, detailing how the temple was brought to Agilkia Island to save it from being permanently flooded after the Aswan Dam was built. It was a wonderful undertaking, he said, but also a tragedy. The sacred buildings were rescued, but Philae Island had been sacred as well. And now it was gone forever.

"The island was sacred," he said in French.

"What island?" Memphis asked.

"Philae."

"Right, it was a holy place, dedicated to Isis," she agreed. "And it's ironic—the temples were built on high enough ground that the yearly flooding of the Nile never reached them. Ancient Egyptians believed the flooding was the tears of Isis over the death of Osiris. And then boom! Modern people build a dam and the flooding stops, and—"

"—the sacred ground of Isis floods forever," he finished. "Drowning her in her own tears."

Memphis smiled at him. "Exactly."

"It's there, the piece," Ash said. "It's on the island." He'd never been so certain of anything. Maybe the god really was speaking to him.

"On Philae?" she asked. "You mean . . . underwater?"

CHAPTER 12

M hugged Dr. Bashir. "I can't thank you enough. I promise I'll bring it all back in one piece."

The older woman waved off the thanks and nodded toward Ash, who was already climbing into the boat. "Are you positive you can trust this boy? I've never heard of him."

"He was doing grunt work researching a Set cult with my dad," M replied glibly. It was true enough, and Dr. Bashir didn't need to know more. "But I'll run the machine, I won't let him touch it."

Dr. Bashir chuckled. "All right then. Have fun."

M climbed on board and nudged Ash away from the ship's wheel with her hip. "I'm driving. She doesn't trust you."

"And she trusts *you* with this kind of equipment?" he replied. "You're a kid!"

M raised an eyebrow. "I'm a legal adult."

"Barely," he muttered, but she could tell he was kidding.

"Dr. Bashir has known me my whole life. She's the one who taught me how to pilot a boat, and how to use the sub-bottom profiler." M headed out into Lake Nasser, the reservoir made by the Aswan Dam. She had the coordinates for

Philae Island—it was obvious where it was—but finding the exact original spot of the temple would require work. Ash theorized the Eye would have hidden the Set piece at the mammisi honoring the birth of Horus. So they were looking for an old portion of the former foundation. "She and my dad went to grad school together."

"Still," he said. "She doesn't own the profiler, her university does. It's a risk letting us take it at all."

M shrugged. "I'm family to her." She glanced at him out of the corner of her eye. Whenever she mentioned family, Ash tensed up. Today was no different. He'd hinted at trouble with his parents, and curiosity was getting the better of her. And maybe if she understood him, she'd know how to convince him to tell her where Dad was.

"Okay, here's Philae," she announced, slowing them over the submerged island.

It took the better part of an hour to isolate the general location of the ancient mammisi and start the sub-bottom profiler. Now there was nothing to do but wait.

"It's using sonar to do what? Find rock?" Ash asked over the whirring of the big machine that took up the entire bow of the boat.

"It analyzes the different layers of sediment to make a map of what's there. We're hoping it will find a block of stone different from the ground it's built on." She sighed. "This is a lot of effort for a hunch. I hope you're right."

"I am. I'm certain of it. I can feel it," he replied.

M refrained from saying something sarcastic. He seemed so rational until he started talking about his religion, then he just seemed nuts.

"Is that a thing with Horus? He talks to his followers?"

"No. I have a . . . special connection," Ash said. "Even so, it's not that he speaks to me. But for some reason, right now, I'm sure. It's like I can feel the piece of Set."

"Can you feel the piece I have?" she asked. She could sense it at the edge of her consciousness—always throbbing at that strange low frequency.

"You mean the sound? I can feel the vibration. But that's not what I mean." He didn't explain further. They sat in silence for a while, listening to water slap against the hull and the occasional pinging of the profiler. M leaned back in the captain's chair, slowly eased the piece of the artifact out of her backpack, and lowered it into the pile of life preservers stacked behind her. The entire time, she watched Ash. He was gazing out across the waters of the Nile, his face utterly motionless, his expression serene. Once she was sure the piece was hidden, she casually tossed her backpack in the other direction. Then she closed her eyes and tilted her face up to the sun.

"You've been there before, huh? To the Temple of Isis?" she asked.

"Philip—my mentor—he began my training there," Ash said.

"Your *training*?" she repeated. "Is that different from just learning the religion? Are you a priest?" How had she managed to miss that? It explained his devotion to Horus, a devotion so extreme he was willing to let her father die for it.

"In a way. It's not quite that simple."

"Are you chosen? Or is it like being a lama—do the older priests just decide when you're born that you were meant for the priesthood?" she asked. "Did you grow up knowing?"

"I didn't grow up in the Eye at all," he said.

M sat up in surprise, opening her eyes. "What?"

"I thought you knew everything about me—didn't you tell me I grew up rich in Sutton Coldfield?" he teased.

"Right, but I assumed you were born into the Eye," she

said. It was the only way a normal guy believing in an ancient, extinct religion made sense.

"No. I joined them when I was sixteen." He squinted at her, blocking the sun with his hand. "I say 'joined,' but it was more like they took me in. They essentially saved my life."

"From what?"

Ash pursed his lips and looked away, not answering.

"So the Eye isn't only your religion. They're your family," she said.

"No." The word was a weapon, sharp and biting. M didn't allow herself to react. She'd really gotten to him.

He took a deep breath and unclenched his fists, turning to look into her eyes. "They're not my family. My family was nothing but shame and misery. The Eye is Horus, and Horus is everything."

"But Horus—" she began.

The pinging of the sub-bottom profiler sped up, becoming an insistent *bing-bing-bing* that put an end to their conversation.

"Rock!" she exclaimed. "Time to get suited up."

The only thing different is you're underwater. It was what her father had said the first time he took her to a submerged dig site. Mike had laughed, but M had understood what Dad meant. The archeology was the same—what mattered, mattered. The only thing different was water. Sea life over the relics instead of rocks or later construction.

As M swam toward Philae, she glanced at Ash. He'd only been scuba diving once, so she had to keep an eye on him. He caught her looking and smiled, giving a thumbs up. There were a few structures left on the island, abandoned to the flood. But her focus was on the spot where the mammisi had stood for over two thousand years. She hadn't told Ash, but the profiler's results had been bizarre, like nothing she'd seen before. Under normal circumstances, she'd have assumed it was malfunctioning. Now, though, she had a feeling they were aiming for the piece of Set itself. She hadn't had much time to examine the piece in her possession—Ash was always around, and the way he'd looked at it back in Paris was the way a dog looked at a steak. But in the brief moments when she was alone, she'd studied the small rock and found it baffling. It wasn't like anything she'd ever seen, and she was certain that's why the profiler had gone wild.

Philae Island was made of syenite, something the machine was calibrated to analyze. Whatever it had found here was unclassifiable.

An enormous blue-silver fish brushed by her—*Nile perch*, she thought—and M glanced over at Ash to see his reaction. Not because the perch was so big, but because the stories about Philae had always said fish wouldn't come near due to its sacred nature. Ash watched the beast swim by, but didn't seem bothered. Maybe the Eye told different tales.

M swam down to the "surface" of the island, skimming what used to be its shoreline, her mind overlaying the original layout of the temple complex onto the lonely space below. Every so often she'd spot a piece of pottery or small carving left behind. This place had been revered for millennia, and now it was lost to time, meaningless. Something about it just made her feel sad.

Checking her coordinates, she slowed. The mammisi had been built ten yards away, but the profiler had found the anomaly here. She pointed, so Ash would know they'd arrived. A layer of silt covered everything, so she gestured for the equipment he carried.

The only difference is we're underwater, she reminded herself again as she set up the vacuum tube to remove the silt. Even the tools were sometimes the same. Within minutes she was able to see a paving stone embedded in the island. She shined her light down, realizing it was part of a subfloor used to even out the ground beneath the temple.

M ran her fingers over the ridges on the rock. It was criss-crossed with small lines, likely from the weight of the temple columns resting on it for so long, and a crack that snaked across the entire thing. *Bingo.*

She put her fingers into the crack and pulled as hard as she could, trying to pry it open. It didn't budge. She turned to Ash, motioning. He grabbed on to one edge of the crack and she took the other. Their eyes met, and she nodded.

They both pulled.

The rock shifted, no more than a millimeter. M caught a glimpse of black, a small bit of stone her mind instantly recognized and categorized—the torso of a Set animal—as it tore through the opening, taking out a chunk of the sub-floor. The piece shot through the water like a torpedo, the power of it forcing M and Ash backward.

She fought to right herself, her shocked gaze tracking the artifact as it rocketed through the water. Within seconds, it had vanished into the murky depths.

Ash took off the same instant she did, swimming full-force after the piece.

M only got about ten feet before a riot of bubbles and whitewater obscured her vision. When it cleared, she was staring at crocodile teeth. Adrenalin took over and M ducked, diving under the creature's sharp jaws. She shoved herself forward, trying to swim past it, but from below she could see how massive it was. It was turning, diving in pursuit of her.

M spun around and kicked its snout, using the force to propel herself up toward the surface. The bubbles meant it had just dived in, and her brain frantically searched for how long Nile crocodiles could remain submerged. It was a long time, she knew. She had to escape or fight it off; she couldn't wait for it to leave.

The vacuum tube was still back at the temple site, but she had a digging tool in her belt. She pulled it out and prepared to attack, wishing she had her bo staff instead.

The croc lunged, and M darted to the side. It was hard to do anything quickly with the scuba gear on, and she had to be careful not to damage the oxygen tank—the crocodile couldn't be allowed anywhere near it.

It lunged again, and she slammed the digger down toward the beast's eye with both hands. She missed, but struck something. It retreated, taking the digger with it.

Ash. Where is Ash?

She glanced about, getting her bearings, remembering the path the piece of Set had taken. That was where she found Ash, hovering uncertainly in the direction it had gone, looking back at her.

It's been less than a minute, she realized. She'd been so occupied by the croc that it felt like a year, but the artifact was still leaving a trail through the water. She swam toward Ash.

A second crocodile burst into the water between them.

M elbowed it in the nose and went sideways, preparing to kick. The first croc streaked back from behind her, the digger sticking out of its head. Without thinking, she jerked it free, but the croc was too fast for her to stab again. The two beasts moved in, surrounding her.

Desperate, she looked for Ash. He hadn't moved. The crocs were ignoring him, and he was still floating in the path of the Set piece. Their eyes met.

He was a stranger. A wild-eyed, strung-out stranger. There was no recognition in his gaze, no concern, nothing but raw hunger. He wanted to chase the artifact. It was the only thing he cared about.

M was on her own.

The betrayal felt like a body blow, but there was no time for emotions. She put Ash out of her mind and focused on the crocodiles. Could she get to their bellies and stab there? They were so big her small tool probably couldn't do fatal damage, but maybe if one was hurt, the other would turn on it. Then she could escape while they fought.

M took the digger in both hands; she had to at least try. The first crocodile lunged. M dove and rolled, but the second croc was there already. Jaws wide open, ready to close around her legs. It was too fast. She couldn't maneuver away. M steeled herself for the pain.

The croc's jaws stayed open.

Time seemed to stop. The crocodile was frozen. The one above her was, too, stuck mid-turn, trying to follow her as she rolled beneath it.

M scrambled to swim out of reach of the snapping jaws, unable to process what was happening. *It's not frozen,* she realized. *Just moving slowly.*

The open mouth was twitching, trying to free itself from something. Its body thrashed from side to side as if to shake off an attacker. But it was all at half-speed, slower even. The croc above was opening its mouth to snap, but again it moved slowly, as if . . .

As if . . .

The water around the crocodiles looked wrong. Not like liquid. More like Jell-O. M swam back further, realizing that gelatinous water had surrounded both crocodiles, forming a protective bubble around them. The lunging beasts were panicking now but couldn't move fast enough to break free.

Through her confusion, M became aware of her heart slamming against her chest, her pulse pounding in fear. She turned to swim to the surface.

Ash was there.

He floated behind the crocs, his hands out, the strange

gelatinous water streaming from them to form the bubbles around the attacking beasts. Somehow, Ash was creating this bizarre protection.

M gaped at him, astonishment rendering her mind blank.

Ash's eyes rolled back in his head. His body went slack.

M snapped out of her shock. She sped toward him as he began to sink, wormed her arm around his chest, and pulled him as fast as she could toward the surface, all the while hoping the crocodiles were still trapped.

The sunlight grew stronger as she swam, until she could see the bottom of the boat. Her head broke the surface and she stroked hard toward the boat, dragging Ash with her. When she reached it, she grabbed a clip and attached it to his suit. Pulling off her scuba mask as she climbed, she got on board, then turned to Ash.

He was dead weight, but she had to get him out before the crocs came back. Using all her strength, she hauled him up and over the side, letting them both fall to the deck. She rolled him over and pulled his mask off.

"Ash," she said loudly, resting her hands on his cheeks. "Ash!"

For a terrible moment, nothing happened. His dark skin looked gray and his eyes remained closed. His lips were parted, slack.

Then he drew in a deep, shuddering breath. His eyes opened and he shot up to a sitting position.

"Easy," M cried, grabbing his shoulders. "You passed out."

He nodded, crumpling back against the side of the boat, his body leaning on hers. They sat in silence for a minute.

"Are you okay?" M asked.

Ash nodded again.

"Good," she said. "Now tell me what the *hell* just happened."

It was as if she could see his resistance vanish. He was too weak to sit up straight, much less keep lying to her the way he'd obviously been lying all along. "The crocodiles would have killed you. I used the power of Horus to save you," he said.

"The power of Horus," she repeated. When he didn't answer, she realized what he meant. "Power? As in *magic*?"

"I'm not supposed to let outsiders know. But you were in danger, and I couldn't let you . . ." His voice trailed off.

"You're spent. Whatever that was, it exhausted you," she said.

"Yes."

"Thank you," M said, pulling him into a tight hug. Had she even bothered to say that yet? "For saving me. I thought you were just going to go after the piece of Set."

"M," he said, reproach in his voice. "I never even considered that."

She smiled into his neck. "Well, thanks."

"You're welcome." He brought his arms up, weakly hugging her back.

Again, no one spoke. The hot midday sun beat down on them, and the water plunked against the boat.

"Seriously, what the hell?" M exploded, pushing him away. "Magic? That was magic? Your cult teaches you, what? Telekinesis?"

"They didn't teach me. I was born with it," Ash said. "All my life I could access this power. I tried never to use it, but sometimes, when I was afraid or angry, I couldn't stop myself. It just . . . came out."

Something about his expression made M lean closer. His voice shook. "Why didn't you want to use it? Does it hurt people?"

"No. Well, yes. It can hurt people, but that's not why. I was taught it was wrong. My parents said the power was the work of— They said it was wrong, that I was a disgrace for having it."

Was this why his parents had treated him poorly? "Did they think you were possessed by the devil or something?"

Ash closed his eyes, and when he spoke it was in a monotone. "They punished me when I used the power. They hated me for having it. I was considered an embarrassment to them. They threw me out when I was fourteen."

M drew in a sharp breath. No wonder Ash didn't understand her devotion to her father. "What did you do?"

"I went to Paris." He laughed, a thin, choking sound. "Like Baptiste told you, and tried to be an artist. I don't know why. I guess I finally felt free to be who I wanted."

"What happened?"

"Being free meant that for the first time I felt allowed to use my power." Ash opened his eyes and turned his face to her. "I had fun with it; I'd never done that before. But I also needed it to live. I used it to scam people for money, food, a place to live. I felt justified. But I also liked it."

"Well, you'd been powerless all your life. Of course you liked it," she murmured.

He looked startled. "Right. Anyway, I had power but I was also a dumb kid. I attracted the wrong kind of friends, and I let them talk me into using it for more hardcore things."

"Like what?"

"At first just a lot of partying. Epic parties." A smile played about his lips. "But then they decided to rob a store. And I went with them." He paused, glancing away.

M concentrated on peeling off her scuba suit, sensing he didn't want her to look at him.

"I'd only ever had one friend before, Hugh. He was the only one who didn't treat me like a freak. He didn't listen to my parents. He stuck by me. But when I was in Paris, I had all these new friends. They didn't hate me for the power; they loved me for it. And then, when they were in the store, and the police came . . ."

"What did you do?" M whispered, afraid to hear the answer.

"It's more than just that thing with the water. I can do a lot of stuff. I used it to keep the police back while my friends got out. And one police officer was hurt. Not killed. But really hurt. I didn't mean for it to happen."

"They caught you? Baptiste said something about prison," M said.

Ash nodded. "They caught me, and they caught my friend Jack. He wanted to be an artist too, taught me a lot. The rest of my friends scattered. I never saw them again."

He sounds less bitter about that than I would be, M thought.

"In jail, they called my parents in England, but they said to let me rot. I had no money, no family, and I was considered a freak. That was the end of my life. Then Philip came."

"Philip from the Eye?"

"Yes. He'd been aware of me for some time. He and the other high priests of Horus can feel the magic. They know when the power of the god has been used, though they cannot use it themselves."

"So it's only you?"

"Philip explained I was a god channeler. A vessel through which Horus may flow. It is a rare gift. I had been taught it was a curse, so to hear it described as a gift was invaluable to me. Philip took me out of jail and brought me into the Eye. He taught me that Horus had given me the gift out of love. He trained me in the ways of the god. But for all that, still the most wonderful thing he did for me was explain that my power was good, not evil. That I was not evil."

"That's why you're so loyal to the Eye," she said.

"No. It is Horus I am loyal to," Ash explained. "Once I allowed myself to accept the power, it deepened and grew, and

I understood it was the god I felt within. I realized the greatness of Horus."

And there he goes again, sounding like a zealot, she thought wryly. She'd never imagined Ash to be abused, but he obviously had been. His lack of normal family life made it difficult to think of him as an adversary—until he started talking about his religion, the whole reason he wouldn't help her find her father.

It sounded like lunacy, this idea that he let a god work through him. And yet, the crocs in their suddenly solid water bubbles had not been normal. Her brain had been going over and over it, desperate for a scientific explanation for what she'd seen.

But there was none. She didn't know what to think or how to interpret the event, a new feeling for her.

What Ash did wasn't natural, she thought. *It was supernatural.*

"If you can channel a god, why can't you just ask him where the pieces are?" she said, asking the first thing that popped into her mind.

His brow furrowed. "I don't know. We've tried. It doesn't work that way. Horus has not granted that power to the Eye."

"Well, then, why didn't you just use your power to smash your way out of the building where my father is being held? If you wanted him and his map, why not just burst in, grab him, and leave?"

Now Ash was sitting up again, leaning toward her. "I am a god channeler, not a god. There are limits. To use any power exhausts my body. I could not take on the cult of Set single-handedly."

"Why? Do they have powers too?" She gasped, thinking through the implications. "Is there a person who can channel Set? Is my father being held by people with that sort of magic?"

"No. Power comes from Horus alone," Ash said, but she was barely listening. Dad was captive to much darker forces than she'd realized. Did he know?

"That piece of the artifact—it shot out of the ground like a bullet. Why? Did you move it with your power to keep it away from me?"

"What? No. Why would I do that? I have not used my powers on you at all," he protested. "I told you, it weakens me."

"So why did the piece go flying away? Does it have its own magic?" M demanded.

"I don't know! We have lost much of—"

"—much of your lore, I know," she cut him off, frustrated. "Maybe there's some kind of magnetic pull near Philae—it was always rumored to be an odd island, where fish and birds didn't go and even the waters behaved strangely. Before it was flooded, I mean."

"Whatever happened, the piece is now free in the world, which is extraordinarily dangerous." Ash climbed heavily to his feet. "We must go back down and find it."

"We can't," M protested. "Crocodiles, remember? But the sub-bottom profiler found it last time. We can use that to track it!" She leapt up, planning to start the machine again. Her next step landed with a splash.

The entire deck was wet.

"We're taking on water!" she cried.

"Over there. Did something hit us?" Ash pointed to a small, jagged hole in the hull. M felt a strange tightening sensation in her stomach.

She stumbled over to the stack of life preservers where she'd hidden the other piece of Set, pawing through them until she found the small leather pouch where she kept it. There was a hole in the bag, as well. A buzzing filled her ears as she opened it.

Inside lay the Set artifact—arms and torso as one, as if it had been that way all along.

"The torso shot up here and attached itself to the arms," she whispered. "It tore right through the boat."

"I don't see a crack or a joint," Ash murmured, peering over her shoulder. "Nothing to show they were separate pieces."

M turned it over in her hands. "There isn't one." She pulled and twisted, but the pieces didn't budge. It was one statue. One piece. Inseparable. "How is that possible?"

Ash's expression was grim. "The power of Set."

CHAPTER 13

Ash stared out the window of the plane as it ascended. His shoulders relaxed as he let himself lean back in his seat, Egypt becoming smudges of muted color beneath them. He was sure the high priests of the Eye had felt the burst of power he'd used. They always felt it when he used the power of Horus. If Philip could trace the power accurately enough to get even a rough location, he and the others would come for Ash immediately.

They would come for M.

He turned his head so she entered his frame of vision. Her long hair was loose—she only let it down on planes, as far as he could tell. A shame, really, to keep such beauty tied up in a ponytail all the time.

M didn't seem to have made the connection that the Eye could be tracking them. He didn't see any reason to worry her now.

But he couldn't shake his own concern. All he'd been able to think about since Philae was getting as far away as possible from the place where he'd exhibited power. It was an old habit—to run from the scene of the crime. Now that they were safe, though, the enormity of what had happened was sinking in.

Philip must be furious. Obedience without question had been one of Ash's first lessons in the Eye. It had been a relief to turn himself over to Philip's teachings. Philip respected the power instead of hating it. His only goal was to help Ash reach his potential, to open him more fully to Horus. Obeying Philip was a way to obey Horus.

I should end this now, Ash thought. He could subdue M and take the two Set pieces. The one Set piece. He felt sick every time he thought of them fused together. The entire reason the Eye existed was to prevent those pieces from joining again, and thanks to him, they had.

Is there a way to separate them? He wanted to ask Philip, but that would mean betraying M. And surely that knowledge had been lost. Everything else useful seemed to have been lost, so why not this?

Ash felt a stab of guilt. M's influence, he knew, yet it was also the truth. The Eye had never taught him that the pieces would reunite themselves. He'd always assumed there had to be a ritual. He'd learned as much, in fact. What had M said? That facts get forgotten over time, and stories get twisted.

The pieces had to be re-hidden. It was far too dangerous to carry them around this way, even more so to look for another piece. What if that one fused with these two? Could Ash live with himself if he was the reason the Set statue reunited?

Could I live with myself if Philip took M, he wondered, closing his eyes against the very idea of it.

He'd told Philip she would never translate the map for them. But the Eye could force her to give them the locations of the other Set pieces. She would fight with everything in her, but ultimately the Eye would break her.

M nudged him, bringing him out of his thoughts. "Do

you want something to drink?" The flight attendant had reached their row. "Water, please," he told the man.

"Are you okay?" M asked. She used her teeth to open a small bag of pretzels.

"Fine, yes, thanks," Ash told her.

"That was not even a little bit convincing," she replied. "Jellying those crocodiles took a lot out of you. You should try to sleep while you can."

There was no hint of revulsion or fear on her face. She was treating him as if nothing had changed; as if he were still the same person he'd been before she saw what lurked inside him. She wasn't even trying to figure out what his power could do for her, like so many others had.

It was unexpected. She was unexpected. Even with Philip, there were times when he had obviously been calculating how to use Ash's gift to his advantage. Being Ash's mentor had allowed Philip to rise quickly within the Eye.

"You realize you're staring," M said. "What? Do I have a bat in the cave?"

"Pardon?"

She laughed. "Never mind. Your ever-so-polite Britishness sometimes brings out my crude American. But you *were* staring."

"My thoughts were elsewhere. I didn't mean to stare," he explained. He looked out the window again.

"The pieces are still fused," M said quietly, as if she'd known what he was thinking all along. "Why? Are they some kind of freaky strong magnets?"

Ash knotted his hands together. "I don't know anything about them," he admitted. "At least not about their physical properties. At one time they are said to have been part of a completely ordinary piece of statuary. Then, many thousands of years ago, a group of five priests bound Set to the statue."

"Horus priests?" she asked.

He nodded. "After, the priests broke it into five pieces, and each went in a different direction, to hide them as far apart as possible. They got the idea from him, from what he did to his brother Osiris."

"I still find it impossible to believe," M said.

"Even after what you saw me do? Even after the way the pieces joined?" Ash asked.

"It's easier for me to think magnetism, and some kind of telekinesis on your part," M said. "After all, you're telling me actual gods chopped each other up and squabbled over who got to be in charge of Egypt."

"Squabbled?" Ash repeated. "You're trivializing what Set did. He murdered Horus's father and dismembered him. That's hardly a squabble."

"And I'm supposed to take it as literal truth?"

"I do," Ash said.

They stared at each other in silence. M sighed. "If I'm supposed to believe myths are true stories, why are they only about gods? I've always been more interested in the real people of ancient Egypt than two gods having crazy fights. There wasn't much about humans in the Contendings of Horus and Set."

Ash opened his mouth, but there was nothing to say. For him, it had always been the opposite. What was important to him were the gods, and knowing which god he should dedicate himself to. He'd never questioned what he'd learned of Horus's relationship with Set. He'd never asked himself if either god cared for the people doing the worshipping.

For Philip, the actions of Horus weren't to be questioned. Philip was similar to his father that way—though Philip wouldn't slap Ash for asking questions. He would just sit silently, cold.

"The Eye's mission is to keep Set from destroying the world," Ash pointed out. "Perhaps Set and Horus didn't consider how their actions impacted humans. But if Set is freed, it *will* mean the death of every human on the planet."

"You really believe the world will be destroyed if the pieces are put together?" M asked.

"Yes," Ash answered without hesitation. "And you? After what you've seen, it must at least seem like a possibility, theories of telekinesis and magnetism aside."

"Let's say I do believe in the gods. And I accept that you corralled those crocs through the power of Horus. I still don't understand why everything would be annihilated. Why would Set want to destroy it all? Wouldn't he just want to enjoy being back in the world?" She kept talking, speeding up. He could tell she was working hard to keep her terror at bay. "And Set isn't always portrayed as evil. The pharaohs called on him for help during battles. He's also supposed to help people ascend to heaven. Set and Horus were often thought of as two parts of the heavens, Horus as the daytime sky, Set as the nighttime sky. What does the Eye say about that?"

"That if the Set animal is reassembled, Set will become incarnate and the world destroyed. Something I believe with every fiber of my being. Maybe I'm wrong, maybe we're all wrong, but are you willing to risk it?" Ash asked.

Her eyes filled with tears, but she blinked them away before they could fall. "You and the Eye can worry about saving the world. All I care about is saving my father. Our deal hasn't changed."

Didn't she understand that if the world ended her father would die? She would die. That Mike person of hers would die. Everyone she'd ever met would die. But she was willing to risk it all to save her father.

What was it like, to have such loyalty to another person? To defy all logic just for the tiniest possibility of helping them? He couldn't imagine taking such a risk for anyone, not Hugh, not Philip.

And yet, hadn't he just done the same thing? Staying with M, making sure she was safely away from the Eye? And for what? To keep her safe a little bit longer, until he had to betray her himself? It defied logic.

"I'm worried about the pieces. They joined together without even a prayer, or a ritual," he said, surprising himself. He hadn't meant to tell her his concerns. "My mission is to prevent them from joining, but now I've found two pieces and in effect helped them unite. It's dangerous to keep looking. I need you to tell me the truth."

"What truth?"

"I know when we go to the map locations you're finding clues where to look for them," he said. "Is that the code? Does the map tell you where to find these clues, or are you just getting lucky?"

She didn't answer right away. Telling him this secret gave her less power. But hadn't he proven himself by saving her from the crocodiles? He hadn't known the piece was going to end up attached to the one they'd already found. He could have gone after it and left her to die.

Ash studied her face. Was she going to trust him?

"Okay," she said, and he let out a breath he hadn't realized he was holding. "My father's map isn't the most recent one. The pieces have been moved since it was made."

"What?" He gaped at her. Could that be true? "Is that . . ."

"That's why nobody has found the pieces at any of the map locations. They haven't been there for, well, I'm not sure how long. Sometime after Notre Dame was built and when the Eye lost the ancient language," she said. "But, so far, at each spot on the old map, there's been a signpost—glyphs that give the new location of the piece. It's pretty smart, actually. They made maps, but they also had a backup plan. The people who moved the pieces left directions behind for those who knew how to read them." She gave Ash a poke in the chest. "Which you don't. But I do. You still need me."

"That's all but impossible to forget," Ash answered. "So why are we going to India? Your father sent the cult of Set there already, to some old temple. They didn't find a sign-post."

"They didn't know they were looking for one. I got lucky finding the one in Baiae," M admitted. "And I wasn't even sure I'd translated the next part of the map correctly. But if my dad sent the cult of Set there, I did it!" Her face glowed with triumph. "I *knew* I figured it out—there were glyphs for *one, temple, creation, ram,* and *axe.* I got stuck on the one for axe for months. I'd been thinking the axe was a lotus flower, because my father had. But then I realized it could be an axe. My dad must have realized it too. Once I got axe, it gave Mike an idea."

"Hold on. Your boyfriend knows about this, but you've only just told me?" Ash couldn't believe it.

"Mike's not holding my father's life over my head. You are," M shot back. "The Eye could have saved my dad. We could both be helping you right now, but you wouldn't do it."

He looked away. She was right, but she should also understand saving everyone on earth was more important than saving one person, even her father. Not that he would know. His father hated him. Ash wasn't sure he'd feel anything except relief if his father died.

His relationship with Philip was a lot closer to what M had. But Philip would be willing to kill himself to stop Set from rising. Hell, Philip would kill Ash if necessary.

"Ash, I can't not try to save him. You'd understand if you loved your . . ." She trailed off.

He flinched, then felt himself soften. "Once we find the pieces, we'll save your father," Ash forced the words out. It was harder to lie to her now. He liked her too much. Maybe he could find a way to make it true. Philip hadn't even entertained the idea of a deal, but Ash had been acting as if it were real.

She gave a quick nod, a mix of emotions playing at her face. "Good." She cleared her throat. "Mike suggested the Thrissivaperoor Vadakkunnathan Temple in Kerala. It was the first of a hundred and eight temples to Shiva consecrated by Lord Parasurama, whose name means 'ram with axe.' If my dad already sent the Set people there, it means Mike came up with the same interpretation he did."

"But the cult of Set found nothing," Ash said. "Which means the piece was moved, and we're looking for a signpost?"

"Exactly. The Eye would have left one behind when they moved it," M confirmed. "I've been assuming the signposts are in the exact spot that was vacated, though. So we still have to figure out exactly what the map referred to."

"You said it referred to this temple."

"Right. But there's one part we haven't figured out yet." She frowned.

"Well, now that you've finally confided in me, maybe I can help," Ash said. He had to at least be as useful as her high school boyfriend. Unless the boyfriend was older? Was he an archeology student? Someone M had met through her father?

"The five glyphs form a circle. Around the outside of the circle are four dots. The top dot is larger. I don't know what the dots mean. Neither does Mike." She grabbed a napkin and made a little sketch.

He immediately pulled out his phone and Googled the temple, determined to prove he was as sharp as Mike, before groaning inwardly. That wasn't important. Finding the signpost that would take them to the next piece was.

"This might be something," Ash said, partway through

the third article he found about Thrissivaperoor Vadakkun-natha. M leaned close so she could read along. "There are four gates—gopuras—leading to the temple grounds. North, south, east, west. The dots on your sketch are evenly spaced around the circle. Maybe they each indicate a cardinal point of a compass."

"The biggest dot is the one on top. That could mean we'll find the signpost in the north gopura!" She held up her hand. He felt a little silly, but he gave her a high five.

"You're looking pretty pleased with yourself," M commented, smiling at him.

"I solved that quite handily, you have to admit," he said. "It's a good thing you decided to trust me."

"It is," she agreed. "We make a good team. You with your shady French connections and me with my knowledge of the secret language of Horus priests—which the Eye has forgotten. Oh, and my extensive knowledge of world, not just Egyptian, mythology."

"You forget that I also contribute money. Brat." He felt a grin spreading across his face. Something had changed in Philae. He hadn't thought it possible, but it felt as if he and M were on the same side.

He tried to push away the knowledge that it was only temporary.

CHAPTER 14

M's heart thudded in her chest, as if trying to join the hundreds of pounding drums. Her eyes were dazzled by colored floodlights, rows of flashing neon decorating the buildings around the train station, and the fireworks blazing across the sky, which had barely started to darken. The whole city of Kerala was having a celebration that was part religious ritual, part mega-party. It would have been thrilling, except it was going to make it nearly impossible to get to the temple.

It hadn't occurred to her they would arrive during the Pooram festival. It didn't always fall on the same date, but it was always right around now, and she hadn't given it a thought. Since she'd found out Dad was alive, ordinary things like knowing the date, eating meals, and sleeping every night had become inconsequential.

"Which way?" Ash shouted.

She shook her head. She didn't know. She'd looked at a map, but felt dizzy and disoriented. It felt as if the masses of people on every side of her had already taken all the oxygen. She tried to pull in a deep breath. Someone knocked against her, and for a wild second she thought she was going down. *When your brain is anxious, give it something to do.*

She bent her elbows for protection against the crowd and scanned the area in front of them. High above the people she saw brightly colored silken umbrellas decorated with tinsel, huge peacock fans, and what looked like massive white feather dusters. She had a vague memory of them from when she'd been to the festival with her parents as a little girl. Or at least she had a memory of her father telling her about the trip, and how they'd thought it might be too overwhelming for her, but instead she had loved every minute.

"Come on!" She grabbed Ash's hand so they wouldn't get separated, and launched in the direction of the dusters, fans, and umbrellas. They would belong to men standing on top of a procession of elephants. The lead elephant would be carrying an idol from one of the city's temples, traveling to be blessed by Lord Shiva at the Thrissivaperoor Vadakkunnathan, exactly where they needed to go. All they had to do was follow the procession.

She moved several steps before being blocked by a solid wall of people—which would be fine if she was there to see the festival. But she needed the next signpost.

M pressed her hands together, jamming them between the man and woman directly in front of her. Pushing her hands apart, she created an opening to wriggle through, trusting Ash to stick close. She had to keep shoving and stomping on feet to make any forward progress. She got some shoves back, but most people just kept on dancing, brought to a near frenzy by the stimulation of the drums and exploding fireworks.

Finally, she and Ash were close enough to the elephant procession to feel the hot gusts of air generated by slow flaps from the animals' enormous ears, close enough that she could see the details on the golden headdresses they wore, and hear the tinkling of their decorative bells. "We should circle around to the east gopura," she shouted, unsure Ash would hear her. The elephants would enter the west gopura and come out the south. Most of the crowd would be waiting there.

Once they were able to move past the south gate, it became easier to make progress. As soon as they could, M and Ash broke into a run. But M pulled up short when the east gopura came into sight.

"What?" Ash asked.

"Dress code," M explained. "Most of the Indian temples have them. Look. All the men going in are wearing dhoti, and the women have saris. My father was able to tour the temple through contacts with other archeologists, but usually non-Hindus aren't allowed in."

Another thing she'd forgotten. Would she ever get back to her normal, careful self? Maybe once she saw Dad alive with her own eyes. Still, she had to be better at thinking things through. "We'll be okay if we blend. There are street vendors all over the place. Let's find something."

They found what they needed between a stall heaped with raw dates, grapes, and oranges and one selling Nilgiri tea. M decided on a half sari, which she put on over her clothes, and also a dupatta to wear as a head covering. Ash bought a white dhoti and wrapped the length of cloth around his waist and legs, not bothering to remove his khakis.

"You have to take off your shirt, though," M told him. All the men going in had been bare-chested. He yanked off his tee and jammed it in his back pocket. M took a few seconds to study him, unable to keep from noticing his strong shoulders and chest, then nodded. Now he looked like most of the men around, especially with his black hair and dark skin completing the look. "Am I okay?"

Ash gave her a longer look, letting his eyes wander over her body slowly. M punched him in the shoulder. "That wasn't an invitation to leer at me. Do I look okay to go into the temple?"

"I wasn't leering. I was simply . . . evaluating." The beginnings of a smile tugged at one side of his mouth. "Roll up your jeans a little, so they don't show, and shove your hair further under the cloth," he told her. "Then you're good to go." He bent and began rolling up the legs of his own pants.

M quickly adjusted her clothing and made sure her backpack was zipped. The pieces of the Set animal, fused together in their torn leather pouch, were buried deep within her clothes. Still, it made her nervous to be in a crowd with them on her back. *As long as I feel the throbbing, at least I know they haven't been pickpocketed*, she thought. Who knew there would be a silver lining to such a constant annoying sound?

"Ready?" Ash asked.

"Ready."

They hurried to the east gopura. There was a line to go through the gate, but it wasn't long. Most people wouldn't want to miss the Kudamattam. It would take place right outside the south gate. The exchanging of the umbrellas was one of the highlights of the festival and accompanied by a jazz-like concert played on traditional Kerala instruments.

M forced herself not to fidget as she waited. She couldn't go pushing and shoving through a line of people waiting to worship. "As soon as we enter, we find the north gate and see if we can get into the temple from the inside."

"Yes. The same plan we came up with on the plane," Ash replied with a mix of exasperation and amusement. He stepped in front of her as the line moved forward. M's breath caught in her throat. His back was crisscrossed with old scars, most flat, but a few raised and puckered. Was self-flagellation a part of Horus worship? Or were these older? Had his parents done this? Reluctantly she pushed it from her mind. She needed to focus.

Soon they entered the gopura. It was called a gate, but looked nothing like one. Instead it was a tall building with multiple tiled roofs and ornate gables. Round globes of light had been strung around the eaves of each level, and the whole building was washed in a golden glow.

The interior was several degrees cooler than the hot, humid air outside, and M finally felt like she could take a deep breath. They were close enough that she could see through the door on the other side. The first thing that struck her was the spaciousness. In the distance was the wall their research said surrounded the inner temple. It was lower than the massive one circling the grounds of the entire temple. To the left was a low brick building with a lot of short columns and a huge sloping roof made of copper squares that reflected the light of the fireworks.

"The theater," Ash said. "Where the gods and goddesses are supposed to dance."

In a different life, M would have explored every inch of this lovely place, but in this life there was no time. As soon as she stepped through the doorway, she began, "Now we need to find the—" She stopped, shocked. Something inside her backpack had *moved*. Shifted. It felt like there was something alive in there.

"Keep going," Ash said. "We're blocking the exit."

M hadn't even realized she'd stopped walking. She hurried out of the way, then pulled off her backpack and unzipped it. Had someone tried to pickpocket her? She knelt, frantically searching for the leather pouch. The throbbing had stopped. How was it possible? How could anyone have gotten to the pieces of Set without even unzipping her bag?

But the pouch was still there. M tore it open, and gaped.

"I . . . Look at this," she said. She held up the little pouch so Ash could see. The Set animal remained inside. But the pieces were separate again. They'd both tried to pull them apart, and it had been impossible. There'd been no seams, no anything to indicate they'd ever been two pieces. And now—

Ash reached forward, and she jerked the pouch away. "How did that happen?" M asked. She wanted an explanation that wasn't magical, but knew there wasn't going to be one.

"I don't know." He stared at the pieces. "I don't know," he repeated. He sank slowly to the ground next to her, all the tension leaving his body. "Thank the god."

"Why?" She carefully retied the pouch, wrapping a loop of the tie around the hole to close it.

"The pieces have come apart. They *can* come apart," he said. "I feared that when they joined, it meant . . ."

"Set was already doing his thing, moving toward incarnation?" she guessed.

"I've been afraid to look for further pieces," he said. "I cannot risk more of them joining. When you told me we wouldn't find the next piece here, I knew we could come. But I also knew we could not go to the next location, not carrying the pieces we have. We could not risk adding a third piece to the whole."

M blew out a breath, frustrated. He hadn't mentioned he felt that way. What had he planned to do before the next step? Take the Set pieces from her by force? She should've known better than to trust him, even if he had saved her life.

"But now I'm not worried," he went on. "Now I know the pieces *can* come apart. It is not the rejoining of the artifact. Not the permanent one, anyway."

"Right . . ." she said. Thinking about this would have to wait. "Well, good, let's find the signpost."

She secured the pouch within her backpack and stood, glancing around. It was easy to see all four gopuras. They towered over the grounds at the four compass points. She led the way north, not pausing to look at shrines where others had stopped to pray.

When they were close enough to see the details of the gate, M's mind went into gear. The ground level was made of molded granite, just like the one in the east. There were narrow slits carved in it, but nothing a person could squeeze through. Maybe they could climb to one of the roofs, but she didn't see any windows, only a few small square openings, which were much too small for her to climb through, forget about Ash.

The top levels of the building were made of wood. They could smash a hole through, but she hated the idea of damaging an ancient building. "Any ideas for getting in?" she asked Ash. It was good to be able to talk without yelling. A concert was being played somewhere on this side of the massive wall, but it was softer and had a different rhythm from the music outside.

"Door," Ash said. "Maybe the lock will be easy to break. And that won't be too hard for them to repair."

"Oh fine, pick the obvious route," M snorted, but followed his lead. When he gave the door an experimental touch, it swung open easily. M was so surprised she let out a little gasp.

Ash raised an eyebrow. "Perhaps Lord Shiva is blessing us too," he said, stepping inside.

He stopped so abruptly that M slammed into him. "Wh—"

Ash turned and pressed one hand over her mouth, blocking the rest of the word. He jerked his chin toward the ground. It was dim inside the gopura, so it took her a moment to realize they were standing next to a body.

Slowly Ash slid his hand away and knelt next to the man on the floor. *A guard,* she thought. *Here to make sure no festivalgoers came through this gopura by accident.* He pressed his fingers against the man's neck. M's hand nervously fiddled with her necklace while she waited. Ash stood after what felt like eons. "Alive," he whispered, his lips brushing her ear. She shivered and was annoyed to realize it wasn't because they found the unconscious man.

M struggled to reach under her sari to remove her bo staff from where it was tucked into the waistband of her jeans. When she had it in her hand, she crept forward, this time Ash following her. When they were about halfway through the gopura, she hesitated. She heard voices ahead. She listened hard, trying to filter out the sounds of the concert and the exploding fireworks. At least two people were in here with her and Ash.

Slowly she began moving forward again. They had to be the ones who knocked out the guard . . . but why? She took another step, all her attention on the voices. One male, one female.

British accents.

M's heart ricocheted off her ribs.

She spun around and pointed back to the doorway they'd come in. Ash followed her without question. They retraced their steps quickly and quietly.

They needed to get away, fast. "Over there." M gestured toward a circular structure and they ran to it, skirting a pond, and went inside. A few people were paying their respects in front of the idol of the goddess Parvati that dominated the room.

M whispered so she wouldn't interrupt their devotions. "Bob and Liza! My guardians. They were in the north gopura. But how? They can't be tracking my cell. So how?"

Ash didn't answer. His body was rigid and his face was blank.

"Did my dad send them? Maybe they don't even know we're here. What do you think?" When he didn't respond right away, she gave his arm a little shake. "What do you think?" she asked more loudly. One of the worshippers glared at her.

"The Set cult already checked here," he whispered. "The only reason he'd have sent them back is if he'd found out about the signposts, which he wouldn't have been able to do without visiting the sites himself."

Ash's words were reasonable, but he still had that blank look. It was as if something had terrified him and he was trying not to show it. He'd told her Bob and Liza were dangerous. Was that it? Were she and Ash in danger?

"I know you said they were a threat," she told Ash, squeezing his hand. "But, you know what, we are too. I can fight, and you have the Horus mojo. We can handle them." It was pep talk bullshit, but only in part. She and Ash *were* a good team. Maybe they couldn't take down the entire Set cult, but against Bob and Liza? They had a real shot.

Ash gave a forced smile. "I was just trying to think things through. Your guardians were in the States while I was working for the cult. I'm sure they've been told I disappeared from the Set compound right around the time you took off, but they don't know I made contact with your father. They have no reason to think you're with me. I can distract them. That will give you a chance to find the signpost."

He turned and strode away without waiting for a response.

Ash didn't look back. M was sharp, and good at reading people, good at reading *him*. He didn't want her to see how shaken he was.

Maybe she was wrong about the voices, he thought wildly. *Maybe it isn't them.*

But M knew their voices as well as he did.

"Meet me back at the east gate!" she called after him.

He raised his hand in acknowledgment. He had to focus on the task at hand: get them out of the north gopura so M could find the signpost. But how?

I could just say "Hey, let's get some tea and catch up," he thought. As if he would need to do anything. As if they wouldn't race after him the instant they saw his face.

Ash stopped at the pond. Gazing into it, he tried to see past the reflections of the fireworks into its dark depths. He needed stillness. He needed Horus. He breathed in, then out, trying to match the stillness of the water. "Help me," he whispered. "Guide me."

Then he returned to the north gate and strode inside. He spotted the guard lying on the ground in the dimness, stepped over him, and continued on.

When he was about halfway through the gopura, three narrow beams of intense light struck him, momentarily blinding him. He blinked rapidly until he could see the three figures wielding the flashlights.

His father. His mother.

Hugh.

Ash struggled to hold on to the stillness. He'd been expecting his parents; M had said they were here. Hugh's presence threw him. *Horus is with me,* he thought. *Everything I do, everything I did, was for my god. Even betraying my oldest friend.*

"I should have known it would be you," his father spat, his first words to Ash after years apart. For as long as he could remember, he'd felt the man's disgust. And still his father's hatred was like a fist to the gut.

"I don't know what you mean," Ash replied, pleased to hear his voice coming out flat and calm. The last thing he wanted was for his father to know the effect he'd had.

"You know perfectly well. You're trying to find the sacred body and keep it from us," his father shot back. He tightened his grip on the small metal suitcase he held.

"You're right. I am here to find one of the Set pieces," Ash said, feeling a strange freedom in finally telling the truth without apology. "And yes, I plan to keep it from you." His eyes bore into his father's. This man was no longer in charge of him. "I won't let you obliterate the earth by allowing the God of Darkness to become incarnate."

"Blasphemy," his mother hissed. Ash finally allowed himself to look at her. His mother's face was pale except for two vivid splotches of red on her cheeks, and her eyes glittered with a zealot's fervor and revulsion for him, her only child.

Ash struggled to come up with a response. Some small part of himself still wanted to make her see, make her understand he wasn't evil, that he was using the powers granted to him to do good.

Before he could find the words, Hugh was on him, shoving him backward. "Traitor!" he shouted. "I was happy to see you when you came back. I believed you when you said you were ready to return to Set. I used my influence with the Asim to convince him you were repentant."

"I'm sorry I lied to you—"

"You said the magic had ruined your life! You said you were done using that filthy power." Hugh shoved Ash again, slamming him against the granite wall. Ash didn't fight back. Hugh had been a true friend to him always, and he'd done everything possible to make Ash's return to Set easy. He had a right to feel betrayed.

"I didn't want to lie to you. You were the only one with Set I cared about," Ash said. "But I had no choice."

"Stop!" his mother cried. "Not one more word." Ash and Hugh both turned to her. "I can't listen to you justify what you've done. You don't care about anything. Not your oldest friend. Not your family." Her voice caught. "We were right to send you away. Your magic is profane, and it corrupted you from the moment you were born. I hate that I brought you into the world."

Ash had heard this his whole life, how he was tainted, contaminated, evil, bringing shame and dishonor to his parents. How the power from Horus was disgusting, a source of humiliation to them, something that made the other Set devotees mistrust them.

The anger he'd worked so long to banish overcame him, stunning him with its strength. With his back braced against the wall, he kicked out both legs, smashing his feet into Hugh's chest. Hugh went down and Ash ran. He needed to get them out of the gopura. And he felt as if he'd burst into flame if he allowed himself to stay in their presence another second.

Before he reached the door, he heard footsteps behind him. Ash put on speed, racing around the pond and past the shrine where he knew M was waiting. The farther he lured them from the north gopura, the better.

The sound of drums, trumpets, and cymbals grew louder as he ran alongside the lower wall that surrounded the inner temple. Ash tried to head in the direction of the music. There would be a crowd where he could lose the Set acolytes. It was easier to think of them that way, as acolytes, and nothing more. If he disappeared into a mass of people, they'd have to hunt for him, giving M time. Right now he could still hear them close behind him.

As he wheeled around a curve he saw a line of about fifteen elephants moving through the temple grounds. Men with drums walked beside them, and several men with umbrellas were positioned next to each animal. Ash slipped between two of the drummers and squeezed between two of the immense beasts, putting the procession between him and his pursuers. Muttering an apology, he lay one hand on the closest elephant's warm, wrinkled hide and released a small jolt of power, just enough to startle but not hurt it.

The elephant jerked its head up and down, its ears slapping against its body with a thunderous clap. The elephant in front let out a sound that was more roar than the usual trumpeting. Another whipped its trunk to the side, hitting one of the drummers and knocking him off his feet. The elephants' handlers began to shout. The drummers scattered.

Ash ran. He ran until his lungs burned and his legs cramped. As long as he kept moving, they would be coming for him, and M would be safe. Finally, he slowed to a walk, gasping for air. The sky had gone completely dark since he and M entered the temple, and he would be harder to see. The number of men dressed almost identically to him would also help.

He let half an hour pass before taking a circuitous route back to the east gate, constantly checking to make sure he wasn't followed. Had they given up? It was unlikely. Even after the Asim had allowed him back into the Set cult, his parents had never acknowledged him. They'd been off with M by then, but still, there had been no calls, no emails, nothing to welcome him home to the community he'd been raised in. Nothing to apologize for trying to beat the power of Horus out of him as a child. Nothing to say they'd forgiven him for being a heretic from the moment of his birth.

He hadn't let himself dwell on their coldness. He was there for Horus. His parents were right. He *was* a heretic to his birthright. He'd been born to Set, but his gift had come from Horus.

Ash hid under the branches of a huge banyan tree and waited, trying to absorb its peace. This place felt sacred, just as the pond had. Although the temple was dedicated to gods he didn't believe in, somehow he felt closer to his own god here.

His years of training with Philip kicked in, and his breathing slowed. Soon he was able to return to the state of calm readiness that was his constant as a worshipper of Horus. The chaos and frenzy of the celebration dulled around the edges, fading as he focused his attention on spotting M. As soon as she appeared, he had to get her out of there.

His eyes moved in even sweeps from side to side. He wasn't sure if she would come from the north or take a less direct route. Occasionally a woman of M's size in a full sari or a head covering that matched hers would approach the gate, but he dismissed them immediately. It was as if he were attuned to her frequency after being constantly near her.

His heart lurched when he saw her. She was full-on running—and his father, mother, and Hugh were closing in. At some point they must have decided to go back to the north gopura. He should have known. He should have gone back to M once he'd lost them.

Ash sprang out of his hiding place and reached M in seconds. He grabbed her arm and helped propel her to the gate and all the way through.

"Let her go," he heard his father yell close behind them. "You can't—"

The sound of a detonation obliterated the rest of his words, louder than the nearly continuous fireworks, louder than the dozens of drums, than the roar of the crowd.

He twisted to see what had happened. His father was gripping the metal suitcase with both hands, and Ash could see the tendons in his arms straining. The sound came again, like a grenade, and it was as if an iron fist had punched the suitcase from the inside, causing it to protrude. When another explosion came, something shiny and black burst partway out of the case.

"It's a piece of the Set animal!" M cried. He could barely hear her. His ears were throbbing, even his joints were vibrating in the aftermath of the last blast.

His father, mother, and Hugh all leapt for the suitcase, using their bodies to press it to the ground and keep the Set piece inside. Ash tore his eyes away. This was their chance. "Come on!" He grabbed M's arm again.

"Memphis!" His mother's shriek cut through the noise.

M turned toward her, one hand reaching for her bo staff.

His mother moved apart from the others, letting them fight to keep the piece in the briefcase. Her face twisted in a sneer as she spoke. "We have your father."

M hurled herself toward his mother, but Ash grabbed her around the waist, holding her back. "We have to get away. Now," he barked.

His mother's eyes met his, then moved back to M. "I'll give you a week to come to your senses," she called as he dragged M away. "One week for you to bring me that piece of the Sacred Body. Or else I start taking pieces of your father instead."

M turned into a wild animal, legs pumping, fists clenched, fighting to get to his mother. He tightened his arms around her and half pulled, half carried her into the crowd, forcing his way between the bodies until the mass of people thinned and he could deal with M.

"I'll kill her," M snarled.

"No, she'll kill you. And me. And your father," he yelled, pulling her to face him. *And with the pieces of Set, they'll kill everyone else, too,* he thought.

"Let me go!" She was sobbing.

"No. It's not safe."

She kept fighting, twisting to get away from him as tears streaked down her cheeks. From rage or fear, he couldn't tell. "Let go."

"No." Not knowing what else to do, he wrapped his arms around her, holding her tight. "We have to get away, they probably already called for backup. We'll figure out what to do. I promise," he said into her hair.

She became quiet. Then she pulled in a deep breath, stepped back, and wiped her eyes. "Okay. Let's go."

She sounded completely normal, as if the past few minutes hadn't happened at all. He'd never met anyone so self-controlled in his life—he had to call upon Horus to help him find stillness, and she'd done it in about thirty seconds.

"Motorcycle!" M pointed over his shoulder.

Ash ran over to the guy smoking a cigarette next to the bike. He thrust a wad of cash at the man. Without asking if they had a deal, he yanked off the dhoti tied around his waist and jumped on. M shimmied out of her sari and climbed on behind him, wrapping her arms around his waist. A second later, they sped off. He couldn't go as fast as he wanted, not on the crowded streets, but he headed toward the mountains. As soon as he found a dirt road, they'd be gone, and he was never going to let the cult of Set find them again.

CHAPTER 15

M climbed off the bike and used both hands to comb her fingers through her wind-tangled hair. *Don't think about Liza,* she told herself. *Don't think about Dad. Focus on getting out of India.*

"They're going to be checking the airports," Ash said. His T-shirt was still jammed in his pocket, so he pulled it on. "Maybe we can buy tickets for multiple flights from different airports. That would slow them down. Where are we going, by the way?"

"London," M told him. "Somewhere in London. We're going to have to work the rest of the glyphs to figure out the exact place."

Ash nodded, taking out his cell. "I'll start booking flights."

"Wait. I got this." She called up Joel's number and typed in a text. She should've thought of this earlier. *Focus, M, focus,* she thought.

"Mike again?" Ash complained. "Does he moonlight as a travel agent?"

At first M hadn't wanted to tell Ash anything about Mike because she didn't trust him. But now she kind of enjoyed the little jealous spark he seemed to get whenever the subject came up.

"Mike *is* multitalented," she drawled. "But no. I'm texting a guy who pilots a private jet. My dad and I would hitch rides with him sometimes when he had an empty leg."

Ash raised his eyebrows. "You think this guy just happened to recently drop off clients at Kerala International and also just happens to be flying empty to London for his next pickup?"

M glanced up at him, surprised. She was the one whose family had just been threatened, but he sounded more on edge than she was. "No," M said. "But Joel knows a ton of pilots. One of them might know somebody who knows somebody who can get us out of here." She glanced at her cell. "He says he's on it." She glanced over at two huge glassed-in tubes that formed the airport terminal. She was thirsty. They'd been running for half the night. "I would kill for an iced latte, or, actually, anything caffeinated. But I guess going in probably isn't a good idea."

"Probably not," Ash agreed. "But I'd almost risk it for a beer."

"It's not even six a.m.," M said.

"And?" Ash said.

"It's not even six a.m.," M said.

"You clearly don't go to the right kind of parties." Ash grinned tiredly, and again M saw a flash of who he must have been before Horus. When he was just the arty guy who hung out with Baptiste in Paris.

M plopped down next to the motorcycle, and Ash dropped down next to her.

"Bob and Liza. Those people. Those were my guardians, and they're here. They're—" She struggled to come up with an appropriate word, then gave up. "Liza wouldn't even watch *The Walking Dead*. Too violent, she said. She used to make my lunch sometimes, even though I kept telling her I'd just buy it. And he'd ask about homework."

Ash rubbed at a streak of dirt on the back of one hand. "Were you . . . did you feel close to them?"

"No. They tried. But my dad had just died. I thought he had just died," she corrected. "And I didn't want to talk about it with strangers. After a while, we kept it to surface stuff. What movie should we stream? Please pass the salt. Need any help with physics? That kind of thing. Sometimes they tried to push it further, but mostly they seemed to accept that I didn't want anything more."

"Sounds lonely." Ash looked over at her.

"It would have been lonely anywhere those first months without my dad," M said. "He was my person, the one who just got me. I have friends and all. But ever since my mom died, it was just me and Dad." Her eyes brimmed with tears. She blinked them away. Bad enough she'd let herself freak out instead of just kicking Liza's ass. She didn't need to be blubbering.

Ash returned to rubbing his hand, though the streak of dirt was gone. Was he thinking about his own parents?

"Sorry. I know your father—"

Ash put his hand on her wrist, stopping her. "Don't apologize. It's not like it would make me happy if you had a family as fucked up as mine." He slid his hand away.

M sat up straighter. So much had happened in the last few hours that she wasn't thinking clearly. "Did you know the Set people already had a piece of the artifact?"

"Yes," Ash said. "They've had it for thousands of years. Nobody even knows exactly where they found it anymore. The mouth of Shambhala, wherever that is."

"Shambhala's a place where only the pure of heart can live," she said. "A place with no suffering where people live forever. The most popular theory is that it's in the Dhauladhar Mountains, way up in the Himalayas." Why was she giving a history lesson? Who cared where they had found it? "Is there a reason you never told me?" she asked.

"It didn't seem like it mattered," Ash said. "Getting the other pieces is what the Set cult cares about. That's why they have your father."

"It matters. If you know it, I need to know it," M said, wondering if there was more he wasn't telling her. She'd started feeling close to him. Too close, maybe. Too comfortable. They didn't have the same agenda. For now, they needed each other, but it wouldn't always be true. "Any chance they could have another one of the pieces?"

"Absolutely not."

"Pretty confident, aren't you? You said you were just doing grunt work for them. Why'd they tell you anything about the pieces at all?" M studied his face, waiting.

"Most of the information I got from your father," Ash said. "I was someone he could talk to because I was an outsider. And I overheard things. People weren't that careful with what they said around me. I was kind of invisible. Just the help."

"Just the help," M repeated. "Why did they chase you back there then? You said Liza and Bob weren't even there when you were skulking around the cult. But they sure seemed to know you weren't on their side today."

He hesitated. "The other guy who was with them. He knew me when I worked there. He recognized me."

M nodded. She got the feeling there was something more. But she didn't push. Her cell vibrated and she quickly read the text from Joel.

"If he and my so-called guardians hadn't thrown themselves on the suitcase, we might have ended up with their piece, too," M went on. "It wanted to join with ours. It was hurling itself toward us, just like the torso did when we released it from the ground in Philae."

"Except ours came apart," Ash reminded her.

She frowned, suddenly aware of the deep throbbing that came from the Set animal. It had stopped earlier, but now it was back. M opened her pack, pulling out the leather pouch to check on the pieces. "They're not separate anymore." She held up the single, solid shiny black piece.

He gaped. "When did that happen?"

"I'm not sure," M answered. "I didn't feel it. But when Liza— Well, I wasn't paying attention to anything else, I wouldn't have noticed it. The pack was bouncing around. And when their piece was trying to get out of the suitcase, my whole body felt like it was vibrating."

"Mine too." Ash reached for the melded piece, but M slid it into her backpack. She had no intention of letting him touch any of the pieces until the Eye had rescued her father.

"I don't think the other piece was trying to punch its way out of the suitcase when we were in the temple, though." M zipped the pack and put it back on. "Not with those sounds it made. I would have heard them."

"Everybody would have heard them," Ash agreed.

"Maybe it was only when they got close enough to the other pieces?" she said doubtfully. She couldn't shake the image of them holding their briefcase down. Of Liza coming after her, threatening Dad. *Pieces of him,* that's what she'd said. M rubbed her forehead, trying to push the memory away.

Ash put his arm around her, drawing her close. "It's a bluff. They won't hurt him. They need him to translate . . ." His voice trailed off.

"He can still translate even if he's missing *pieces,*" she mumbled into his shirt.

"M . . ."

"Don't worry. I can compartmentalize." She pulled away and took a deep breath, letting the fear fill her whole body. Then she blew it out, breath and fear together. She didn't have time to be afraid. She had to save her father. *Wallowing doesn't get work done.*

"Let's go find those pieces for the Eye," she said, waving her cell. "We've got our ride."

M closed her eyes and forced away the image of Liza's face. She had to focus on finding the Set pieces. It was her only option—get the pieces, use them to make the Eye go after her guardians and their cult. The Eye had resources—Ash never seemed to run out of money. They'd be able to save Dad. She just had to get the remaining pieces in time.

"Are you enjoying the latte? Did the coconut milk make it extra creamy the way our flight attendant promised?" Ash's voice drifted into her thoughts. He was trying to distract her, make her think about anything other than Dad.

She stretched out her legs as far as possible, just because she was on a plane where she could, then opened her eyes and looked at Ash. His hair was slicked back from his shower—private jets were the way to travel—and she had a crazy impulse to reach over and mess it up. Instead she took a long sip of her latte.

"We still never figured out why Bob and Liza were at the temple," she said, happy her voice didn't shake with the rage she felt. "My father had already sent the Set followers there. So why were they back?"

"Possibly they thought you were following the map and they were looking for you," Ash said slowly.

"But why look only at the temple?"

"Maybe it wasn't only the temple. Maybe they sent people to all the places your father already identified," Ash suggested.

M frowned. "That doesn't really make sense, though. They don't know I have the original of the map, right?"

"Right. Your father told only me." There wasn't even a hint of hesitation in his answer. "Maybe they think you already knew something about the map." He shook his head. "But I doubt they'd have thought you could get to Egypt or India on your own. Your guardians probably didn't give you access to a lot of money."

"I got an allowance. Seriously, an allowance. I was supposed to get my inheritance from my dad when I turned eighteen. Liza was supposed to take me to the estate lawyer, but she said the meeting got pushed back. Probably never was a meeting. Money would give me freedom, and she wouldn't want that," M said. "And it's not like I have friends I could borrow cash from, at least not enough to get me to Kerala."

"Well, now that they've seen you with me, they know you have access to all the money you need."

"Why?" M asked sharply. Ash had worked for the Set cult as a field tech/gofer. There was no reason for them to think he had a lot of money at his disposal. She felt a prickle of unease. There always seemed to be pieces of his story that didn't quite add up.

"Why?" He looked confused for a second. "I was thinking when they saw us together they would presume I was with the Eye."

"Why?" M asked again.

Ash took a sip of his coffee before he answered. The jet had a huge selection of beverages, including the beer he'd claimed to be dying for, but he'd gone for coffee. Black.

"We know who most of the higher up people in the Set cult are. I'm sure they've found out who some of our leaders are. I doubt they know more than that about members of the Eye," Ash answered. "But they know I left my job right before you disappeared. Then they saw me with you at one of the map sites. It's logical for them to assume I am with the Eye."

His explanation seemed reasonable. "Were you scared going in that they'd realize what you were? When you . . . went undercover, I guess. What would they have done if they'd figured you out?"

Ash shrugged. "I tried not to think about it. Philip felt it wasn't a much of a risk."

M snorted. "It wasn't Philip walking in there." She finished her latte and rattled the ice around the glass. "Will they be waiting for us in London? That's the big question."

Ash's hazel eyes flicked back and forth as he thought. "The only way they'd turn up in London is if they'd found out about the signposts, if they'd found one in Kerala, and if they got your father to translate it fast enough. That's a lot of ifs. I think we have to assume they were in the temple on the very slim chance you'd show. They're getting desperate."

"They have my father, so why would they even care about getting me? I'm sure they tell him I'm under constant guard. I'm the same leverage I ever was." It still made her nauseous to think of Dad helping those people because of her.

"Unlike your father, you're free to search for the pieces," Ash said. "They must have thought there was a possibility you knew enough about the map to go to the temple."

"And now they know I have at least one of the pieces. Great," M said. "On that happy note, let's move on. We need to figure out the glyphs."

Ash slid closer, his fresh-from-the-shower scent prickling her nose. She inhaled deeply. "Let's see what you've got," he said.

M pulled up the best picture she'd gotten of the glyphs in the gopura, holding it so they could both look at it. "There were phonograms for *Gog* and *Magog*. I figured those out right away. But I have no ideas on the rest."

"Gog and Magog?" Ash asked, his expression a blank.

"I keep forgetting you know everything about ancient

Egypt, and almost nothing about anything else." M smirked. "Except an assortment of drugs, if Baptiste is to be believed."

"And a few other things." He smiled at her then, in a way that—to her annoyance—made her face flush.

"In medieval legends, Gog and Magog are giants defeated by Brutus, a Trojan war hero. He made them guard his great hall, where Guildhall is now," M explained, keeping her eyes off Ash and glued to her phone. "Here's what we need to figure out. See these glyphs forming the big circle? They're a phonogram for *Henry* and then the number *two*. There's a glyph for *temple* in the middle of the circle. This one." She pointed. "And one for *money*." She tapped another glyph. "But I have no idea what the other one means."

"I do," Ash announced. "It's a symbol for the Knights Templar."

"No." She studied the glyph. "It's a lot more intricate than the Templar cross. It's similar, but . . ."

"Trust me," Ash said. "You know more history than I— more than most normal people—do. But when it comes to Horus, I know everything there is to know. There are ancient Egyptian artifacts that were discovered by the Knights Templar when they were exploring the ruins of the Temple of Solomon. I've studied those artifacts. I *know* this cross."

M felt a buzz of excitement. "Are there any connections between the knights and money? Obviously there are a lot of connections with temples and churches."

"Actually, yes. You may not know this, but the Knights Templar were the first bankers. They—"

"Of course!" M exclaimed, shaking her head. "I need another latte. My brain isn't fully functional." The flight attendant disappeared into the galley. "They had all that money from looting—"

"You're forgetting gifts from the faithful," Ash interrupted.

M waved him off. "They had tons of land, too, and eventually they had banks all over the world."

"With excellent security, because they had members of the knights to guard them. Even royalty used the Templar banks," Ash said.

"So we're looking for a bank with a connection to the Knights Templar in London. And somehow there is a connection to Henry and the number two—probably Henry II, don't you think?"

Ash nodded. "Google it up."

M quickly typed in all the keywords. "Henry gave a pension to his daughter that was payable at the Templar bank." She read a little more. "But it was in France."

"Try that one." Ash pointed to a link and M clicked. "Wrong Henry," she said. "This is about Henry III. He paid the Templars in London eight pounds a year to have some masses said. Which was a lot of money then. I think he made a bad deal there."

She chewed on her lip, thinking. "It's a glyph for *money*. That doesn't have to mean bank. The Templars ran banks, but maybe it's about some other financial situation they were in. Didn't they take a vow of poverty?"

"Yes," Ash said.

She shot him a smile. "I guess your order didn't think that was necessary, huh?"

"The Eye has been in existence for thousands of years, and must be for thousands more. Forever, really. We must be able to afford it," he told her.

The flight attendant plunked down another latte. "I'm going to search connections between the knights and Henry II," M decided, taking a grateful sip. "You keep looking for banks."

By the time she took her last swallow, she'd found a fairly good lead. "It's not exactly money, but Henry II gave the Templars land."

"Land is money," Ash said. "Real estate is how the Eye makes most of our money."

"Okay, then. The Knights Templar used that land to build a church on the River Fleet."

It didn't take long from there. The church on the river later moved and became the Temple Church, headquarters of the Templars in London. Henry II was at the consecration and said he wanted to be buried there, though he later changed his mind.

"So we're off to the Temple Church, then?" Ash said. "Good. We should get some sleep."

M stood and stretched. "Sleep. Yes."

Ash started for the back of the plane. There was a bedroom there with a queen-sized bed. M hesitated. They'd mostly slept in the same bed lately, when they had a chance to rest, but something about it felt different now.

She dropped back down on the long sofa, stretched out, and gave an exaggerated yawn. "You go. I'm too tired to move. I'm going to sleep right here."

Ash gazed down at her, catching her eyes for a long moment, then turned away. "Okay, cheers. Goodnight—or whatever time of day it is now."

M exhaled.

She stared at one of the effigies in the silent circular nave of the Temple Church. The sightless eyes of the stone knight stared back. M had always wished irises and pupils had been carved on this type of effigy. It was supposed to look like the man was sleeping, but to her it always looked like the eyes were open and blind. Mike said she had no imagination, but then, Mike loved everything about the history of the Catholic Church.

M pulled herself over the iron railing and knelt next to the figure. She ran her hands firmly over the cool stone, hoping to find some kind of trigger that would slide the top off the tomb or allow the knight's shield to be raised, anything that might reveal a hiding place for a piece of the Set animal.

If only the piece would behave like the ones before, rushing to join the others. It might destroy a priceless holy artifact, but it would be easy. But as soon as she'd stepped into the church—Ash had picked the lock—the pieces in her backpack had fallen apart again. They weren't attracting each other, so it was doubtful they'd be attracting another piece.

After she'd gone over the effigy a second time, she moved on to another of the stone knights. This one was a little different, its palms pressed together in prayer. She was just as careful as she slid her hands over the ridges of the carved chain mail, the lines of the tunic, the hands, the lips, even the creepy sightless eyes, but she didn't find a way to open or activate the effigy.

"Can you ask Horus for another bird helper?" she called to Ash, her voice echoing in the empty church. He was examining a knight nearby. They'd been at the church for hours before moving on to the knights and had found nothing. And before, when it was light out, they'd walked the grounds, taking in the outside of the building from all angles.

"You said the bird was just a bird," Ash reminded her.

"And you said it was a divine messenger of Horus sent to aid us in our sacred quest," M shot back sarcastically.

"Now, I know I didn't say it like that," Ash replied. "But prayer isn't a bad idea." He lowered his head, still as one of the knights. It felt wrong to watch him, but she couldn't stop herself. She didn't find praying strange. But Ash was praying to a god M had read about in mythology books, as if he truly expected to receive help.

What about the bird, though? It could have been help. But

it could have a completely logical explanation as well. And the mistletoe could be coincidence. And maybe, just maybe, there was a rational explanation for the way the Set pieces melded and fell apart. Although it was hard to believe science could explain the force of the piece slamming inside Bob's briefcase.

But there was no ordinary explanation for what Ash had done to the crocodiles. It was beyond her understanding. Maybe it was psychic ability. Or, she had to admit, maybe it was the power of Horus.

M quickly glanced away as Ash lifted his head. She moved on to the next knight. After more than an hour, she finished her side of the room. She stood and stretched. Where to search next? Ash had moved on to one of the columns, so she decided to check the gargoyles that ringed the inside of the round nave.

These gargoyles were much easier to see than ones usually found in buildings because they were lower to the ground, only about fifteen feet up. There were so many of them—some cheerful and laughing, some shocked, others horrified. One grimaced in pain as a monkey bit his ear; another pulled his own lips wide like a kid trying to gross out a friend; another crossed his eyes—whether the act was a joke or an affliction, M wasn't sure.

By the time she'd circled the room, her eyes were burning from staring at the stone faces so intently. She rubbed at them, stars clouding her vision. On her way to join Ash, she passed under the vaulted arches, to the font. She meticulously examined the carvings on the limestone base. Two panels showed a knight slaying a dragon, the next some kind of large cat, and the last an eagle.

Dragon slaying wasn't a typical subject for a carving on a baptismal font, but it didn't seem to have anything to do with Horus. Same with the cat. But eagles were a standard font carving. There was an old story about an eagle that singed its wings on the sun, then dipped them three times into a fountain of pure water, returning to its youth. It could be considered a reference to Horus's father, Osiris, who was a resurrection god. She studied every feather, but found nothing.

"Anything?" she asked Ash. The quiet was getting to her, and she wanted to hear a voice, even if it was her own.

Ash turned toward her, resting one hand on the column he'd been investigating. "No. But it's a big church."

M frowned. "That's the problem. This place is huge." She pulled a couple of bottles of water out of her backpack and tossed one to him.

"Pieces still apart?" Ash asked.

"Yeah." They'd split apart as soon as M entered the church—she'd learned to recognize the feeling, a snap instead of the usual slow throbbing. M opened her water and took a swig. "Onward."

"Onward," he repeated, shooting her a tired smile.

M felt a rush of gratitude that he was with her. Doing this alone would be hard. But it wasn't just the backup Ash provided. It was the feeling that they were a team, in this together. She knew she needed to keep on her guard with him, be wary, but a part of her didn't really believe that anymore.

They searched until the reds, yellows, and blues in the stained-glass windows began to glow. It was dawn. "Maybe something is hidden in one of the windows," Ash suggested.

"The originals didn't survive the air raid," M reminded him. Some of the church had been damaged during World War II. They couldn't be sure everything they were searching was even around when the Set piece was hidden.

"You checked all the niches behind the altar?" Ash asked.

M nodded. "Those are definitely from the medieval part of the church. The piscina, too."

"Piscina?"

"Where they washed the chalice, and where the priest washed his hands before sanctifying the communion offerings."

"Oh."

M watched him, a new thought taking shape in her mind. "Do Horus worshippers have communion? Not communion, obviously, but rituals like that? Or is the Eye about protecting the pieces of Set and nothing else?"

He hesitated.

"Sorry, is that knowledge for worshippers only?" she asked.

"No, I'm just not used to people asking about my religion," Ash said. "We have a few rituals, I suppose. The main one is every year we celebrate the resurrection of Osiris by eating bread baked into his shape."

"I've seen tomb paintings in Egypt with Osiris's body sprouting grain and his spirit floating above it. There are a ton of paintings depicting bread left as offerings in tombs," M said. "It's funny, isn't it? How bread shows up in so many different religions. When we were in Kerala, in the temple, there were offerings of food. Do you know what 'prasada' is?"

"Horus and recreational drugs. That's it for me, remember?"

"Well, you said there were a few *other* things you knew about. I thought prasada might be one of those," M joked. "It's when food is prepared as an offering for Krishna, then it has a spiritual quality when you eat it. It isn't just food." M pushed a stray strand of hair away from her face. "Coming here, to that temple, the sibyl's cave, and Philae so close together . . . I don't know, it feels like maybe they're all the same. Not the same, exactly, but good in similar ways. In intent, maybe." She shook her head. "I don't know what I'm saying. I'm sleep deprived."

"I know what you're saying. You went from the piscina to communion to foods that are holy," Ash told her. "When I was young, I read the *Chronicles of Narnia*. I'm embarrassed to admit, I had no idea it was Christian allegory. I just liked books with magic in them. They made me feel less like the aberrant little freak I thought I was."

"You really felt that way?" M asked.

"Hear it enough times, and you believe it," he replied, not quite meeting her eye. "In one of the books, the last one I think, Aslan, the Christ-figure, tells a character that a good deed done in the name of the evil god is actually devotion to Aslan. And vice-versa. Basically, it was the intent that mattered, not the god."

She smiled. It was so weirdly normal to hear him talking about books. "I guess that's what I was trying to say. But is that sacrilegious to you?"

"We don't talk much about other religions. Philip barely acknowledged their existence." Ash shrugged. "Ask me whatever you want," he added. "We don't try to convert people, which is obvious, since most people don't even know there is present-day Horus worship. But I can say that I've never felt anything like the power Horus gives me."

If she had the power to stop a crocodile attack, she'd probably feel that way too. "It's getting late." She gestured to the windows. The colors were brighter now. "We don't know when someone will be coming. There could be an early service."

"I think we've covered this floor as well as we can," Ash said. "There are stairs behind the door over by the organ. Let's check it out." He led the way over, opening the door for her. M stepped through and began to climb up the narrow circular staircase. The first thing she noticed was a depression carved into one of the thick walls. Holes had been punched all the way through in two places.

"This has to be the solitary confinement cell we read about," Ash said, joining her.

"It's so small. I know people used to be smaller, but still." M squeezed into the cell. "I can see the altar from this side."

"So the monk being punished could hear the service," Ash said. "A few days with you and I'm learning all kinds of new things."

"Same with you. Like how to dance in the sewer." He cracked a grin as she scrambled back to the floor. Together they studied the cell from the outside. There were no cracks, no seams, nothing that looked out of place.

"I don't see anything up here," Ash said. "We're sure this is where the signpost led, right?"

"As sure as I can be." M turned in a slow circle, searching hopelessly. "But we've looked everywhere and there's just no piece here," she admitted. "It's a dead end."

CHAPTER 16

M sat on a bench beside the church, leaning against the wall. The pieces of the Set animal dug into her back, so she took off her backpack and cradled it in her arms. She must have dozed off for a few minutes, because she jerked awake as Ash dropped down onto the bench beside her.

"Provisions, as promised, from the best street cart in the city." He opened the brown paper bag he held, pulled out something wrapped in greasy paper, and sniffed it appreciatively. "Ah, sausage roll, I've missed you."

A guilty expression flashed across his face. Was he one of these people who never ate junk? She took her own sausage roll out of the bag. It smelled amazing. She took a big bite and chewed happily.

"Somehow food tastes better outdoors," she remarked. Ash hadn't started in on his breakfast yet. "What's the problem?"

"No problem." He took a bite, but his enthusiasm seemed to have drained away.

"Not enough ketchup?" she asked, though she knew it likely wasn't anything quite that simple.

"No it's fine." He took another bite, a bigger one.

"What happened to the guy who was practically writing an Ode to the Sausage Roll ten seconds ago?" M asked.

Ash glanced at her, and she raised an eyebrow.

"You're not going to stop, are you?"

"Do I ever?"

"Fine," he said. "Part of my duty as a devotee of Horus is to control my appetites."

"You mean like fasting?"

"Sometimes I fast," Ash agreed. "But it's more than that. I need to keep my—" He seemed to be searching for the right word, then started again. "Physical pleasures can pull me away from my connection to Horus."

"You're talking asceticism," M said. "Does Horus think pleasure is wrong?"

"It's not that. It's about self-discipline," Ash explained. "It's about clearing the way for Horus to enter. It's part of my . . . gift. Part of accepting it."

"Is body mortification part of it?" she asked without thinking, remembering the scars on his back. She'd met monks who would sleep on a bed of nails as religious duty.

"Not as much anymore," Ash replied easily. "In my training, yes, sometimes. It helped me control my power—Horus's power," he corrected himself. "It helped me see that the power should be Horus acting through me. I had to be open to understanding his intentions."

"Those scars on your back helped you understand Horus's intentions?" M couldn't keep the sharpness out of her voice. She'd always had a hard time with gods who wanted their followers to be in pain. Was that really what Horus required? Or was that Philip's interpretation?

"No, those are— They were from before I joined the Eye." Ash took another bite.

So his parents, then. M put down the sausage roll, suddenly not hungry. They'd had a little fresh air, eaten, it was time to get back to work. "I'm not sure what to do about our missing piece. We've searched everywhere."

Ash seemed relieved at the subject change. "There was the bombing. But the pieces of the artifact are indestructible. So it couldn't have been destroyed."

He was right. It was time to stop explaining things away with rational thought. The Set pieces were *magic*. Ash was magic, or had magic, anyway. Hiding the pieces from him in her backpack was silly. He could take them whenever he wanted. Her bo staff was nothing against the power he could channel. Although now that they were kind of friends, she had a feeling he would think it was rude to just grab the pieces. And he was far too British to do something rude.

"I suppose the bombing might have destroyed the hiding place, though," Ash went on. "In that case, somebody could have found it."

"And currently has it on their mantel," she agreed. "Or is using it as a doorstop."

"It may have ended up in a museum or a private collection," Ash suggested.

"Way to be an optimist. In any case, how are we supposed to track it down?"

"We'll come up with something," he said.

M felt itchy—they'd been here for too long. Every wasted second could mean Dad's life. She only had a week, that's what Liza had said. She stood up, bouncing on her toes. "We're wasting time. I'll ask Mike to track down any artifacts found in this church, or any known fragments of a Set animal. If it was sold or ended up in a collection, there will be some kind of trail."

Ash looked skeptical. "Your boyfriend's a multitalented kid. Is there anything he can't do?"

M's lips twitched at the annoyance in his voice. He really was jealous. "Honestly? Mike can do pretty much anything," she answered, just to goad him. "We should move on to the next location and try to find that piece. Well, signpost, anyway."

"And where is that?" he asked.

"Indonesia. What's the fastest way to Heathrow? Tube?" M slung on her backpack.

"This time of day it's quicker to take a cab," he answered. "Come on." He ate the rest of his sausage roll in a few bites. He was fueling up, nothing more. No pleasure in the food. It made her feel sad for him.

As they stepped out of the churchyard, M felt movement in her pack. "The pieces are back together. Again." She frowned. "They separated when we went onto the temple grounds in India, and separated when we got here, to the church. But as soon as we stepped off the grounds, they fused back together. In both places." She flashed back to Kerala. "And as soon as Bob got through the gopura, his piece went crazy trying to burst its way out of the briefcase. The very second he stepped off temple grounds."

"Trying to get to our pieces," Ash said. "Trying to fuse with them. Our two were back together then, yes? So they must have had more pull than his one. That's why his was trying to get out of his bag, instead of ours trying to get in."

"Whatever the pull is, it was deactivated on the church and temple grounds and switched back on as soon as we left them," M said. "In Philae, once we freed the piece from the stone, it responded to the pull of our piece on the boat."

"Sacred places." Ash looked at M, eyes wide. "They were all sacred places—the Temple Church, the Thrissivaperoor Vadakkunnathan Temple, Philae."

"And we found the first piece in the ruins of St. Stephen's Cathedral. The Set pieces have all been hidden on sacred ground." Excitement coursed through M like electricity, energizing her. "There's no way that's a coincidence."

"But they're not sacred to Horus," Ash said. "Philae was, of course. But the others . . . none of these gods were even known when Horus and Set ruled in Egypt."

M shrugged. "The pieces have been moved many times through the years, you said. And the places on the map, the old hiding spots, those were sacred too. The sibyl cave and an oak sacred to Thor!"

"In Indonesia, where are we going?" he asked.

"The Borobudur Temple." She grinned. "A sacred place."

"The members of the Eye must have known sacred ground neutralized the pieces. It's what keeps Set from taking form." Ash shook his head. "More lost knowledge."

"Well, it wasn't lost when they moved the pieces a thousand years ago," M pointed out. "When they couldn't find places sacred to Horus anymore, they improvised."

"And I can do that too," he said, relief flooding his voice. "I can prevent the pieces from fusing together just by going to a holy place."

"Black cab." M pointed to the car coming toward them. The "taxi" light was on.

Ash stuck out his hand to hail it. When they were inside, he turned to her. "M, Borobudur is one of the places your father sent"—he glanced at the driver—"people. If we're right about why they found us in India, it means they're going to be there. Waiting."

"Too bad the hotel closest to the temple is such a dive," M said sarcastically. She slid off her backpack and flopped down on the cushy bed near the window, then looked over at him. "The chilled towel and complimentary beverage on arrival didn't offend Horus, did it?"

"It's not about offending Horus. It's about making myself an empty vessel that the power of Horus can pass through,"

Ash explained. Again. "Worldly pleasures can become a distraction, that's all." He lay back on the other bed—he had been relieved they had a room with two available—and stared up at the dark wood ceiling fan slowly turning overhead. It was safer than looking at M. She was becoming a fairly big distraction in her own right. He focused his attention on the fan, letting the circling settle him.

"Sorry," M said. "I shouldn't tease you. It's the obnoxious American in me."

"Yeah, it is," Ash joked, eyes on the fan. "You only do it because you know it doesn't actually bother me."

"You've discovered my secret," she agreed. "I don't mock people unless they can take it." He heard her stand and slide back the sheer curtains. "We have an amazing view of the rice fields. So green, the greenest green."

He used the toes of one foot to push off the shoe on the other, then switched feet. Next he used his feet to slide off his socks.

"You do know what separates us from other beasts is opposable thumbs, right?" M asked. A second later a pillow bounced off his chest. "And don't fall asleep. We have work to do."

"We haven't even been here five minutes," he grumbled. But he knew she was worried. She was doing a good job pretending to be okay after what his mother said. But she wasn't. She wouldn't be all right until she knew her father was safe.

And that was never going to happen.

He sat up.

M was rummaging through the drawers of the desk. She pulled out a thick binder of information for hotel guests. "I know it's the temple, but there were other glyphs too. Dad thought they marked a specific spot inside, a place for rituals. He got taken before we could figure it out."

"The hiding spot," he guessed.

She nodded. "We need to figure out those glyphs, so we need to know as much about the temple as possible."

She brought the binder over to Ash and climbed on to the bed next to him, her knee resting on his. "I'm sure there's a ton of stuff in here. The glyphs we're trying to figure out are *sun, road, speak,* and *god.*"

M had worked on the translation on the plane, consulting her father's notes, the annoyingly ever-present Mike, and the jottings she'd made over the last year. As far as he could tell, she'd spent most of her time while living with his parents translating the map. He got the feeling she hadn't had much time left over for a social life. He also got the feeling she didn't care. She wasn't exactly the type of girl who wanted to spend her time making small talk at keggers.

What had it been like for her, living with them? It seemed as if they had made an effort to create some kind of normal life for her. It had only been a pretense, making a home for M was just their way of guarding her, a vital asset for the cult of Set. But he resented that they were able to give a stranger even sham affection and caring, when they'd never bothered to do it for him.

The old scars on his back started to itch, the way they often did when he thought of his childhood in England. His parents had tried to beat the power of Horus out of him, exorcise it. When it hadn't worked, the beatings had only gotten more severe. As far as they were concerned, that he had been chosen by Horus was a sign of his poisoned soul.

"Are you listening?" M demanded, grabbing his face and bringing it close to hers.

"What? Yes! Of course." He fidgeted. She was way too close.

"Ash, any of this could be important. You never know which bit will lead you to an understanding of a glyph," she said, releasing him. She resumed reading him highlights about the temple. "It was buried for centuries under volcanic ash. Only local people knew about it."

"If it had stayed buried, the Set piece probably would never have been found," Ash said. "It would have been better that way."

"Well, one of your countrymen is to blame. The British ruler of Java heard people talking about an ancient monument and investigated." M snorted. "And after he had workers dig it out, the Dutch colonial government gave eight containers of statues from Borobudur to King Chulalongkorn of Siam. That was in 1896. I guess when the investigation started, the Brits were in charge, but by the time everything was dug up, it had gone back to the Dutch."

"Let's just hope our signpost wasn't in those eight containers," Ash said.

"Seriously. But this says it's all still in the National Museum of Bangkok. We could do a little B and E, right?" M asked.

"Prison time in Bangkok is not on my bucket list," he replied. "But if it comes to that, we'll figure it out. The museum part, not the prison part," he added. "Go on."

"It's not a completely Buddhist temple," M read. "It was planned by Hindus as a Shiva temple in around 775 C.E. They completed the first two terraces, then Buddhists finished it."

She paused. "*Sun, road, speak, god.* That's what we're trying to get to. The *god* part won't be much help in giving us an exact location. Not with a thousand images of Buddha. Nothing so far has made me think of the other glyphs."

She stood, walked to the window, stared out for a few seconds, and then sat in the desk chair briefly before returning to her place next to him on the bed. He'd seen her like this before, so filled with nerves and the need to *do* something that she could hardly stay still.

"Let's go down to the dining room," he suggested. He

knew it wouldn't help. M wouldn't feel settled until she got her father back. It was different for him. They had two pieces of the Set animal. The pieces weren't completely safe, but knowing the cult of Set didn't have them allowed him to relax in a way M couldn't—especially now that he knew how to keep them from sealing together permanently.

"We don't have time," M protested. "You said the Set people would be here. What if they find the signpost before we even figure out where to look?"

"They don't know they're looking for a signpost," Ash reminded her.

"But if they see hieroglyphics in a Buddhist temple, they're going to know they have something to do with the piece," M argued. "Although not all the signposts have been in hieroglyphics. But the ones here could be." She jumped up again and began pacing.

"The signposts have been so well hidden in the other locations that I didn't even know you were finding them," he said. He picked up the binder. "And they aren't just going to stumble on them. The temple is huge. This says it's made of nine stacked platforms, plus the central dome." He grabbed her hands to still her.

"It's going to take forever to search. Liza said my dad has a week. Less now," M said quietly, curling her fingers in his.

"We'll figure it out. I promise. We'll just eat while we figure it out," Ash assured her. "There's supposed to be a view of the temple in the dining room. Plus, I'm sure everyone who works here knows all about the place. It's basically why the hotel exists. We'll ask our waiter to give us a rundown."

M nodded. "Okay." She glanced down at herself. "I don't even want to think about how many days I've been wearing these jeans. I'm going to change." He released her, and she disappeared into the bathroom with the bag with the clothes she'd bought at Cotton On during the layover in the Singapore airport.

Ash had bought some clothes too, and quickly switched his old khakis for new ones and his T-shirt for a button-down. He heard the shower run for about forty-five seconds—clearly even in the shower she couldn't stand still.

About two minutes later she reappeared. On the hanger the dress she'd bought looked like a long gray T-shirt, but on her it was perfect. Beautiful. "You look nice," he said.

"You too. Of course, you'd have looked more than nice if you'd gone for the pants I picked out," she teased, grabbing her backpack and heading for the door. The idea of talking to the locals had calmed her down a little, thankfully.

"I'd have looked like a bloody moron," he muttered, following her. M had tried to convince him buy one of the truly astounding selection of slim-cut pants with elasticized cuffs about four inches wide.

They were on the early side for dinner, so easily got a table overlooking the temple. It seemed more like a fortress than a place of worship.

"It looks spiky. Like it's designed to keep you away," M commented, echoing Ash's thoughts. They both stared out at the gray stone structure in silence until the waiter appeared.

M waited until he'd handed them menus before jumping right in: "What can you tell us about the temple?"

The waiter smiled. "It is the largest Buddhist monument in the world, constructed with over two million stone blocks. It is estimated construction began in the Sailendra dynasty, around A.D. 750, taking roughly seventy-five years to complete."

Ash knew the man must have answered the question hundreds of times, but his tone remained pleasant. "The temple was almost lost to us. It was covered in volcanic ash during—"

M interrupted, speaking what Ash could only guess was Indonesian. He blinked in surprise. How many languages did she speak? He wondered if she had any idea how truly exceptional she was.

The waiter's face became more animated as he started to answer. M held up a hand and said something in an apologetic tone, and when the man began to speak again, it was in English.

"Your friend tells me you intend to make a pilgrimage to the Candi Temple," the waiter said.

"I explained we were interested in the spiritual aspect of the temple, more than the historical," M explained.

She was trying to find out the most sacred place, assuming the artifact would be hidden there for safekeeping. Ash was still trying to wrap his head around the idea that areas dedicated to Buddha, Christ, Shiva, and Thor could all have power over an artifact that contained an Egyptian god.

But now wasn't the time. When he had recovered all the pieces and returned them to the Eye, he could discuss these questions with Philip. If Philip ever forgave him, that was. He focused in on what the waiter was saying. He knew no detail would escape M's notice. Her father had been the same way, asking Ash about small things he'd said weeks before, remembering that Ash had used his left hand to write on one occasion even though he usually used his right.

"As pilgrims to Candi Borobudur, you need to understand that the monument itself, the way it is constructed, is part of the teaching," the waiter explained. "It forms a mandala. As you walk through it, you are symbolically following the path from samsara to nirvana. It is important you walk clockwise. The carved reliefs of the life and teachings of the Buddha will guide you toward enlightenment. At the top, you'll see the central stupa. It is empty, a symbol of the enlightened mind."

Ash noticed a couple being seated several tables away. The waiter turned to leave. "I'll be right back to take your order. I'm happy to answer more questions as well."

"Thank you," Ash and M said together.

"I think we found our road," M commented when he was out of earshot. "The path you walk through the temple."

"What is 'samsara'? Nirvana is total happiness, right?" Ash asked.

"Pretty much. It comes from a root word that means 'to blow out,'" M began.

Ash laughed.

"What?"

"Nothing," he said. "It's just that you know far too much for a schoolgirl."

"Tell me about it. I was counting the days until I could get out," she replied. "So nirvana—it's when you blow out greed and hate and delusion. You don't have any more personal desires, and you break free from the cycle of samsara. That's the cycle of birth, mundane existence, death, and rebirth."

"Okay, so besides the spiritual, we have an actual road we can walk with actual feet. The waiter—"

"Sarip," M told him.

"Sarip. Sarip told us we have to walk clockwise. So in a circle. Could the glyph for sun have to do with that?" Ash said. "Like following the path of the sun?" He pulled out his cell to Google it, ignoring the five new texts he'd received from Philip. He was sure they all said variations on the same thing—"Get back here with the pieces of Set and the girl."

There was no point in reading them. He knew M, and Philip didn't. That made Ash the expert. And if Philip thought he could force M into translating the glyphs of the last signpost if Ash brought her to the Eye, he was very, very wrong. It was clear to him that M could stand up to anything, any torture, if it meant she could save her father. He wasn't sure it was possible, though. The Eye was powerful, but so was the cult of Set.

Ash's stomach twisted. This hunt for the Set pieces required so much focus and energy that he usually managed to keep himself from thinking about what would happen when they had all the pieces in their possession. Would he be able to convince Philip and the rest of the Eye to rescue M's father? Would they be too furious to even try?

"Find anything?" M asked.

Ash jerked his head up. "What?"

"I thought you were looking up a possible connection to the sun," she said.

"I was. I am." He did a quick search for "Borobudur," "sun," and "path." "Walking the path is about moving from darkness into light," he read, before skimming ahead. "And listen to this—the movement around the central stupa, which represents the cosmic center, mirrors the path of the sun. When you come out of the dark galleries of the temple and into the open air of the upper walkways, you literally come into the light."

"Enlightenment," M murmured. "Of course! 'Clockwise' is an adaptation of a Sanskrit translation that meant 'sunwise.' I should have thought of that as soon as Sarip told us which way to walk. So we've got *sun,* and *road.* We still need *god,* and *speak.*"

"And a plan to escape the Set acolytes who will be waiting for us," he put in.

"Well, you'll be able to use your power, right?" she asked.

"Right," Ash said, forcing himself to sound casual. He didn't want to use any power. If he called on the power of Horus, every priest in the Eye would feel it. And Philip would come for M and the pieces. Ash sighed. It was getting harder and harder to keep lying.

Sarip returned to the table. "Did you decide what you'd like?"

"We haven't even touched the menus," M admitted. She smiled at Ash. "Trust me?"

He nodded, and she turned to Sarip. "Do you have kerak telor?"

"Yes, miss," he replied.

"Then that's what we'll have. And an answer to another question, if you don't mind."

"Not at all," Sarip said.

"Is there one Buddha in the temple that's special?" she asked.

"Besides the friezes, there are ninety-two statues of Buddha in small stupas all around the central one. Unfortunately, many are damaged—looters took many of the heads in the last twenty or thirty years. They go to the collections of the wealthy." He paused, thinking. "Each of the Buddhas has one of five different mudras, hand gestures . . ." His words trailed off and he gave a slight frown. "I'm not sure what you mean by special."

"I'm not sure either," M said, smiling. "Just one that has a story to it, or one that stands out from the others somehow."

Sarip shook his head.

"The hand gestures, what significance do they have?" Ash asked.

"There are mudras for blessing, meditation, calling the earth to witness, fearlessness, and teaching," Sarip replied. He glanced at the other tables in the dining room, which were beginning to fill. "Excuse me, I must see to the other visitors. I will return with your kerak telor." He winked. "It is my favorite too."

"Blessing, calling to witness, and teaching could all connect to the *speech* glyph, I guess," M said, but she didn't sound hopeful.

Ninety-two statues divided by five hand positions. That was a little over eighteen Buddhas per mudra. And there were three mudras that could connect to the *speech* glyph, so fifty-five possible Buddhas to check.

"Speech, god, speech, god, speech, god," M mumbled, brow furrowed. "Speech, god, speech, god, speech—"

"What's your favorite band?" Ash interrupted her.

"What? Why?"

"Sometimes when you're not trying to think of an answer, that's when it suddenly pops into your head. I'm trying to get you to not think of the answer," Ash explained.

"All right. Twenty-one Pilots," she said. "You?"

Ash hadn't listened to music in years, not since he left Paris. He heard it when he was out, whatever was playing in taxis or shops. But he didn't go to concerts or download music. It was one of a long list of distractions Philip believed would make Ash a less pure vessel for Horus.

"Daft Punk," he answered. They'd been his favorite back then.

M laughed. "Really? That doesn't seem like you."

"I'm full of surprises," he said.

"My turn. Favorite movie?" M asked.

Why had he even started this conversation? He tried to think of movies he'd heard people talk about. It wasn't as if he lived in a cave. "Uh, *Me Before You*," he tossed out. He'd heard some girl on the bus call it "the most intense thing she'd ever seen."

M laughed so hard that she snorted. "If that weepy chick flick is really your favorite I'm going to have to move to another table."

Ash held up his hands in surrender. "Okay, I haven't seen it," he admitted. "I never go to the movies anymore. But I flipped for *The Hangover* back when I was a fourteen-year-old hooligan." He left it at that.

"TV?" she asked.

He shook his head.

M's eyes grew serious as she studied him. "It's like the sausage roll, right? Nothing to distract you from Horus?"

"Yes," he admitted. "But you have to understand, it's what I want. It's what gives my life meaning, my devotion. Do I wish it didn't require so many sacrifices? Sometimes. But movies or music or food are nothing compared to the feeling of the god letting his power flow through me."

"What about sex?" M asked.

Ash coughed, feeling his cheeks grow hot. At least with his dark skin, she wouldn't be able to tell. "Same thing."

"But still worth it?"

Ash nodded, although there'd been times he had trouble keeping his eyes off M, something he'd mastered with other women.

"Speech, god, speech, god, speech," M murmured again. Ash was glad she let it go. He looked down at his phone—a voicemail from Philip—and found another article to read about the temple.

When Sarip came back with the food, Ash asked, "Is there a place around here to buy or rent climbing equipment?"

"Ah, you're planning a visit to Siung Beach! There are more than two hundred climbing routes. You can rent equipment here at the hotel and you can also arrange for a guide," Sarip said. "Is there anything else I can get you?"

"Not right now, thank you. You've been very helpful," M told him. "Climbing equipment?" she asked after he left.

"Going straight down the outside of the temple may be our fastest escape route," Ash said. "I want to be prepared for anything. We don't know how many people to expect—not after what happened in Kerala. And I can only use so much power before I pass out."

"I'm all for preparation," M said. She took a bite of her food and rolled her eyes with pleasure. "Perfect. Try to enjoy it. Just this once. I'm not saying abandon . . . everything. But kerak telor on Java. You might never have the opportunity again."

They locked eyes, and for a brief, crazy moment he wondered what other opportunities the two of them might never have again. He forced himself to look away and took a bite of his food. He let himself savor the blend of egg, shredded coconut, and dried shrimp, all flavored with a hint of the charcoal they'd been cooked over. Just this once he would allow himself to take pleasure in eating. How big a transgression could that really be?

An hour and a half later, they returned to the hotel room with their rented climbing equipment. They had decided to begin walking the path through the temple at dawn. It wouldn't be open to the public yet, and M hoped the rising sun would show them something they were supposed to see, something that would clarify the meaning of the last glyphs.

"I'm going to take a shower," he said as she set the alarm. He headed into the bathroom, stripped, and turned on the cold water. He needed discomfort in his body to return his mind and soul to Horus. He stayed under the stream until his fingers were wrinkled and his skin had gone to gooseflesh.

He was careful to be quiet when he returned and slid into the bed across from M's, but she was still awake. "We're halfway there," she said. "We have two. We need two. Two pieces until I can save my father." He heard her roll over and he could feel her staring at him through the darkness. "You have it all arranged, right? The Eye knows they have to rescue my father before they get the pieces."

"Right." Ash's stomach twisted. He flipped onto his back and closed his eyes, letting his breathing go slow and deep.

If she said anything else, he wouldn't answer. He'd just pretend he'd fallen asleep.

He didn't want to reassure her again. He didn't want to lie to her again. He wanted to keep going the way they had been, getting along, having fun, building trust.

Until he had to betray her.

CHAPTER 17

The sun wasn't up yet when they started out the next morning, but the sky had lightened to a pale gray. A low mist hovered above the ground, and the darker gray of the squared-off pyramid shape of the temple loomed in the distance. M couldn't shake her impression that it looked ominous, even though it had been built to teach visitors the path to enlightenment. Maybe she just felt that way because she knew worshippers of the dark god Set would be waiting.

If she was captured, would they take her to the same place as Dad? It would almost be worth it if— No. She was desperate to see him, but being taken prisoner would make everything worse. She needed the Set pieces. They were the only way she'd have the leverage to save them both.

Just two pieces to go, she thought as they walked across the manicured lawn. The grass was wet with dew, and her sneakers and the hem of her jeans quickly grew damp. There was something about the day's early stillness that made her want to stay quiet. Ash must have felt the same way. In silence, they left the hotel grounds and started on the path to the temple, the only sounds their soft footfalls, the chatter of the birds that populated the rainforest, and the click-clack of palm fronds in the wind.

The canopy wasn't thick. Many of the trees were slender and uncrowded, so plenty of sky showed through. Several looked as if they were standing on tiptoe, balanced high on a network of roots that seemed like they should be underground.

"It's like they're holding up their skirts because they've seen a mouse," M said softly, nodding toward one.

Ash chuckled. "More likely a snake out here," he commented, keeping his voice low.

They fell back into silence, until M spotted several yellow-orange fruits in one tree. She darted over and pulled down two of them. "I can't remember what they're called, but they taste almost like mangos." She bit into one. Sweet. Sometimes they could be a little sour, but this one was perfection.

She held the other out to Ash. "Breakfast," she said, encouraging him to eat it. That wasn't trying to corrupt him, was it? To make him taste pleasure, whether Horus approved or not? Or was it Philip who wouldn't approve?

Ash's life with the Eye sounded lonely and sterile to her—it was hard to understand why he loved them so much. Still, if she'd had a childhood like his, maybe she'd have ended up feeling equally devoted—Philip must have seemed like the complete opposite of Ash's abusive father. Did he really care about Ash, though? Or did he just care about what Ash could do?

"It smells like turpentine," Ash said.

"Doesn't taste like turpentine. Try it." He took a bite, sending a droplet of juice running from the corner of his mouth to his chin. Without thinking, she reached over and wiped away the juice with her thumb. He started, and she suddenly felt self-conscious. "Good?" she asked, pulling her hand away.

"Good," he answered, meeting her eyes briefly. Then he turned and continued down the path. "We timed it about right, I think," he commented as they reached the edge of the trees. The temple was about four hundred feet away. The sky was turning pink at the edge of the horizon and the day dawning hot and humid, even though the sun still wasn't visible.

They both hesitated before stepping from the shelter of the forest. They'd be in clear view the rest of the way. It wasn't dark enough to hide them. But they reached the gate without a problem. Ash did his lock-picking trick, giving the lock a tiny jolt of his power. There didn't seem to be anything he couldn't open.

After they entered, he locked the gate behind them. "No reason to advertise we're here," he explained. "Maybe the Set people slept in."

"Or maybe they'll reach enlightenment while they're here, and they won't want to destroy the world anymore," M joked. But he didn't laugh.

They stepped inside the temple, and M felt her backpack shift. "The pieces came apart again. Just like we thought."

He nodded, the relief in his expression obvious.

They began their first clockwise circuit through the temple. "We were right, it's going to be impossible to search all these carvings." Ash ran his hand lightly over the image of a couple entwined in a passionate embrace—which they were punished for a few carvings later. The theme of this level seemed to be punishment of the wicked.

"All we can do is keep our eyes open for anything that makes us think of one of the glyphs. The *god* one won't be useful, not with the number of Buddhas, but there's still *speech*. Maybe *road* or *sun* has some other meaning we haven't figured out," she said.

They continued their circuits around the temple. "We're

through the part about punishment for stealing and killing and the hardships of basic daily life," M commented.

"Samsara," Ash said. "You can use the big words."

"This one—" She nodded toward a carving of a six-tusked elephant. "I'm pretty sure it's an image of a dream Queen Maya had. Monks told her it meant her son would become a Buddha." They walked a little farther. "And this has to be baby Buddha—Siddartha. The stories say he walked seven steps as soon as he was born, and each place he stepped, a lotus flower bloomed." She touched one of the carved blossoms.

"Are they all stories to you?" Ash asked. "Just stories?"

"I . . ." M hesitated. She'd always thought of myths and legends, even the ones from modern religions, as a way to understand a culture, a people. But then Ash had to go and turn water into gel using magic that came from a god. Her worldview had been upended. "I don't know anymore," she admitted. "So many myths from various cultures have the same elements. I used to think that was a reason not to believe any of them. But maybe it means they're all representations of the truth in different ways. All gods are one god, or something like that. The Set pieces react the same way to all the sacred spaces, no matter which religion the space is dedicated to."

"True." Ash looked troubled. He'd seen some things the past few days that had probably upended *his* view of the world too, M realized. He'd been worshiping Horus since he was a teenager. Now he had to consider that maybe Horus was only one of many gods who deserved worship, or maybe that all the gods of all the sacred places they'd visited were only one god.

M shoved the thought away. Now was not the time to be philosophical. She had a puzzle to solve. What were the glyphs trying to tell her? She took in as many details of each carving as she could without stopping to study any particular one. There wasn't time. The longer they stayed here, the more likely they'd be caught.

They passed scene after scene from Buddha's life as he journeyed toward enlightenment. Once they reached the moment of his enlightenment, they entered a gallery filled with Buddha statues, hundreds of them, with still more images carved on the walls. M froze, overwhelmed. "It would take years to search this place thoroughly."

"Which is why we're not going to try. We're going to keep walking," Ash said. He gave her a gentle push that got her going again, not that she was reluctant. The corridors on the lower levels of the temple had a claustrophobic effect.

When they neared the entrance to an open terrace, they slowed to a creep, then stopped, scanning the area for any sign of the Set followers. Nothing. Maybe they'd been wrong. Maybe the cult of Set wouldn't be here.

Gingerly, M stepped out into the fresh air. She saw how the structure of the temple mirrored the path to enlightenment—coming outside made her feel suddenly free. Tilting her head back, she allowed herself to take in one long, deep breath before she studied her surroundings.

"These are the Buddhas Sarip told us about," Ash said. "The ninety-two with the five different hand positions."

"Ninety-two," M repeated. She wandered over to the nearest stupa. It was shaped like a bell—they all were—the kind with long handles that bell-ringers used. The handle was solid, but the curved part of the bell was latticed. She placed her hands on the cool stones with reverence, briefly thinking about how ancient they were, how long ago the temple was built, eventually leaning forward to look at the Buddha inside. "This is one of the headless ones," she told Ash.

"I guess we could check all the stupas and see how many have heads. That might narrow things down. The speech glyph makes it seem like we're looking for a god with a mouth," Ash suggested.

"The looting was recent, from what Sarip told us," M reminded him. "When the Set pieces were moved and the signpost was left, most of the Buddhas probably had heads."

"Right." Ash jammed his hands in his pockets as he looked around the terrace. "Nice view at least."

The sun had appeared, the mist dissipating. Looking out, M saw green stretching out everywhere, the green rice paddies, the lush green vegetation of the jungle. Smoke drifted from one of the four volcanoes that ringed the temple. "Maybe we should—"

Her mouth snapped shut. All she could do was stare. The sun's position must have shifted minutely, because now the beams of light looked like they were coming straight out of the volcano directly ahead. They hit one of the stupas, bathing it in a golden light so beautiful it was almost hard to look at.

"What?" Ash asked. When she didn't answer, he followed her gaze. "I think we've found our Buddha."

She nodded. "*Sun* meant more than walking clockwise to follow the sun's path. It meant this." M ran, racing toward the stupa. What if there was something they needed to do right now, while the sun blessed the Buddha?

But when she reached it there was nothing obvious.

"*Speak.* That's the last glyph. Maybe there's a sound we need to make." She looked around, hoping to see something, anything, that would be useful. But the stupa was empty except for the Buddha. Ash came up behind her. "Do you think it could be a song? A specific note that resonates?"

"That's not what *speak* would mean to a priest of Horus," Ash said slowly. He moved closer to the stupa, pressing his face against one of the holes in the stone lattice. M could see the muscles in his body tightening, as if he were gathering his strength. Then he spoke, his voice low, but firm and commanding.

The Buddha began to tremble, then with the sound of stone grinding on stone, opened its mouth and began to speak. The voice was inhuman, but M thought the language was Magahi. She'd spent some time in India with Dad and Mike, studying Magahi folk songs.

"I can't translate it!" M cried over the thundering voice of the Buddha.

"Me either!" Ash yelled back.

"Can you tell it to speak in another language?"

"All I can do is command the statue to speak. It's one of the powers of Horus," Ash replied.

M pulled out her cell. "I'll record it. We can get it translated later." But as she held her phone out toward the Buddha, she saw scratches on its stone tongue.

Not scratches. Carvings. Glyphs!

Her heart skipped a beat. *The signpost!*

She took dozens of pictures as the mouth opened and closed. She was still shooting when Ash grabbed her arm, fingers digging into her skin. She jerked her head toward the terrace entrance.

Liza and Bob stood there with a group of people—more Set followers. There had to be at least ten of them. Liza shouted M's name, and the sound sent a sudden fury charging through her, slamming through her heart, searing the blood in her veins. This woman had been her jailer, had made her think her father was dead. She'd threatened to hurt him. M's hand went for her bo staff, the desire to take Liza down, to make her feel the pain M had been feeling all these months almost overwhelming.

But she couldn't fight them all. Ash yanked her toward the edge of the terrace farthest from the entrance. As they ran, he chanted the command to speak again and again, and the Buddhas they passed responded one after another, adding their rumbling voices to the first. The headless Buddhas shook as if the tremendous desire to speak coursed through their entire bodies.

"He's using his foul magic," someone cried behind them. M shot a glance over her shoulder to see that the young Set acolyte who had been in Kerala was leading the group now. "Stop him!"

Ash's steps faltered, as if the man's voice had been a physical blow. *Using so much power is draining him,* M realized. Ash kept repeating the command, but she could feel his fingers trembling on her arm, his grip loosening. It was up to her to get them out of here.

Ash spoke the command again, and although his voice was weak, new Buddhas joined in. The movement off all the stone bodies became so intense the ground began to tremble. A few of the Set devotees screamed. She heard Bob urge them forward.

M wrapped her arm around Ash's waist, taking as much of his weight as she could. When they reached one of the stupas close to the edge, she twisted around and pulled the climbing gear out of his backpack, letting it fall to the shaking stones. Quickly, she looped the rope four times around one of the spokes of the latticework, leaving two long lengths free. It was fast—no carabiners or webbing—and it would hold.

She allowed herself a glance up to check on the Set people. Close. So close. She had the equipment she needed, belay loop, locking biner, everything, but there wasn't time. Years ago Mike had taught her the Dülfersitz rappel, where all you used was a rope. It was a good technique for an emergency.

This was an emergency. She let Ash slump down on the

shaking terrace floor. Struggling to keep her balance, she straddled the two lengths of rope attached to the stupa. She pulled them around her hip, over her left shoulder, then around her neck and down her right arm. She'd use her right hand as a brake.

"Ash, you have to get up." She used her left hand to pull him to his feet and helped him wrap his arms around her. "Don't let go!" she yelled, stepping off the edge of the terrace just as Bob reached for her.

The rope ripped against her hand as she brought them to a stop one level down. She shoved Ash onto the staircase, and scrambled out of the makeshift harness. She hoped the lengths of rope dangling down to the level below might confuse the Set followers about where she and Ash had gone. Quickly, she grabbed Ash and half dragged him into the chamber with the hundreds of Buddhas. She squeezed behind the biggest one she could see, pulling Ash down next to her.

A fine layer of dust rained down from the stone roof, but the shaking had ceased. Maybe Ash was too far from the Buddhas now. "You okay?" she whispered.

He nodded without opening his eyes, but she could feel his body trembling and hear his ragged breath. He'd used everything he had to make the statues speak. There was no way he could make it out of here now, not until he'd rested. Even if he could, there was that stretch of open space between the temple and the jungle. They'd be way too vulnerable.

M shifted and wrapped one arm around his shoulders so he could rest more comfortably against her. All they could do for now was hope Liza and Bob didn't find them.

CHAPTER 18

M's legs cramped from keeping them tightly curled beneath her in the space between the Buddha statue and the wall. Her back ached from being pressed against the stones of the niche behind her for so long. All she could think about was the need to move.

But Ash wasn't ready. He lay slumped against her shoulder still, his breathing uneven and raspy. He'd been wiped out after he'd saved her from the crocodiles, but it had been nothing like this.

Liza, Bob, and the others had run through the room almost as soon as she'd gotten herself and Ash hidden. The rope she'd left dangling must have fooled them into believing she'd climbed down three or four levels, because she heard them hurry past without even bothering to search the area. She'd been afraid they would come back up, but it had been hours with no sign of them.

M wiggled her toes, hoping the small movement would alleviate the almost unbearable urge to scramble to her feet and stretch. Soon the temple would be open and tourists would start to explore. When they did, it would be time to leave, if Ash was able. The people would give them a little protection if the Set acolytes were outside. They wouldn't grab her in front of witnesses—would they?

No point in worrying about it. They couldn't hide here forever. She had to translate the signpost glyphs, which meant getting someplace where her cell—currently trapped in a pocket she couldn't reach—had a signal. M knew the glyphs were Sanskrit, but that was about it. She needed Mike's help.

M's muscles cramped even more. She was going to go nuts if she had to stay still for much longer. She turned her focus to Ash's breathing, which seemed to be getting steadier. If she could will some of her strength into him, she would. That had been some trick, making statues speak. Part of her wondered if she'd dreamed it. She kept thinking she'd adjusted to the fact that there was actual magic or miracles or whatever they should be called in the world. But she hadn't. She wasn't sure if she ever would.

A man's voice broke the silence, coming closer. He was talking about the carvings on the wall. Another voice followed with a question. M relaxed. A guided tour was in progress, so there were other people in the temple now.

Ash gave a little moan as the voices grew louder, accompanied by the sound of footfalls coming toward them on the stone floor. M pressed her fingers lightly to his lips. "Shhh," she whispered into his ear. His eyelids fluttered open. He was looking up at her, but she could see he didn't recognize her.

"It's me, Ash. It's Memphis," she told him. He blinked, but his eyes remained glazed. "Ash, it's M." In that moment she watched him come back to himself, the memory of what had happened on the terrace hitting him. His body tightened, his breath seeming to catch in his chest, as his eyes burned into hers, full of everything he knew about her.

M slowly slid her fingers away from his mouth. The guide pointed out a few of the statues, then ushered his group up the stairs to the terrace where Ash had made the statues talk. He had made the statues *talk*.

"How long?" Ash asked, voice thick, when the gallery was silent again.

"Almost three hours," M said. "I think Bob and Liza assumed we made it out. I thought we could just blend with a group of people leaving."

Ash nodded. He struggled to get to his feet. "Wait," M cautioned. "You just woke up, or came to, I'm not sure which. You were really out of it, Ash. Give yourself a minute. The group will be up on the terrace for a while anyway."

"I'm . . ." He coughed, clearing his throat. "I'm okay."

"At least let me get up first, in case you need help." She twisted around and put one hand on the statue and one on the wall, levering herself to her feet. She wriggled out from behind the Buddha, ignoring the pins and needles stabbing into her legs, then reached one hand down to Ash. She didn't bother pointing out he was unsteady on his feet, and had, in fact, needed the assist.

"Have you ever done that before? Made a statue speak?" she asked, shaking out one leg, then the other.

Ash leaned against the wall. "As part of my training. The Opening of the Mouth is one of the hardest talents, and the one that requires me to be the most open to Horus. I was only able to do it after weeks of purification and prayer. I made a small statue of Isis open its lips. There was a small sound, more of a sigh, and then it was over."

"But what you did up there . . ."

"Maybe my need, *our* need, made it easier for me to allow Horus in. I honestly don't know," Ash said.

M gave him a once-over. He looked better. The grayish tint his skin had taken on was disappearing. "Has using the power ever knocked you out for this long?"

"It's been bad before, but this might have been the worst,"

he admitted. "The more power I have to channel, the more depleted I am after."

"But you're okay?"

"I'm okay."

M was doubtful. She wouldn't mind standing there for a bit, just looking at him and seeing him look at her. That moment when he'd stared right through her had been terrifying, as if he'd vacated his body entirely. But she couldn't gape at him like some whack job, so she raised her arms and stretched. "We need an exit strategy. The Set followers know we were here. Which means if they're smart, they'll be watching the airport in Yogyakarta."

"Where's our next stop?" Ash asked. "Did you read the signpost?"

"No, I haven't even been able to look at the glyphs yet." M gave a helpless shrug. "I have no idea where to go. And I'm going to need serious help on this set."

"So for now we just need to find a place to lay low. Somewhere far from our last known location, which is here." Ash ran his fingers through his dark hair, making it even messier than it already was.

"Voices," M said. "That tour group is coming back. Let's follow them out of the temple, hope nobody's waiting for us, and go from there."

"I wanted to stay longer," a woman complained as she entered the gallery.

"The Buddhas all look alike. What's there to see?" the guy with her asked.

Ash grabbed M's hand and pulled her out of their hiding spot. "I'm with you," he said, falling in step behind the couple. "I have seen enough Buddhas to last me a lifetime."

"See?" the man said, grinning at Ash. "He knows."

The couple continued to bicker as they walked around and around the temple. M and Ash joining in occasionally to make it look like they were a foursome. When they reached the bottom, M was relieved to see a bunch of people milling around. The ticket booth was open, and there was a long line. She was sure everyone waiting to buy a ticket had a cell, if not a huge camera. If Bob and Liza were watching the temple, they couldn't make a move without being caught in a whole bunch of photos.

"I think we're good," Ash said, glancing around.

"Romantics! Harmony, courage!" a man called to them with a giant smile. "Prambanan now, yes? Beautiful. I guide. Harmony!"

Ash shook his head, but M stopped. This could be a good idea. "Prambanan is on the other side of Yogyakarta, isn't it?" she asked in Javanese.

The man's smile widened, something M didn't think possible. "It's not far," he answered, shifting into his native language. "I have a van. You shouldn't miss it. Some think it is even more beautiful than Borobudur. How long will you be here? I also have a speedboat. I can take you to Nusa Lembongan, Lombok and the Gilis, Bali, anywhere you like."

"Really?

"Yes!" He beamed. "It's the best way to travel!"

M turned to Ash. "Ever been to Bali?"

"That's a lot of motor for a vessel this size," Ash yelled over the booming Honda V-8 powering the jacked-up longboat.

"Courage! Romantics!" their guide, Agus, called back.

"Courage," "romantics," and "harmony" were his favorite words in English, and made up most of his conversation with Ash.

"Can't say it's not fast," M shouted. "Or safe."

"Pardon. Did you actually just say *safe*?" Ash tightened the straps on his life jacket.

M gripped the edges of the bench as the boat gave a particularly hard jounce. It was almost as bad as the way Agus's van had jolted and jerked on the road to the harbor. "No one's following us. That's what I meant," she said, hands cupped around her mouth to be sure he could hear her.

He nodded. M took in a long breath. The sun was only starting to set, but she felt as if she'd been awake for days. It only added to the feeling that time was running out. How long until Liza kept her promise to take a piece of Dad?

M pushed the thought away, locking it in the place she kept all her fears. All she could do was find the last two pieces. And she had no idea where to look. She didn't even have a continent as a starting place. The hopelessness must have shown on her face, because Ash reached over, resting one hand on her knee.

"Ah, romantics," Agus said approvingly. Then he gave a yelp. "Harmony!" He pointed. M saw a dolphin arcing out of the water. A few seconds later, another joined it. They swam alongside the boat, whistling, leaping, flipping. Watching them with Ash beside her, M couldn't help feeling a little bit of hope and strength return to her.

"It's rare to see them this time of day," Agus called to M in Javanese. "Harmony, harmony!" he added in English.

The dolphins accompanied them almost to the wharf, then turned and headed back out to deeper water. "Now where?" Agus asked as he docked the boat. "Food? Drinks? Monkeys?" He turned to M, switching to his native language. "You should see the temple and the monkeys in the Sacred Forest. And Tirta Empul, the sacred spring where the priests get their holy water. There are over twenty thousand temples in Bali. I can show you all of them!"

"I wish we could," M replied. If she'd been with Dad, or even Mike, they would have done it. They would have spent the day exploring, urging Agus to take them wherever the locals went, asking a million questions the whole time.

"I will show you the beach borrowed by lost spirits. Or the deaf town where they have their own kind of performing shows." Agus nodded toward Ash. "Or would he like to climb in the underground caves? Or spas? Where you could get a massage by the ocean?"

"We don't have time. But thank you. Thank you so much for bringing us here." M switched to English. "Thank you," she said again.

"Thank you," Ash echoed. He took out his wallet and gave Agus double what he'd asked for.

"Picture!" Agus said in English. M gave him her cell and he gestured for her and Ash to move closer together. Ash rested his arm around M's shoulders, and she slid her arm comfortably around his waist. "Smile!" Agus urged. They both laughed, smiling like they really were a couple off on an exotic vacation.

Agus handed her cell back. "Romantics, harmony, courage!" he said in farewell, and M and Ash waved as he got back on his boat.

Then, turning away from Ash, M checked for service, before shooting a message off to Mike. She attached the photos of the glyphs they'd found inside the Buddha's mouth.

"The Set followers have no reason to be watching Bali. We can fly out of the airport here," M said. "As soon as we know where we should be flying to. I just sent Mike the glyphs. I can start trying to translate them, but I'm not so good with Sanskrit."

"Let's find a place up there to sit. At least we can look at the signpost. I was a bit . . . distracted. I didn't get to see the

glyphs at all." Ash started toward a row of shops and restaurants that ran along the top of the beach.

"Okay. I should be able to work out the actual glyphs, I
just won't understand any of the nuance. Mike's good with
Sanskrit," M said.

"Like the looks of that one?" Ash nodded toward the en-
closed patio of one of the restaurants.

"I'm not in a tablecloth and china kind of mood," M answered. "Too much *ambiance*. How about that one?" She
pointed to a tiny warung a little farther down. Its patio was
open to the street and palm fronds hung from the peaked
roof covering it. The wooden chairs and tables were painted
in bright colors and a large chalkboard listed the specials.

"Fine," Ash said.

As they started toward it, M felt the Set pieces in her
backpack shift. She stopped, surprised—they'd fallen apart.
They had snapped together as soon as she and Ash had left
the grounds of the Borobudur Temple, starting up their
weird throbbing, and she hadn't felt them move until now.

M glanced around, trying to figure out why the pieces had
separated. "What?" Ash asked.

"The Set animal fell apart just now."

"Ah." Ash looked around too. "Perhaps we were wrong
about a sacred space triggering movement?"

"There!" M nodded toward the dashboard of a car parked
alongside them. A metal dish rested on top of it, containing
palm fronds, a mango, some rice, and a frangipani blossom.
She laughed at the baffled expression on Ash's face. "It's
called a canang sari. It's an offering to the gods. It must create a sacred space the Set pieces respond to." She was surprised such a simple, personal thing would make a difference,
frankly. She'd assumed it had be something more official, a
church or a temple.

"It's like the tree in Norway," Ash said. "There wasn't

a church, but you said the tree itself, the whole grove was sacred—"

"Their culture worshipped outdoors—" M began.

"That's what I mean," he cut her off. "It's not about a place, necessarily. What made that oak grove sacred was that people worshipped Thor there. Perhaps that's all it takes to make a space holy, the intent to honor a god."

"Could be," M agreed. They continued walking, and after several steps, she felt the pieces joining together once more. When they reached the warung, she felt them separate. A woman had just placed a woven mat of banana leaves on the sidewalk. Like the bowl in the car it held flowers, rice, and fruit. The woman lit a stick of incense, then stood and waved M and Ash to one of the two empty tables.

"They make offerings three times a day," M said as they sat down. "They're like you in a way."

Ash raised his eyebrows. "How so?"

"Just in how they constantly bring their god into their lives," she replied. "I wonder if—" She was interrupted by her cell vibrating.

"Mike already," she told Ash. "Give me a minute."

M: What do they say?

MIKE: I'm a genius, but come on. I just looked at the pics.

M: How long?

MIKE: Faster if you help. Come to me. You're so close.

M: Really?

MIKE: You have someplace better to be?

M: Not unless you found the other piece.

MIKE: Got a lead on it, but nothing solid yet. Come. I need to see you, sweetie. I want to see for myself you're okay.

M: Ash has to come too.

MIKE: Fine.

M: See you as soon as I can get there.

Heart pounding, M looked up to find Ash watching her. "We can go to Mike!" Just the words filled her with fierce joy. She hadn't seen Mike since Dad died, she'd put even the possibility of it out of her mind.

Ash paled. "What do you mean, go to him? Why? Where is he?"

"Translating the glyphs will take a while, and we still have to track down the missing piece from the Templar church. Plus, we need to lay low and hide from Liza and Bob. Mike's in Thailand. It's not far."

"You're not going without me," he said.

She rolled her eyes. Why would he even say that? They both knew the deal. "I wasn't planning to. And Mike said you could."

She held his defiant gaze until he looked away. "So long as there's nothing more useful we can be doing, fine."

M could tell he wasn't happy, but she felt lighter just thinking about going to Mike's. It was the closest thing she had to a home now.

———

"Mike should be waiting for us," M said as they inched closer to the immigration counter in the Bangkok airport.

Ash nodded. It was the third time she'd told him, and each time she sounded more excited than the last. She didn't seem at all bothered that her boyfriend had been spending time in Bangkok, which everyone knew was famous for the sex trade industry. What was he doing in Thailand, anyway? Ash had assumed he was back in Boston. He wanted to tell M she should be concerned about STDs, but couldn't think of a civil way to work it into the conversation.

He'd refrained from asking any questions about Mike, even though his curiosity was overwhelming. It had been good practice keeping his mind where it should be—on Horus. As part of his training, he'd worked to stay focused no matter what Philip threw at him. Yet M managed to distract him quite often. Too often.

The queue moved again. The unsmiling immigration official waved M forward, and she stepped up, handing him her arrival card and passport, like she'd been through the process a thousand times. She probably had.

The man snapped her picture with a webcam, stamped the passport and card and handed everything back to her. It was Ash's turn. He felt uneasy as he gave his documents and had his picture taken. He wished he and M could move from country to country without leaving a trace. They'd booked tickets to several destinations besides Bangkok in case the Set cult—or the Eye—was tracking flight records, but that was far from foolproof.

The Eye could easily have gotten them fake IDs, but that would only have protected them from Set followers. They needed protection from the Eye as well. How much longer would Philip tolerate Ash being out of contact without taking action? Had he already tried to track them down?

The immigration agent gave a grunt, and Ash realized the man was holding out his stamped passport. He took it, and he and M cruised through the green "nothing to declare" section of customs. They probably could have been leaving trails of cocaine behind them without being stopped. Clearly even the customs agents didn't believe people would try to sneak anything *into* Thailand.

M checked her cell. "Mike's waiting!" The happiness in her voice grated on him. She acted like this Mike guy was going to magically make all her worries disappear.

Ash scanned the signs—Car Park, Medical Clinic, Reception Room for Buddhist Monks, Muslim Prayer Room, Restaurants, Meeting Point, Public Transport, Airport Rail Link—and started in the direction of the meeting point.

"Where are you going?" M asked.

"Meeting point." Ash nodded at the sign.

"No one meets at the meeting point," she scoffed. "Well, most people meet at the meeting point, which is why you shouldn't meet there. Mike's waiting in front of the Family Mart. Come on." She charged off, Ash following cautiously.

When he spotted the sign for the Family Mart, he looked at the people nearby. Which one was the brilliant Mike? He didn't even know how old M's boyfriend was, or what he looked like. Was he that waster with the beard? Or the blond one who looked like he'd been head boy every year of his—

M let out a cry of delight and raced forward, hurling herself at a middle-aged woman in a nun's habit. The woman wrapped her arms around M and rocked her back and forth.

Ash slowed down, baffled. Was this Mike's mother? It couldn't be. She was a nun. Nuns didn't have children.

Maybe Mike was in some kind of church school and this was the headmistress?

Still hugging, M and the nun kept talking over one another, asking questions, interrupting as they tried to answer. Abruptly the nun turned to Ash. "Ashwin. I'm Sister Michael." She stuck out her hand. "Call me Mike."

Dumbstruck, Ash shook her hand.

"Call me Ash," he replied automatically, trying to process that M's boyfriend was a nun. He felt muscles relaxing all over his body, muscles he hadn't even realized were tense. The ever-present, jack-of-all-trades, helpful Mike was a woman. A nun. Middle-aged, her blond hair streaked with gray and the corners of her brown eyes creased with laugh lines.

Mike reached into her bulging Family Mart bag, pulled out a Dr Pepper and a bag of chips, and handed them to M.

M immediately ripped into the chips and tossed a handful into her mouth. "Spicy Chili Squid. Betcha can't eat just one," she said. She shook the bag in Ash's direction. He grimaced. They sounded revolting.

"Ash doesn't believe in finding pleasure in food," M told Mike. "Do you have an IV of glucose we could hook him up to?"

Mike gave her a reproachful look. "Ash, I also have peanuts, crackers with something cheese-like, pineapple cookies, dried bananas, water, Sprite, orange juice, some chocolate, iced tea—"

"Coconut rolls?" M interrupted.

"Of course, coconut rolls," Mike replied. "I spoil her," she told Ash. "And I intend to spoil you while you're here. What would you like? If I don't have it, I'll find it."

"Water and fake cheese crackers, please," Ash told her, a little dazzled. Mike was one of those people who could make you feel like the only person in the world when she talked to you. Philip was like that too, when he wanted to be.

"You must both be exhausted. Let's get you to the car," Mike said, handing Ash his snacks. She looped one arm around M's shoulders and started toward the airport exit. "You didn't tell him I was a nun, did you?" she asked. "His face when he saw me!" Mike bugged her eyes out and dropped her jaw. Ash felt his cheeks heat up. He hoped he hadn't and never would look anything like that.

"Actually, I *may* have let him believe you were my boyfriend," M admitted, grinning. "It was too much fun watching him get jealous."

"I wasn't jealous," Ash grumbled, then wished he'd stayed silent when they both laughed. Maybe he had been a little jealous. Why else had he felt that rush of relief when he'd seen Mike wasn't a bloke?

"Have you ever been to Thailand?" Mike asked as they made their way to the parking garage.

He was glad to have something to think about other than how ridiculous he'd looked when he met her. "No, this is the first time I've been anywhere in Asia."

"Well, you're young. What are you, twenty-two?"

"Yes," he said, surprised she'd guessed so exactly.

"I'd been to Asia by the time I was three," M commented.

Mike ignored her, still focused on Ash. He had the feeling she was studying him, testing him. What would happen if he didn't pass?

"So you've been in England predominantly?" Mike asked. "And France?"

"Mostly," he confirmed. "If you can believe it, I've never even been to the States."

"Except when he came to Boston to steal my map," M said cheerfully.

Right. He'd forgotten about that. "That doesn't count. I was there for less than a day," he mumbled.

M reached into the bag Mike was carrying and rooted

around until she fished out a packet of cookies. It was as if she'd regressed to being a child again. She was playful, giddy. So much looser and more relaxed. Mike wasn't just a friend, obviously. She was a surrogate mother, and a good one.

"I've been showing him the world," M said, mouth full.

"He couldn't have a better tour guide. The car's down here," Mike told them, leading the way into the parking structure and down one of the rows to a beat-up old Honda Civic. She opened the trunk. "You can throw your gear in there."

"I'm going to hang on to mine." M slid the backpack off and hugged it against her body. Ash could see her fear and stress returning. She'd only been able to relax for those first few moments around Mike.

He tossed his bag into the trunk and started to get in the backseat. "Take the front," Mike said. "Your legs are too long for the back."

"I don't mind. You two have a lot of catching up to do," he replied.

Mike rolled her eyes. "She'll be asleep in twenty minutes, thirty at most, and it'll take us more than three hours to get to the convent. Don't worry," she added. "We have several guest cottages that are very comfortable and men often stay in them."

"Good to know." Ash climbed into the front seat and shut the door.

"We should have a pretty easy ride. The highway from here to Chanthaburi is in good shape," Mike commented as she got behind the wheel and M settled in the back.

About a half an hour into their journey, Ash checked on M. "You were right. She's asleep."

"Always happens. She has the gift of being able to nap anywhere, a product of her upbringing. As a kid she didn't exactly have a regular bedtime." Mike used the rearview mirror to glance at M.

With M asleep it was as if he and Mike were alone. He could feel her attitude shift. She wanted explanations, reassurances he couldn't give. She wasn't going to push him, but he had to say something. "I'm sorry Memphis and her father ended up in the middle of a situation they have nothing to do with."

Mike nodded. "He's alive. That's something. That's everything." Her eyes flicked to the rearview, checking on M again. "She's strong. Her dad taught her how to deal with her mother's death, and I think she used what she learned to make it through his. And she's using it for this. Still, making it through isn't the same as being happy."

"I didn't get to know him well, but I quickly came to respect Dr. Engel. He always handled himself with such dignity," Ash said.

"He's one of the best people I know. Salt of the earth," Mike replied. "If she loses him again, I don't know what it'll do to her. She'll blame herself, and I'm not certain she can bear that."

"Nothing about this is her fault. And she's doing everything possible to get him back. She has to know that," Ash protested.

"She won't believe she did enough until he's home with her." Mike slowed to a stop. A tollbooth up ahead had brought traffic to a standstill. A man trotted up to her window holding several garlands of marigolds and what Ash thought were jasmine blossoms.

Mike opened the window and handed him some money. When he gave her the flowers she looped them around the rearview mirror. "They're an offering to Mae Yanang, goddess of journeys," she explained to Ash.

"Isn't it . . ." He searched for a polite way to say sacrilegious.

"Sacrilegious for a Catholic nun to honor a heathen god?" Mike asked before he could think of one.

"Well, yes."

"Nah. It's my way of honoring the culture of the place I'm currently living," Mike said. "I'm sure St. Christopher will understand." She tapped the medal that also hung from the mirror.

Ash wondered what she thought about the Eye. Now that he'd seen how close they were, he was positive M had told Mike every detail. But he didn't want to bring up the Eye. He didn't want to lie.

They both fell silent until they'd made their way past the tollbooth. Mike spoke up once traffic sped up again. "I'm glad M has had you with her. She can handle herself, I know that as well as anyone, but that doesn't mean she should always have to go it alone."

"I didn't actually give her much of a choice," Ash confessed.

"I know," Mike said. "But Greg trusted you. That means a lot. It makes me inclined to trust you too. He's always been an excellent judge of character."

Ash stared out the window as if fascinated by the scenery that was much too dark to see.

Mike shouldn't trust him. Gregory Engel shouldn't have either. Nobody should.

Not Philip. Ash hadn't obeyed his mentor's instructions.

Not Hugh. He'd lied to his oldest friend.

And definitely not M.

CHAPTER 19

"This is so freaking good," M said, slurping her way through her second bowl of pumpkin coconut soup. She shot a sideways glance a Mike. "Clearly *you* didn't make it."

"Brat," Mike said affectionately. She and M sat across from Ash in the convent's cozy kitchen. They'd been invited to eat with the nuns, but Mike had politely turned down the offer, telling the other sisters that M and Ash needed a little down time. "Sadly it's true," she admitted, turning to Ash. "My culinary skills are limited to peanut butter sandwiches and spaghetti with sauce from a jar. Unlike M's father, who learned to make the local specialties everywhere we traveled, seemingly by osmosis."

"Remember the time he spent all those weeks making pidan?" M asked, laughing.

"Pidan's also called a thousand-year egg," Mike told Ash. "Making them takes four or five weeks. But that was fine with Greg. The more complicated a recipe, the better."

"You preserve the eggs with a mix of ash, tea, lime, and salt, then wrap them in rice husks and leave them there for weeks and weeks. If you want to do it the old-school way, which of course my dad did," M continued.

"Of course," Mike echoed. "He treated those eggs like he was their mama duck. I wouldn't have been surprised to see him sitting on them."

"We were sleeping in tents, working a dig outside Qantara," M continued. "So a few days before what was supposed to be the grand unveiling of the eggs, I wake up to this absolute bellow from my dad. A jerboa—you know, those little rodents that look kind of like mice with kangaroo legs and fluffy tails?—got into them."

"The thing that made Greg furious, and Greg is exceptionally even-tempered, was that the jerboa only took a bite or two out of each egg," Mike told Ash. "It didn't even—"

"Appreciate them enough to finish one," M jumped in, snorting with laughter. "He now calls anyone he thinks is ignorant or lacking in discernment a jerboa." Her laughter trailed off, but she still smiled. "It's good to talk about him. After he—after I thought he died—it was just too hard, even with you," she told Mike.

"With time you would have been ready to tell stories about him again," Mike replied, reaching over to brush M's hair away from her face.

Ash couldn't take his eyes off them. Mike had worked her magic again—M was relaxed, dropping her usual wariness. And she smiled, almost constantly. "You were probably named M's guardian, and someone from the cult of Set tampered with the papers," he said to Mike.

"After M's mother died, Greg and I did have a conversation about it, and, of course, I said I would take care of Memphis if anything happened to him," Mike said. "When I found out he'd appointed other guardians, I just assumed he hadn't ever made time to change his will."

"Me too. I couldn't believe he and Mom were ever friends with Bob and Liza, much less made them my guardians," M said. "Guess I was right."

"But they were decent to you, though, weren't they?" Mike asked, her voice sharpening a little. "You told me they were." She glanced at Ash. "M doesn't always like to share how she's feeling, even with me."

Ash nodded. He wasn't the type to share either.

"It was what I was stuck with," M said. "There was no point in whining."

"But I live to hear you whine," Mike teased, refilling Ash's water glass.

"They were fine. Now I know they had to be. They were protecting an *asset*. They just felt so conventional, not like any friends of Mom and Dad's I ever met," M explained. "Most of my parents' friends are like Mike, or Joel," she told Ash. "So I thought Bob and Liza were Mr. and Mrs. Ultra Normal. And then it turned out they're part of a secret society that worships Set. Who'da thunk it."

Mike was frowning. She had caught the glint of darkness in M's eyes too. She was tense again. Ash nudged M's knee with his. "What?"

"I'm good at reading people. I always have been. But I didn't see them, even though I was literally under the same roof." She dropped her spoon into the soup and pushed the bowl away. "Maybe I've lost my touch."

"Or dark god worshippers are experts at being deceitful, more likely," Mike said. Ash started, his eyes going involuntarily to her face. But she just smiled. He forced a smile in return.

It wasn't hard for him to believe his parents acted like decent people while they lived with M. They'd always been good neighbors, friends, citizens. It was only Ash they treated like an untouchable.

"Done, M?" Mike asked, nodding toward the soup.

"I guess. It's so good, but my stomach might burst," M said.

"What about dessert? There's sticky rice and oranges in syrup," Mike offered.

M prodded her belly with two fingers. "Just not possible."

"Ash?"

"No, thank you," he said.

"Let's get to work on the last signpost." M stood up and started gathering the dishes.

"No." Mike took the dishes from M and shooed her away. "You are going to get a good night's sleep. You too, Ash. Neither of you looks like you've had one in a while."

"But—" M began to protest.

"No," Mike cut her off. "I'll do some work on the glyphs tonight. Tomorrow I'll fill you in."

"You said you had a lead on the lost piece. Where—"

"Tomorrow." Mike's voice was as laid-back as ever, but there was an undercurrent of steel to it. "Now go."

M looked at Ash. "I guess we're going."

"Thanks for everything, Sister," Ash said. "You've been extremely kind."

"Extremely kind," M repeated, doing a decent imitation of Ash's accent.

"Good manners are always appreciated," Mike said, winking at Ash. "You might want to remember that, miss." She gave M a little push. "Go."

M took a step toward the door, then turned around and gave Mike a hard hug. "I love you." She said the words quietly, but Ash couldn't help but hear.

"I love you too, Little Elephant," Mike answered. "Get some sleep." She opened the kitchen door that led outside, and ushered them through, shutting it firmly behind them.

"Little Elephant?" Ash asked.

"I used to hold on to the back of her skirt and walk behind her everywhere she went when I was little," M told him as they started up the flagstone path to the cottage where they were staying.

"So you've known her—"

"Always," M said. "She was there when I was born. I call her my big Sister."

Ash laughed.

"Do you have any brothers or sisters?" she asked.

"No." An old memory, old, but still fresh, slammed into him. "When I was six, I asked for a little brother, and my mother . . ." He had to take a breath before he could continue. "My mother said she was afraid of having another child like me."

M fell silent, finding his hand and folding it into hers. Finally she said, "Mike would know exactly what to say, but I don't. That's horrible. It's an unforgivable thing to say to a six-year-old kid. To anybody."

Ash shrugged, trying to act as if he'd put it all behind him. "If I'd been an addict, or transgender, or disabled in some way, anything else, they would have still loved me, done anything to help me, I know that. But they couldn't handle my power. They thought it was evil."

Because they'd known it came from Horus, and Horus was their enemy . . .

"Don't make excuses for them." M's voice was tight with fury. "I'm sure you were a good kid. I bet you did everything you could think of to please them. Good grades, helping out around the house, whatever. If they chose to see evil, that's their true selves being revealed. Not yours."

He *had* tried to be good, at least when he was little, before he gave up on trying to please them. But nothing he'd done had made a difference. "It's in the past. They're not in my life anymore." They reached the small stone cottage and M opened the door, dropping his hand. Ash curled his fingers over his palm, wanting to keep her warmth a little longer.

"You have Philip," M said as they went inside. "Is he your Mike?" She struck a match and lit the oil lamp on the window-sill. The convent was hundreds of years old, but they had put electricity in the main building. The cottages, though, were still stuck in the sixteenth century.

"In a way, I suppose," Ash said. He sat in one of the rick-ety chairs in the common room, and M dropped down onto the floor, folding her long legs into a lotus position. "He never calls me Little Elephant. But, in his way, he's the most impor-tant person in my life. He's been the best teacher I ever had."

Even to his own ears, the words sounded empty. He re-spected Philip. But it wasn't love. Not like what M had with Mike. And he didn't want to talk about the Eye. Not with her. It made him feel like he was coated with greasy sweat. He gave an elaborate stretch. "I'm knackered. I'm going to bed."

She snorted. "Knackered? Have you been away from Philip for too long? I bet he's posh, right? Never lets you use slang, or the wrong fork? Makes you act like a middle-aged man even though you're only four years older than me?"

"It's fair to say Philip would be appalled by your influence on me." He stood. "Good night."

"Good night," she answered. "I think I'm going to stay up for a bit."

He nodded and headed to the bedroom. It was really more like a closet, and the beds were two small cots. He'd heard Mike arguing quietly with M about them staying in the same room. But M had insisted it was the deal they had— so neither of them would betray the other. He cringed think-ing about it, then lay down on a cot, not bothering to take off his clothes or even his shoes, and closed his eyes. Sleep. He wanted to sleep. He needed to shut his brain down.

But sleep wouldn't come.

Instead he tried to meditate, attempting to quiet his mind, except thoughts ricocheted around loudly inside his skull. And when he tried prayer, he didn't feel the connection to Horus he usually did.

Bits and pieces of the evening's conversation kept bombarding him. *You have Philip. Is he your Mike? I love you, Little Elephant. I call her my big Sister. She was afraid of having another child like me. They were protecting an asset. They were protecting an asset. You have Philip.*

Finally, he had to admit to himself why the words kept attacking his brain. He'd lied to M, to himself. Philip wasn't his Mike. Yes, Philip had taken him in. Yes, Philip had corrected his thinking about which god he was meant to worship—not his parents' dark god, but the just god, Horus. Yes, Philip had reassured him he wasn't evil, no matter what his parents had said.

But it had never been out of love. Ash was an asset to the Eye. He was an asset to Philip. Nothing more. Nothing more than what M had been to his parents. Ash was valuable to the Eye because he was a god channeler. It was the only reason Philip had sought him out. Because he had felt Ash's power and knew where it came from. It had nothing to do with helping Ash.

Whereas Mike worried about M. She spoiled M. She listened to M. She made M feel safe. She loved *her.* Not something M could do, just M.

And M loved Mike. It was obvious. It was also obvious that she loved her father. It was there in the way her eyes glowed when she was telling that silly story about the eggs. It was there in the fear and desperation and fierce determination he'd seen in her from the day they met.

Ash had never loved anybody like that. He'd never been loved like that himself. He'd never thought love like that existed.

He sighed, shoving himself off the bed, and walked to the window. M was out in the courtyard, going through a series of moves with her bo staff.

At first her motions were smooth and slow, almost a dance, her body lithe and graceful, but then she launched into a series of quick, brutal strikes. Even though he couldn't see her face, he could imagine the intensity of her expression.

When the time comes to take the pieces, I have to be fast, he thought. *I can't give her the chance to strike first. If she were to knock me out, my god-channeling ability would be for nothing.*

The thought made him feel as if he'd been eating stones, his stomach heavy. Taking the Set pieces would be the end of their partnership. He'd vaguely hoped he could convince Philip to mount a rescue once the Eye possessed the pieces, but he knew it was a false hope. He'd been hiding that truth from himself as much as from M. Once the pieces were rehidden, there was no reason for the Eye to put themselves out on Dr. Engel's behalf. Saving M's father wouldn't gain them anything. Philip didn't do things because they were good, or right. He only did what was useful to the Eye.

And once the pieces were rehidden, the Set cult would decide M's father was useless. So they would kill him.

If she loses him again, I don't know what it'll do to her. She'll blame herself, and I'm not certain she can bear that. Mike's voice pierced his brain, their earlier conversation replacing every other thought.

She had been right. M would blame herself for not saving her father, and it would destroy her.

He couldn't do that. He couldn't destroy M.

And he couldn't pretend it wasn't his choice. He could use his power to take the pieces from her by force. Or he could use the pieces as an asset.

He would give the pieces to Philip only after the Eye rescued Dr. Engel. Not before. That was the bargain he'd made with M, and he was going to stick to it.

If Philip couldn't agree to those terms, he and M would come up with a new plan.

Together.

No matter what, he was standing with her. The love between M and her father was worth fighting for. And he would do whatever he could, use all the power that had been given to him, to save M's father.

He'd worry about saving the world after that.

"Ash is still sleeping," M said when she found Mike in the convent kitchen early the next morning.

"You should still be sleeping too." Mike banged a glass of mango juice onto the table to register her disapproval.

"Thanks!" M said cheerfully, taking a long gulp. "I'll sleep when I get Dad back."

Shooting her a look, Mike sat down next to M. She pulled enlarged photos of the most recent glyphs out of a worn leather satchel, as well as a legal pad covered with notes, then pressed her hands together, resting her fingertips against her lips. Mike hesitated. "I'm concerned about the boy."

"Because he's part of a woo-woo Horus-worshipping cult?" M teased.

"Is that what you think of it?" Mike asked, her tone serious.

M shook her head. "It's what I thought at first. I guess I still want to think of it that way, because the truth freaks me the hell out." She wiped a drop of condensation off the side of her glass. "I told you about the crocodiles. But do you know how we got these pictures from the Buddha's mouth? Ash commanded the statue to speak, and it did."

She saw her own shock reflected in Mike's expression.

"They all did, every statue in the place," she went on. "I thought they were going to shake down the temple. Ash says the power comes from Horus, that Horus is using him as a vessel. But that's impossible, right? I don't know what I think."

"I don't know what I think either," Mike admitted. "One God, revealed to humanity as Father, Son, and Holy Spirit. That is what the Church teaches."

"So, does that mean you think Ash is . . . is somehow against God? That his powers are evil?" M demanded, her voice sharper than she'd intended.

"I'm not inclined to call everything I don't understand evil," Mike said crisply. Then her voice softened. "Some scholars believe Horus was a model for Christ. There are similarities in their stories. But that can be said of many mythological gods—Mithra, Krishna, even Dionysus. Maybe there's a spark of the divine anywhere someone worships with pure intent. It goes against my deepest beliefs, but no human has a perfect understanding of God. I certainly don't have an explanation for Ash's abilities."

"His parents treated him like an abomination. They thought his power came from the devil or something like it. I think . . . I'm pretty sure they tried to beat it out of him," M said quietly.

"Poor boy. Poor, poor boy." Mike slowly shook her head.

"It was the Eye that saved him," M told her. "They taught him his power was from Horus."

"Which gives me even more reason to be concerned," Mike said. She reached across the table and took M's hand, a sure sign she wanted to make a Serious Point. "Ash is going to have to choose between his religion and helping you. Maybe not immediately, but eventually."

"No," M protested. "We have a bargain. The Eye doesn't get the pieces of the Set animal until they rescue Dad."

"And yet, those who worship Horus feel they have a sacred duty to protect the pieces, to protect the entire world. What is one man's safety when you believe the world is at stake? It's hard for me to accept that the Eye has agreed to this bargain in good faith," Mike said. "If Ash has to choose between the duty to his god and his desire to help you, no matter how strong . . . Well, it wouldn't be an easy choice even for me, much as I love you and your father. I feel for him."

M's body went cold. She'd let herself lower her guard. She'd let herself believe all she had to do was find the last two pieces—with Ash's help. But Mike could be right. Ash's religion, his connection to his god, was as deep as her connection to her father. Could she really be sure he would honor their deal? Would it be possible even if he wanted to?

And Liza was going to start hurting Dad soon. There were only three days left in the week.

"I can't afford to feel for him," M said. "If he tries to break our bargain, I'll do anything to stop him."

Mike studied her, as if taking an X-ray of M's soul. Then she slapped her palm on the legal pad. "Fine. Let's get started. I'm a lot stronger in Sanskrit than I am in the Horus language, so I've made good progress. See these words written in a jagged horseshoe?" She traced the marks on the enlarged photo with one finger.

M nodded.

"There are several words repeated: *fire, earth, shudder, ash,*" Mike explained. "The words, and especially the shape they form, made me think of the Ring of Fire."

M snorted. "That doesn't help us much. If you're right, we know the piece is located somewhere along the Pacific coast of New Zealand, the Philippines, Japan, North America, and South America. Doesn't exactly narrow it down."

Ash came in just in time to hear Mike say "Patience."

"Asking M to be patient?" he joked. "Good luck with that."

"Mike just told me the next piece is somewhere in the Ring of Fire." Ash gave her a quizzical look. "It's where seventy or eighty percent of active volcanoes are, and where the worst earthquakes happen," she explained. "This is New Zealand." M pointed to the bottom of half of the horseshoe. "And this." She stabbed the bottom of the other half with one finger. "Is Chile."

Ash sank down into one of the chairs. "Mango juice?" Mike offered, rising to her feet.

"Please. Cheers," Ash replied, staring at the photo. "That's got to be around forty thousand kilometers."

"Patience," Mike said again, putting a glass of juice in front of Ash. "Those are only part of the glyphs. "Right here"—she showed them a glyph—"this says *mud cat* and the one next to it says *child*."

"That's around where Central America would be on the Ring," M said.

"You've lost me. What does that mean?" Ash asked.

"That, my friend, is what we have to figure out," Mike told him.

"Every hiding place so far has been sacred. Temples, churches, a sacred grove," M said. "Anybody ever heard of mud cat worship?" Ash and Mike shook their heads. "Anybody ever heard of a mud cat at all?" They shook their heads again.

"We have much work to do, but while we work, how about some rice porridge? Not made by me! Promise," Mike said. She began filling dishes from the pot on the stove without waiting for an answer.

"Mud cat, mud cat, mud cat," M muttered. "Mud. Cat. Mud. Cat. It's already getting to the point where the words don't sound like words."

"Do you think it meant a brown or black cat?" Ash asked. "Mud-colored?"

"Possibly." M looked up "cats" and "Central America" on her cell. "Most of them seem to be spotted. Except the cougar, which is tan. Oh, and one called a jaguarundi. Its fur is supposed to be unmarked, but the color goes through stages—black, brownish gray, and reddish brown. So I guess part of the year, it's mud-colored. It's not much bigger than a house cat, and has a tail that's more like an otter's than a cat's, if that's useful to anyone."

Mike gave M and Ash their porridge and sat down, flipping to a new page of her pad. She began to draw spots all over it.

"She can't think well without doodling," M told Ash. Maybe that's where she'd picked up her own doodling habit.

"What are those spots?" Ash asked.

"Mud puddles, of course," Mike answered, without looking up.

Distraction, M thought. *What's your favorite band? What's your favorite movie?* "What did you find out about the piece from the Temple Church?" she asked. "The piece that should have been there but wasn't?"

Mike looked surprised at the sudden subject change, but didn't question it. She raked her hands through her short hair, giving it what M used to call the porcupine do. "I have a contact who has another, somewhat shady contact who sometimes, but not always, deals in stolen artifacts. He specializes in—"

"We don't need his CV, Mike!" M interrupted.

"I was finding it quite interesting," Ash put in.

M glared at him. "Quit the polite British thing. Unless you're wondering if you knew him from your time as a criminal—"

Ash's face began to color. "Stop it," Mike barked.

M went silent. Part of her would always be a little kid around Mike, and that little kid knew when to obey.

"Here's the short version," Mike went on. "An artifact matching your description turned up in an acquisition by the British Museum. It was lumped in with a collection of minor Egyptian artifacts, catalogued, and stuck in a box somewhere. The only remarkable thing about the piece was that it resisted carbon dating, and, in fact, the material couldn't be identified. The attempts to analyze it were made in 1969, and shortly thereafter, the piece disappeared."

"Disappeared?" Ash repeated.

"My contact's contact has heard mention of a similar piece in New Orleans. And, interestingly, a young lab assistant from New Orleans was working at the British museum in '69. He quit soon after the piece vanished."

M found herself staring at Mike's legal pad. The top sheet was now covered with black spots. "Spots!" she cried.

Ash looked at Mike, and Mike shrugged. "I usually have a good idea what she's thinking, but not this time."

"Wasn't there a myth about a jaguar getting its spots by using its paw to daub mud on itself?" M asked. She jumped up, almost tipping over her juice glass. Ash caught it.

"Yes!" Mike cried. "A Mayan myth. The Maya revered jaguars. The jaguar was their god of the underworld. It helped the sun travel under the earth at night, so it could rise again in the morning."

"They believed in were-jaguars, too!" M exclaimed, her Mayan mythology coming back to her. "Dad and I went to an exhibit once that had all these statues of parents holding half-jaguar, half-human babies. Some researchers thought they were showing deformed children being offered to the gods. But some thought the statues memorialized a child born to the Jaguar line who would be a successor to the throne."

"The glyphs! 'Child' and 'mud cat' together." Mike raked

her hands through her hair again. "It seems we're looking for a temple where the were-jaguar was worshipped, somewhere along the Central American coast."

M felt the smile spreading across her face just as one beamed back from Mike's. "Dr. Verela," they said together.

"If there's a Mayan were-jaguar temple, he knows about it," M explained, turning to Ash.

"On it!" Mike hurried from the room.

M let out a deep breath and sat back down. "We're getting so close."

"No one will be waiting for us in Central America or in New Orleans," Ash said. "Neither place was on the map."

"Great. Then it will be easy-peasy lemon-squeezey."

"I'm sorry?" He blinked in confusion.

M laughed. "You're right. I can't believe I just said that."

Ash gave a mock frown. "I can't believe I've been traveling the world with someone who would utter such a thing."

"I can't believe I've been traveling the world with someone who would utter the word 'utter,'" M shot back.

"'Utter' is a perfectly—"

Ash was interrupted by Mike returning. "Dr. V. came through. He's going to email me the location of a temple in Guatemala where there is a throne with a statue of a huge golden jaguar standing behind it."

"How is that not in a museum?" Ash asked.

"The locals think it's bad luck. And, for whatever reason, many of the people who have tried to study, in many cases loot, the temple have been killed," Mike replied, staring hard at M. "Even Dr. Verela is unwilling to go inside."

"But Dr. Verela is incredibly superstitious. Every time he hears about a new superstition, he takes it on," M reminded her.

"Even so, there are real dangers behind some old superstitions. You have to promise me you'll be careful, both of you."

"We will," M and Ash said together, and Mike handed M a slip of paper.

"The coordinates," she said, her voice cracking a little.

"Don't you dare cry," M warned her. "Or I'll cry too, and I don't want to cry."

Mike wiped at her eyes with the back of her hand. "I wasn't crying."

"As soon as we finish this thing, Dad and I are going to be expecting a visit from you, a long one," M said. Mike nodded. M was afraid they'd both be full-on crying momentarily. She threw her arms around Mike, and Mike squeezed her back so hard it hurt M's ribs, but she didn't want to let go. After a long moment, she forced herself to step back. It was time to save Dad.

She turned to Ash. "So where first? Guatemala or the Big Easy?"

"Do you ever want to go to college?" M asked as they walked across Loyola's Peace Quad. The day was warm, and kids were hanging out all over the place, flirting, studying, talking, playing Frisbee, sunbathing, napping.

"Not particularly," Ash said.

"You don't need to know about anything but Horus?"

"Which includes studying linguistics, history, philosophy, and archeology with some of the most knowledgeable people in the world," Ash retorted.

M wondered if the Eye would even let him go to college if he wanted. She decided not to ask. They were in New Orleans with no reason to think anyone from Set knew it. Why spoil this little bit of time they were safe?

"What about you?"

"I'm deciding between Boston University and the University of Sheffield," M told him.

Ash let out a low whistle. "Not bad."

"Yeah, well, everyone in those archeology departments knew—knows," she quickly corrected herself, "my dad. And that he and Mom took me with them whenever they possibly could. So I have the life experience factor. So I'll probably go. When all this is over."

"You don't sound so sure," Ash commented.

M glanced around at the college kids again. "It's hard to imagine fitting in. They feel like an alien life form."

"You've experienced more, survived more, than most of them," Ash said. "You know, when I first met you, I was expecting a spoiled American teenager. You're anything but. At least, *most* of the time."

"That's sweet. You've defied my expectations of a foaming-at-the-mouth cult member too," she said.

He smirked. "I only foam when I brush my teeth."

M grinned. Crap. She was really starting to like him. And what if Mike was right? What if when it came down to it, if the Eye demanded the pieces, Ash just took them from her? Could she really expect him to go against his god?

They reached Bobet Hall, and Ash opened the door for her. M glanced at her cell. "His lecture should be wrapping up in a few. Wonder what made a lab tech decide he wanted to teach philosophy."

"Very few people end up doing what they expected they'd do when they were twenty," Ash replied.

"There you go again, sounding like a middle-aged man," she teased.

"It's still true," he grumbled. They climbed the stairs to the second-floor lecture room and waited outside until all the students had left. When they walked in, M was surprised to see an old man gathering papers at the lectern. He was probably in his twenties back in 1969, she reminded herself. "Dr. Ferguson? Would you mind answering a question for us?"

He glanced up at them and smiled. "Is it the Hegel? I know it's a challenge. Just get through the reading before class, and we'll start hammering it out."

"We're not in your class, sir," Ash said. "We thought you might have some information regarding a piece that was once part of the collection at the British Museum. It would look something like this." He brought up a picture on his cell of the Set arms. They had photographed the pieces while they were separate at the convent.

The professor swallowed. Then smoothed down one eyebrow with his pinky. M narrowed her eyes. He was about to lie. "We don't care how you got it. We just want to know where it is now," she said quickly. "It's important. Really, really important." She hated that she sounded like she was begging.

The professor's genial manner dropped away. "I sold it to a man who calls himself Papa Ozee. He has a shop in the Quarter. Anything else you want to know, you'll have to ask him." With that, he pushed past them and out the door.

"I'm surprised he told us," Ash commented. "Even years later, stealing from the British Museum could ruin his career."

M nodded, already searching on her phone. "There's a Papa Ozee's House of Voodoo on Decatur Street. The St. Charles Streetcar should take us most of the way there."

"It's like stepping back in time," Ash said as they found places on the mahogany seats of the streetcar.

"It is," M agreed, gazing at the brass fittings and exposed lightbulbs. The kids on campus had made her feel like such an outsider, but here, sitting on the streetcar with Ash, she suddenly felt like a tourist out for a fun day. "You can tell Mardi Gras wasn't that long ago," she commented, gesturing at the brightly colored beads that still hung from the power lines and the giant oak trees.

Ash leaned across her to get a better look, his soapy scent catching her off guard. She inhaled deeply. "I wonder how it compares to Kerala?" he asked, straightening up.

"Fewer elephants, more alcohol, more boob flashing," M answered.

"Then by all means we should go," Ash joked.

M played along, deciding, temporarily, to put her worries on pause and pretend they were just normal friends who could make plans for the future. "Definitely. We'll stay there." She pointed to one of the huge old mansions, layered like a wedding cake, with a gallery running along the second floor.

"Is it a bed-and-breakfast?" Ash asked. "There's no sign."

M gave her hand a dismissive flick. "Doesn't matter. For us, they'll make an exception. We'll sit up there and drink mint juleps out of silver cups. No, silver vases!"

"Big drinker, are you?"

She shrugged. "It's Mardi Gras."

"Vases it is."

M was almost positive Ash didn't drink anymore. It didn't fit with the whole being a vessel thing. But he'd started the Mardi Gras game, and she was glad he was still playing. "At midnight, we'll go to a masquerade ball," she added. "I'll wear some grotesquely expensive gown and a fabulous mask. You'll wear white tie and tails, with white gloves."

"I thought I'd be dressing up," Ash said. "That's my usual weekend wear."

She laughed.

"And of course, we'll dance," he went on, a slight rasp in his voice. "You'll look too beautiful in your grotesquely expensive gown for me to resist dancing with you."

Heat flooded her body. "Of course," she said, trying to seem casual, like she wasn't reacting to what Ash had said, how he'd said it, or the way he'd looked at her. She started to turn away, but her gaze caught on his, and she couldn't.

"Right," he said.

"Right," she repeated.

She wasn't sure who'd moved, or if they both had, but somehow they were closer together. M felt paralyzed, unable to pull herself away from him.

The streetcar shuddered to a stop, jerking M back against the seat, breaking the lovely daydream she and Ash had created together. There was no time for this. Her father's life was on the line. She couldn't let herself forget that, not for a single second.

She checked the streetcar map on her cell. "Our stop is the one after this."

"Bourbon Street runs parallel to Decatur. We need to take a right on one of these streets," M said.

Ash took in a deep breath as they walked. "Smells a bit like London. Piss, river water, diesel, food cooking."

M laughed. "You're right. There must be a bakery nearby. Smell the bread and some kind of pastry?" She took another sniff. "And somebody's definitely smoking pot."

"We can do a guidebook. Instead of the city sights, the city smells," Ash said.

"Did you notice the smell of the elephant pee when we were in Kerala?" M asked, glad Ash was acting normal, as if their moment on the streetcar hadn't happened. "It was like black licorice."

"That's definitely going in." Ash came to an abrupt stop. "One moment." He disappeared into a small shop.

M followed him. "That mask in the window, the deep green one with the crystals and the feathers on one side? I'd like to buy it," he said to the woman behind the counter.

"Lovely," she replied, her face lighting up. "It's the only one we have. Handmade, one-of-a-kind." She smiled at M. "He has good taste. It will be striking with your green eyes."

"It's not for—" M began.

"That's exactly what I was thinking," Ash told the woman.

"You're buying it for me?" M asked.

"For our masquerade ball," he said, winking at her. After he'd paid, he handed the bag to M.

"Thank you." She felt like she should say more but couldn't figure out what.

"Pleasure," Ash said. He held open the door and waved her outside. "Less of a piss smell on this street," he commented.

"Um, yeah." M was flooded with confusion. She was used to pushing emotions away, locking them in an airtight compartment. She'd assumed that was what they were doing with *whatever* that had been on the streetcar. But Ash seemed perfectly happy to lean into it. He was acting as if flirting and present buying could fit right into their normal relationship. She didn't know what to think or where to look. M might be able to break thousand-year-old codes written in ancient languages, but right now she was squarely out of her element.

Focus, M.

They walked in silence until he pointed to a round sign outside a store with peeling blue shutters. "There it is. Papa Ozee's House of Voodoo." He led the way inside.

The amount of *stuff*—too much to identify at first—assaulted M's senses as they walked into the dim interior. Hundreds of necklaces hung from the ceiling. Wooden masks that looked African were hooked on the beams. Voodoo dolls in surprisingly bright colors cascaded down one wall next to shelves crammed with large candles. Were those Buddha statues on the floor? She leaned closer. Yes. And some of the Virgin Mary, too. Bags of herbs lay heaped next to a display of bow ties. M felt like she could stand there for an entire day and not see everything.

A young redheaded woman pushed through a doorway heavy with strings of beads at the back of the shop. Only a few years older than M, she wore a long gauze caftan of all white, with, M was pretty sure, nothing on underneath. It was hard to tell because the room was shadowy and the caftan was floaty. She shot a glance at Ash. He was trying to look anywhere but at the girl.

"What can I help you with?" the girl asked him, and only him, her voice almost theatrically low and throaty. She brushed her long, curly red hair away from her face.

"We're here to see Papa Ozee," M told her.

"And what is your business with Papa?" she asked, resting a hand on Ash's arm. M blinked in surprise. Was she this full-on ridiculous with all the male customers?

"We'd like to ask him about an artifact he might have for sale," Ash replied. "It would look something like this." He showed her the picture.

The girl took it, letting her fingers slide slowly over Ash's, then turned and hip-swayed her way through the bead curtain. "Seriously?" M muttered.

"Hmmm?"

M trailed her fingers down his arm as suggestively as possible, while staring into Ash's eyes. "I think she must work on commission," she said, mimicking the girl's husky tone. "If not, she's definitely still selling something."

"Jealous?" Ash asked, the corners of his mouth twitching with amusement.

Before M could respond, the girl returned with an elderly man, his dark head bald and his beard gray.

"I was expecting you days ago!" he exclaimed, his own loose white clothing billowing around him.

M frowned. Was this a dramatic way to offer a private reading or something? "Are you Papa Ozee?" she asked.

"Obviously," the redhead said. Then she smiled at Ash. "I'm Veronica."

"I have what you're looking for," Papa Ozee told them. "And it no longer wants to be here."

"I'm not sure what you mean," Ash said.

"It tried to escape," Papa Ozee answered. "Come on to the back. If it wants to go to you, you may have it with my blessing."

"Papa, do you really want to sell a power object?" Veronica asked as they followed him through the beaded curtain.

"Not sell, give. I don't need power that strong." His expression darkened. "I pray I never will." He opened a weathered wooden cabinet altar mounted on the wall. It was crammed with objects, but M's eyes instantly locked on the small black Set piece. Papa Ozee reached for it.

"Wait!" Ash demanded. He turned to M. "Take off your backpack."

She understood. As soon as the piece was off the altar, it would want to join the others, and it could hit her with enough force to fracture her spine. She quickly took off the pack, unzipped it, slid the fused Set piece free, and lay it on the floor. Then she backed away.

Ash stepped back too. "You don't want to be between the altar and this statue."

Papa Ozee quickly positioned himself to the side of the cabinet instead of in front of it. Veronica hesitated, staring at the piece on the floor as if mesmerized, before slowly moving away.

"What is that?" she breathed. "I can feel its power. It vibrates in my bones. The other gives a tingle, but this . . ."

"Don't know," M said abruptly. "We were just hired to find it."

Papa Ozee looked at Veronica, Ash, and M in turn. "Don't try to hold on to it," Ash warned. The old man nodded, then gingerly lifted the piece from the cabinet. As soon as he did, the piece jerked free and hurtled across the room. It fused with the other pieces so quickly that M heard the click, but didn't see the motion.

Gasping, Veronica stepped forward, picking up the statue. Her blue eyes were wide, her face so pale that her freckles looked black. "Don't!" M ordered. "Give it to me."

It was as if Veronica hadn't heard. She reverently turned the piece over in her hands. "It's . . . complete. There's no sign of where the connection was made, no crack, no seam."

M stepped up to her, hand out. Veronica continued to caress the piece—arms, torso, and legs now. "Give it to her," Papa Ozee instructed. Reluctantly, she handed it over. M returned the Set animal to the backpack and slid it back on. She'd felt naked without it, missing the feel of the small weight and the strange throbbing.

"Mine knew yours was on the way. That's why it tried to escape. It knew its brothers were coming," Papa said.

"Do you mean it moved? When?" Ash demanded.

"About a week ago, I took several objects, including that piece, off the altar to clean them. I put them on the table." Papa Ozee indicated a table covered with a brightly patterned cloth. "Then six days ago, it began twitching. It skittered off the table and started jerking across the floor. I managed to get it back in the altar, and it quieted. And I waited for someone to come."

"Six days ago we broke open the foundation to the Isis temple, and the two pieces fused," M murmured to Ash.

"But that would mean the pieces attract even when they're on different continents," he replied. His eyes went wide. "What if this is how they've been tracking us? We thought they'd sent followers to places on the map, but maybe that's not what happened."

"What are you talking about?" Veronica asked, her voice sharp now, the purr gone.

M and Ash locked eyes. "We have to get out of here," M said, adrenalin pulsing through her.

"Now," Ash agreed.

They rushed out of Papa Ozee's, breaking into a run. As long as she had the artifact in her backpack, they were in danger. They passed shops, restaurants, a cemetery.

M skidded to a stop, whirling around. "I have an idea." She grabbed Ash's hand. "In here," she gasped, pulling him through the black wrought-iron gate of the cemetery. She felt the Set pieces shift as soon as they entered.

"Sacred space," she said.

"But we're still standing out in the open."

She glanced around, searching for a hiding place. "Over here," she pointed and took off. Ash raced behind her to a mausoleum near the center of the cemetery, where she hopped over the low fence, then ducked inside.

"The pieces . . ." She had to pause to suck in a breath. "Don't attract in here. They fell apart."

"And if they don't attract one another, they won't pull on the piece the cult of Set has."

"It's the throbbing, the vibration," M said, realizing it even as she spoke. "The pieces only do it when we leave a sacred space, the same way they suddenly attract. That throbbing is some kind of signal the Set animal sends itself."

Ash's nostrils flared. "It wants to be complete. Set wants to rise again."

She pushed aside how fanatical he sounded. No matter how much magic she saw, she couldn't believe there was an actual god involved. "If we're right, the reason Bob and Liza were at the temple in Kerala was because they already knew we were there," M said. "Except they were already in the gopura when we spotted them."

"Right." Ash said, thinking. "Say they were tracking us. At some point, they would have seen we were heading toward Kerala, and your father had already sent them there once. It wouldn't be a big leap to assume that's where we were going. They just got there first."

"I know why we were safe at the convent. Can't get more sacred than that," M said. "But why didn't they nab us in Bali? We thought going by boat would make us hard to follow, but the pieces would have been signaling all the way there." She sunk down onto the cool granite of the mausoleum floor. Ash sat beside her.

"Remember how the pieces kept falling apart and coming together in Bali?" Ash asked.

"Because there were offerings and altars all over the place, even in cars!" M exclaimed. "Almost the whole island was sacred."

"Mike even had some kind of holy garland hanging from her car—along with a St. Christopher's medal—most of the way to the convent. Maybe the pieces stopped sending the signal before we even got there."

"Do you think we're safe here?" M asked, worried. "If they know how sacred spaces affect the pieces, and our trail ends at a cemetery, they wouldn't have to be geniuses to know we're here."

"Maybe not," Ash said. "We've seen the way the pieces act on sacred ground, so we eventually made the connection. The Set people didn't know we were in a sacred wood when they lost the signal—if that's what happened. Or that we'd gone into a church."

M chewed on her lip. "We don't know how the tracking

process works, either," she added. "Is it like a paranormal GPS, where they know precisely where we are? Like you said, if they knew we were around Kerala, it made sense to go there. If they knew we were on Java, it would make sense to check the biggest temple. Even if they don't know how the pieces react to sacred spaces, they must have figured out the places on the map are holy."

"So it's likely they know we're in New Orleans. But not precisely here."

"It's not like Java, where there was an obvious place to start, either." M fingered a piece of moss that had pushed its way through a crack in the floor. "The map didn't send us here, so they wouldn't start out with a location. They could be searching random churches or whatever, but there's no reason to think we were at a voodoo store with an altar."

"So we stay put," Ash said. "When we leave the cemetery, the signal starts up again. On the other hand, if they were able to track us to the cemetery gates, well, like you once said, I have my power, you have your bo staff."

"And that ain't nothing," M agreed. "But we can't stay here forever. We have another piece to find, and my dad . . ." Her voice wavered. She didn't want to say it.

When Ash spoke, he spoke slowly. "The jaguar temple in Guatemala isn't on the map either. We got that location from a signpost." He hesitated. "We have to split up."

"No," she said.

"It's our only choice, M."

"Not happening."

"It's the safest way," Ash insisted. "One of us stays here, hidden, with the pieces. One of us goes to Guatemala—with no possibility of being tracked."

"Then I stay." The pieces were Dad's life. She wasn't letting go of them. But even as she said it, she realized that if the Set devotees did search the cemetery, her bo staff wouldn't be enough to stop them. She'd seen what Ash's power could do. He at least had a shot.

"I know you don't want to leave the Set pieces with me—" he began.

"Those pieces are all I have to guarantee my father's life."

"I know," he said. "M, I know. He means everything to you, and you don't trust the Eye to rescue him unless you can bargain with them. And . . . I think you're right. I don't believe Philip will save your father if he has already secured and rehidden the pieces."

She stared at him, astonished. "You said we had a deal."

He nodded. "We do have a deal. You and I, we have a deal."

"But you're admitting the Eye can't be trusted?"

"I don't know who to trust anymore," he said as he took her hands, intertwining her fingers with his. "Except you. I trust you, M."

His eyes hadn't left hers for a second.

"I trust you, too." The words escaped M's lips without her deciding to say them. They came from her gut. Mike was right. There were reasons, huge reasons, for Ash to betray her. She was on one side, his god the other.

But her gut told her to trust him, and her parents had taught her to trust her gut. She pulled her hands from his and slid the pieces out of her backpack, knowing what she was about to do could get her father killed, but believing—or at least hoping so hard that it was almost like believing—that Ash would keep his word.

Ash took the pieces and stowed them in his pack, looping a strap around his arm like she always did. His eyes slid away from hers, and he suddenly looked guilty. "There's something I need to tell you."

"What?" M demanded, every nerve crackling.

"Nothing that changes our deal," he answered quickly, his gaze jerking back up to meet hers. "But I don't want you to leave with any secrets between us."

She just nodded. Her throat felt too tight to speak.

"M, your guardians? They're my parents." His words were rushed. "I know it might make you hate me."

M stared at him, too shocked to speak. What was he talking about?

"They're . . . they're with Set. I was born to Set, raised to worship Set," Ash said. "I'm sorry."

Bob and Liza? Those disgustingly normal people? They had nothing in common with Ash. *But it was a lie, everything I knew about them was a lie,* she thought. She still hadn't adjusted her thinking on them enough. None of this computed.

"That's why they hated me. It wasn't my power. It was because my power came from the enemy of their god." His throat convulsed as he swallowed hard. "I don't know why I didn't tell you. I'm an idiot."

M's brain whirled as she tried to take in what his confession meant. "So when you went undercover . . ."

"I had to pretend I wanted back in. I had to make my oldest friend believe I'd realized my power was an abomination," he replied.

It had always nagged at her that the Set cult had let some grunt get close enough to her father to speak to him. Now it made sense. "You got back in as the prodigal son."

Ash nodded. "I should have told you."

A reluctant smile tugged at M's lips. "Well, if you'd told me you had any connection to Set that first night, you would have been saying hello to my bo staff."

He didn't smile back. His face looked haggard, his expression haunted. M frowned. He really thought this would change her opinion of him.

"Ash, you're not them," she said. "Bob was the one who . . ." She gestured toward the scars hidden beneath his shirt. "And Liza, she said those horrible things to you. They're horrible. I hate them. I don't hate *you*."

He nodded, lips pressed together as if to hold in a sob. "Thank you," he whispered.

She reached out and took his hand, unsure what to say. She'd known his family life was bad. But apparently it was even worse than she'd realized. Of course he hadn't trusted her with the truth. How could he ever trust anyone when his own parents thought him a monster?

"You should've told me, but I know why you didn't," she said. "We've never completely trusted each other. Until now."

"I'll keep the pieces safe," he promised.

"I know."

They sat in silence, staring at each other. Finally M sighed. They had work to do. "There's not much food. Should I—"

"No, when you leave the cemetery you need to run. You can't risk being seen." Ash smiled wanly. "I have water. And I'm used to self-deprivation, you know."

She smiled. "Horus likes that, I hear."

"Just don't be gone too long." He reached into his own bag and pulled out a wallet. "There's enough in there to get you to Guatemala and back."

"Okay," she said. "Thanks." She got to her feet. All that was left to do was say good-bye. It shouldn't be so hard. She'd only known him for a matter of days.

Ash stood up too. "It'll be okay. I'll be here when you get back. The pieces of Set will be here."

She felt a jolt of surprise. She should be thinking about the pieces. But she'd only been thinking of him.

"I have to go." She started toward the mausoleum's narrow door, then turned and launched herself at Ash, hugging him tight. His arms came up, crushing her to him. "Be careful," he said.

"I have to go," she repeated, mumbling into his chest. Then she pushed herself away and left.

She didn't let herself look back.

CHAPTER 20

M checked to make sure the needle on her compass was perfectly aligned with the orienting arrow. Then she aimed in the direction of the traveling arrow, chose a tree in the distance, and started toward it, silently thanking Mom and Dad for teaching her navigation skills. She wouldn't have been able to find her way through the jungle to the jaguar temple without them.

After three hours of hiking, she was also thankful she'd decided to buy two pairs of thick, comfy socks along with her new hiking boots and small scythe, all paid for with Ash's money. *I guess it's the Eye's money, actually,* she thought.

She had mostly managed to wall Ash-related thoughts into one corner of her brain. But apprehension kept slipping through. She knew wondering if she'd made the right decision was pointless. It had been more than a day since she left him. If he were going to take the pieces to the Eye, he was already gone.

She'd made her choice. She wasn't going to think about it anymore. Distractions were something she couldn't afford. If she got off course by as little as fifty feet she might walk right past the temple.

After another half hour of hacking her way through the jungle, she found it. Vegetation had begun creeping over the carved jaws that served as the temple's entrance, enormous teeth designed to incite fear. She stopped and a shiver slithered through her.

Her gut was telling her she was in danger. Her brain knew the mouth was a carved rock and not at all threatening. But her gut couldn't be ignored. It believed stone teeth should be avoided. And soulful eyes should be trusted. When she'd first met Ash, she'd known to be wary, she'd—

Stop, she ordered herself. Just because she'd successfully navigated the jungle didn't mean she could stop paying attention to her surroundings. Ruins could be extremely dangerous. And her gut was telling her the temple should be avoided. She had to be careful.

M straightened her shoulders and walked through the monster's mouth un-chomped. The temperature dropped several degrees inside the stone building, and as she moved deeper, she was struck by the silence. During her hike through the jungle, insect whirs and buzzes, screeches and monkey chatter had been incessant, but no living creature had taken shelter in the temple. Even the mosquitos that had been biting her all day hadn't followed her inside.

She took a large flashlight from her backpack. Her fingers brushed against the feathers of the mask Ash had bought her, a silly thing to take to a jungle, but she couldn't bring herself to leave it behind. It had been so unexpected, so sweet.

Was he waiting? Was he— She sighed, not finishing the question. She flicked on the flashlight and studied the narrow passageway in front of her. Looked good. Nothing to climb over or squeeze around.

She slowly walked down the passage, playing the flashlight beam along the wall carvings as she went. They all seemed to be of warriors, but many had lines carved across them, slashing through the images.

The grooves were deep, clearly made by a sharp blade, because the cuts were smooth. M ran her fingers down three parallel grooves, her nails making a light scratching sound. *They're supposed to be claw marks,* she realized. Well, she was in the Temple of the Jaguar. Did the slashes indicate warriors who had somehow angered or disappointed the god? Her fingers itched to pull out her cell and document what she was seeing, but she wasn't here as an archeologist.

The passageway widened, and she saw another carved mouth. This time she stepped through without hesitation—but the small circular room she'd entered was a dead end. At the far side was a raised stone altar. On top sat a cracked statue of a man with the ears and teeth of a jaguar, and beside it a bowl. The walls on either side showed paintings of the gradual transformation of a man into the great cat. The paintings only used two colors, red and black. To the Maya, red represented initiation, and black represented transformation.

She ran her fingers along the walls, hoping to feel something her eyes had missed, some way to get deeper into the temple, but there was nothing. She studied the altar. It was unadorned, made of the same stone as the walls. The were-jaguar statue and the bowl were both ceramic.

Could the statue hold some kind of trigger mechanism that would open a door? Or set off a booby trap? Dr. Verela was superstitious, but that didn't mean there weren't real dangers here. There had to be some reason the people who had come to the temple ended up dead, a reason these two artifacts had been left untouched.

Before last week, M would never have considered a supernatural explanation. But now she wasn't so sure. And if she had to face down an actual were-jaguar to get the last Set piece, so be it.

She gently ran her hands over the ancient statue. There didn't seem to be a way to move the ears or mouth, the jaguar's feet or the man's hands, at least not without powers she didn't possess. Who knew, maybe Ash could make it dance a jig, but she was on her own. She tried pressing on the jaguar's spots, but nothing happened.

She put down the statue and picked up the bowl. There was a series of pictures painted in red. The first showed a figure cutting its tongue and letting blood drip into a bowl. The one she held?

The next showed the figure adding a flowering plant to the bowl. Then there was a picture of the figure drinking from the bowl. The final image showed the figure curled up under the altar M stood before, complete with bowl and statue on top.

M returned the bowl to the altar. The instructions were for a ritual of some kind. Likely an initiation. M looked inside the bowl. There was a yellowish residue, maybe powder from the decaying clay, but maybe something else. Could it have been left behind from something mixed in the bowl, remains of the plant shown?

M thought back to the sibyl cave. The lore had said to bring an offering of mistletoe, and mistletoe had helped them get to the room with the signpost. The bowl was telling her what to do.

In her backpack, she had the Swiss Army knife her mother had always carried. Dad had given it to her when she turned twelve. Mom had believed every woman should have one, and since then, M had used it for a million things—gutting fish, disgorging a fish hook from her dad's cheek, pressing the reset button on her cell, getting spinach out of her teeth, making a new tent peg, killing a scorpion, cutting moleskin for a blister, sharpening a pencil, opening a can. M had never done anything as cool with it as save a life, but her mom had. She'd used the knife to perform an emergency tracheotomy once.

The most important thing the knife did was make M think about Mom. Every time she used it, she made sure to remember something, even if it was just something from a story someone had told her about her mother.

M took out the knife and selected the small blade. She opened her mouth. Was she really going to do this? Yeah, she was. At least the blood didn't have to come from a penis, like in some rituals. She'd have been shit out of luck.

With a quick motion, she nicked her tongue and leaned over the bowl, squeezing the tip of her tongue between her fingers until a few drops of blood mixed with the powder residue. She used her pinky to mix in her blood, then licked the concoction off. It burned where it touched the cut she'd made, but didn't have much of a taste, just the usual salty tang blood had.

I may have lost it, she thought as she crawled under the altar and curled up to match the position of the figure on the bowl.

She closed her eyes, waiting for . . . *something.*

Swirls of red and black appeared beneath her eyelids. Her scalp began to tingle, burning, the sensation flowing down her skin. The pain went deep, stabbing now, burrowing under her skin, blazing.

She tried to scream, but she couldn't pull in any air. She couldn't even open her eyes. It was as if her eyelids had melted into her cheeks. Her arms had fused to her sides, her legs bonded together.

Then she was falling.

Falling.

Falling.

She landed with a thud. And lay there. The fire in her body extinguished. The pain was gone.

It took her a second to realize she couldn't feel her heart beating. Or her chest rising and falling. Was she breathing? Was she alive?

Terror threatened to overwhelm her. She shoved it back with everything she had in her.

I'm alive, she told herself. *Of course I'm alive. I'm thinking this, so I'm alive.*

If she could just open her eyes . . . just see where she was . . .

What would Mike do? Or Ash? Pray. But M didn't know how. Or who she would pray to if she did.

So what would Dad do?

She called upon one of his favorite expressions: "Let's review."

Okay, M, let's review, she told herself. *What just happened? You—intentionally—ingested the residue of what was most likely a hallucinogenic plant.*

And then? Let's review. You felt as if your body turned molten and fused into a somewhat person-shaped lump without a pulse.

The logical answer? You are tripping.

What should you do? Wait it out. Because, let's review, you don't have a choice.

She felt fractionally calmer. She pretended she was taking yoga breaths, in through the nose and out through the mouth, nice and slow and controlled. Maybe that's even what was happening. It felt as if she weren't taking in air, but it was impossible. Because she was alive.

Although, if she couldn't move, she wouldn't stay alive forever. She'd starve. Was that what had happened to the people who died in this temple?

Not a useful thought. She did some more pretend breathing. In out, in out, in out.

After some amount of time—M wasn't sure if it was minutes or hours—she heard a faint cracking sound. Had she been able to hear before? The cracking continued, along with a new sound. The pounding of her heart!

She tried to open her eyes, and felt her eyelids give a little. They didn't open, but they'd responded. She tried again, managing to open her eyes a slit, enough to turn the terrible blackness into a deep gray.

M concentrated on her lips, trying to wrench them apart. There was a louder crack, and her mouth opened slightly. A fine grit slid inside.

What she needed was her hands. She struggled to yank her arms away from her sides. It was as if she were encased in a hard shell. She felt something crack, then crumble, when she tried to jerk her arms free again. It was working. The knowledge gave her a blast of strength, and she wriggled and twisted and wrenched her arms until, with a crack as loud as a gunshot, her right arm burst free.

She shook and flexed her hand until she had control over it, then brought her fingers to her face. It felt hard and smooth, like ceramic. She tapped on her cheek with her knuckles, first tentatively, then harder. The cracking sound again. She explored with her fingertips and discovered a fissure. She pried at it until shards began to come off.

Gently, she worked her eyelids free. Opening them felt miraculous. She couldn't see much. It seemed like she was lying on a mound of dirt. As quickly as she could, she cracked the area around her mouth until she was able to work her jaw. Opening and closing it caused more of the hard shell to fall off.

Chipping away at the ceramic was taking forever. She wanted out. Now. She used her free arm to give herself a push, then another. She managed to get herself rocking and was soon tumbling over and over, rolling down the mound. When she hit bottom, she felt large pieces of her casing break off. She arched, and flexed, and bucked, until she was able to stand. She looked down. Chunks of ceramic painted with a complex pattern of red and black were scattered around her.

Her breath caught as she turned. At least a dozen bodies, in varying degrees of decomposition, lay behind her. Each had been pierced by at least one jade-tipped arrow.

M crouched down and examined the floor she'd rolled across, before stretching out on her belly, pressing down on one of the stones. Wffft! An arrow shot out of a hole in the wall to her right and flew over her head.

If she had walked across the floor instead of rolling in her ceramic casing, she would probably be dead. Those who had died down here must not have followed the whole ritual, so the ceramic cocoon hadn't protected them when the arrows shot out.

What had just happened hadn't been a hallucination. It had been real. She'd seen equally strange things—talking statues, the behavior of the Set pieces—but still couldn't quite believe it.

She turned away from the bodies and saw that the only way forward was a tall, narrow staircase. She began to climb. At the top was something she'd seen in Mayan ruins before—a ball court. The Maya were believed to have played a game somewhat like basketball. There was a clear space about the size of a football field with a twenty-foot-high black wall running along one side. Stone rings carved with snakes protruded from the wall at either end. The openings in the rings were positioned out to the side, rather than parallel to the floor the way a modern basketball hoop was. But the object was the same—get a ball through a hole.

A strange phosphorescent light poured down on the court from globes, hundreds of them, arranged around a stone throne at the top of the wall. A massive golden jaguar sat there, towering protectively above everything. *Maybe the globes are coated with jarosite,* M thought, unable to stop trying to come up with logical explanations for a situation where logic clearly didn't apply.

The jaguar glyph they'd found inside the Buddha's mouth made the golden jaguar the most logical place to start looking for the Set piece. M had brought along climbing gear, but the wall was absolutely smooth. Could the whole thing be made of polished obsidian? Mayan royalty had used that for their mirrors, tezcatl.

How was she going to get up there? A small stone pyramid sat on either end of the court. They weren't high enough to help her, but M walked over to the closest to see if it might be useful in some way.

From a distance it had been invisible, but there was a pit in front of the pyramid, circled with flat stones. The stones were covered in more red-and-black paintings, this time of male warriors playing on the court. Well, some were playing. Others were almost entirely enveloped in snakes twining around their bodies.

Peering inside, she saw that the pit was deeper than she realized, and filled with bones. Bones of the defeated warriors? But not all of the bones were human. A long skull with large, pointed canine teeth made her think the others were jaguar. So there was a connection with the were-jaguar worship. Maybe the game had something to do with picking the new king, something the jaguar was supposed to be involved in.

M walked back across the court until she was even with the golden jaguar and the throne it guarded. Someone used to sit in that throne. There had to be a way up. If she could get a rope through one of those rings, she might be able to use it to walk her way up the wall. She snorted. "Easy-peasy."

She smiled, the goofy expression making her think of Ash. Instead of sending a spike of worry through her, this time she found the thought of him comforting. She wasn't completely alone in this, even if he wasn't with her right this second.

Okay, rope through ring. Could she tie the rope to a piece of bone? Or maybe go back and get one of those arrows? Before she could decide, a sound split the silence she'd grown so used to.

It came from above, a noise like the grinding of gear teeth.

She looked up and saw the jaws of the golden jaguar jerking open inch by inch. Then something came hurtling down at her. A black ball. It struck her on the cheek, hard. A drop of blood trickled down her face and plopped onto the stone floor.

A crack appeared in the spot where the blood hit, and a long, slender red snake slithered out.

"Holy snakes," she whispered, her hand on her cheek. It had all happened so fast that she felt a little stunned.

The snake slithered toward her, but she stepped out of its way. Snakes under the floor. Not her biggest problem. She picked up the ball that hit her. It was made of hard rubber, and was just a bit smaller than the holes in the stone rings. Clearly it was designed for the game.

M rolled the ball between her hands, thinking, before taking her mom's Swiss Army knife out again. One of its features was a hook that turned the knife into a package carrier. The hook was also useful for guiding a line through a tight spot. She got to work removing the knife's outer casing and unscrewed the tiny bolts, carefully putting them in a pocket of her backpack. Then she removed the hook, and with the help of the small blade, managed to gouge a hole in the ball and jam the end of the hook into it. Next she attached one of her climbing ropes to the hook. Now all she had to do was throw the ball through the hoop. If a Mayan warrior could do it, so could she.

M eyed the ring, took a few running steps, and hurled the ball at it. Not even close. The ball hit the stone floor with a *wham*, making a new crack. Another red snake wriggled up and out, its tongue tasting the air. She threw the ball at the ring again. Missed. *Wham.* Crack.

And there came another snake. It stayed nearby. So had the other two. "I really don't need spectators," M muttered. She took another shot. "And I win another snake!" she cried, throwing up her arms in frustration as a new snake came out of a new crack in the floor.

She stomped off to retrieve the ball. The newest snake followed, and as she picked up the ball, twined its way up her leg. *Oh, hell no.* She grabbed its neck, right behind the head so it couldn't bite her, and yanked. It tightened its coils until she gave a yelp of pain. The snake hadn't looked big enough to be this strong. She returned to her backpack, the snake still bearing down on her calf. She took out the knife blade and cut off the head. Its body twitched and tightened its grip.

Warriors with snakes twined around their bodies. Now the red-and-black pictures made sense.

M let out a howl of frustration and fury. Without even taking aim, she threw the ball in the direction of the ring as hard as she could. Didn't make it. The floor cracked as the ball landed, and another snake appeared. This one immediately headed for M. She backed up, but it was too fast. It twined itself up her other leg. Killing the first one had just made things worse. The headless body was squeezing harder than the living snake. She left the new one where it was.

M threw the ball again and again and again. The stone floor looked like the epicenter of an earthquake, cracks everywhere. Snakes wrapped themselves around her thighs, her waist, her left forearm, and her right upper arm. Another had encircled her throat, not tightly enough to constrict her breathing. At least not yet.

As she went after the ball so she could try again, she stumbled over one of the cracks in the floor. The snake around her neck hissed, its tongue flicking against the tip of her ear. This was impossible. Impossible. But she couldn't stop trying. That would be the same as saying, "Go ahead, kill my dad, I give up."

"The only way I'm stopping is if I die first!" she shouted. In response, the snakes tightened on her body. M forced herself to take time to center herself in front of the ring. Ignoring the snakes, she aimed and threw, not too hard, not too soft.

The ball flew through the stone ring, taking the rope with it. Before the ball even hit the ground, the snakes dropped off her body. They slithered back into the cracks, even the one that should have been dead. The cracks sealed behind them, leaving the floor of the court as she'd found it.

M tied the ends of the rope together so it wouldn't slither out of the ring like one of the snakes. Then she took off her heavy boots and thick socks, figuring her bare feet would get more purchase on the slick wall.

She locked her eyes on the golden statue high above and climbed straight up without pausing. She strode over to the jaguar. The head of the Set animal lay between its shining paws.

M's breath caught in her throat. The black stone piece was facing her, its eyes staring directly into hers. Was Ash right? Was the Egyptian god of the underworld trapped in this piece of stone, looking right at her?

She didn't care.

"I'm coming for you, Dad," she whispered, grabbing the Set piece. "Hang on just a little longer."

CHAPTER 21

"M?"

Ash sat up, shaking off sleep. M couldn't possibly be back yet. This was his second night in the mausoleum, but a flight to Guatemala would take six hours minimum, not to mention all the other travel time. He had no idea how far the were-jaguar temple was from civilization, nor how M planned on getting to it. He couldn't expect her for at least another day, and that was if everything went smoothly. He hated to think of her navigating the jungle alone, even though he knew she would do a better job than he ever could. She'd probably been in a hundred jungles in her life.

He looked around. There was enough room to stretch out on the floor between the two columns of stacked crypts, but not much more space. At a glance he could see he was alone. But something had woken him.

Instinctively, he reached for the backpack. His hand hit cold stone.

All remnants of sleep vanished instantly.

It was gone! He'd fallen asleep with it right beside him, and it was gone. The Set pieces had been stolen.

He jammed on his shoes and bolted for the door, then forced himself to slow down. If someone had just taken the artifact, they were likely to be nearby. He crept outside and pressed his back against the cool stone wall, surveying the cemetery. The moon was nearly full, but it was obscured by clouds. When he was sure no one was in sight, he inched down the wall.

How had this happened? The pieces shouldn't have been giving off a signal. They couldn't have, or his parents would have shown up before now. He wouldn't be surprised if they had people stationed all over the city, waiting for a new signal. But it didn't make sense that they would just happen to search the mausoleum where he was hiding. Nor that they would leave him sleeping. His parents would kill him if they had the chance, and so would Hugh.

He peered around the corner of the mausoleum. Three dots of light flickered in the distance. Keeping low, he moved toward them until he could make out three candles set on a grave. Someone knelt over them. Silently, he stole closer, using mausoleums for cover when he could.

The wind kicked up, and the clouds shifted. Now the moonlight illuminated the figure. It was the girl from the voodoo shop, Veronica. She was naked, kneeling before the Set pieces, her pale skin almost glowing. She sprinkled something over them. The three candle flames flared, and Ash could see the ardent expression on her face.

He launched himself toward the pieces, but before he could reach them he heard a sound that sucked the air out of his lungs. Click. Click. Click. The Set pieces had fused. Somehow Veronica had desecrated the cemetery. It no longer acted as a sacred space.

Ash snatched up the Set animal, kicking over one of the candles. Veronica let out a high screech of outrage. But he didn't waste time demanding to know what she'd done. He had to get the piece to another sacred space before the cult of Set tracked him.

The cemetery gate was swinging on its hinges. Ash knocked it open with his body. He didn't know the city. He had no idea which way to run. So he just ran, dodging around a group of people coming out of a bar carrying red plastic cups.

Should I go into a bar, he thought wildly. No. Hiding in a crowd wouldn't help him. The pieces would just be constantly signaling where he was. He needed another cemetery, a church, a mosque, anything.

He spotted a spire with a cross in the distance. Maybe he'd find something closer, but at least it gave him a direction. He locked his eyes on it as he hurtled on, cradling the Set animal tighter against his chest.

Ash heard tires squeal and shot a glance over his shoulder. A dark van was coming toward him, fast. He took the first turn he came to. An alley. A dead end. His eyes flicked around wildly. Black iron fire escapes zigzagged up the five stories of the brick building.

The van couldn't follow him up there.

The bottom platform was about six feet up. Ash used the momentum of his run to hurl himself toward it, but his free hand was too sweaty and slipped right off.

When he landed, a pair of hands grabbed his shoulders and something heavy slammed into his skull. Everything went black.

M drove her rental car one-handed, her other hand resting on the backpack that held the last Set piece. She should be exhausted after being turned into a life-sized ceramic figurine and battling undead—or at least undying—snakes, not to mention hacking her way back out of the jungle. Instead, she felt amazing, flying on an adrenalin high and the knowledge that she had what she needed.

Unless Ash—

Nope. She wouldn't doubt him. He'd promised he would be there, and she believed him. She trusted him.

She slowed to take a curve on the winding road. A particularly elaborate animita came into view. The roadside shrine was backed by some sort of triptych with niches in all three sections holding statues of saints. There were also a couple of potted plants, and what looked like a solar lighting system. Someone was taking exceptionally good care of the memorial.

M had seen a few roadside memorials in the U.S., usually just a cross with some plastic flowers or maybe a stuffed animal. But in Latin America, the shrines were incredibly common. She'd passed one every hundred feet along the narrow two-lane road, most commemorating someone who'd died in a car accident, but some honoring the victims of drug or political violence. They were placed on the spot where the soul and body separated.

Dad had consulted on an ancient Olmec site when she was thirteen, and she'd mostly just hung around with the students. They'd told her people would visit the animitas and ask the souls of the dead to intercede for them. She'd found the shrines fascinating, especially the way that portable animal kennels were often used to hold a loved one's favorite things. Now she saw them differently; she saw them as sacred.

M spotted a road sign. A little over fifty miles to Flores, where Joel had hooked her up with another private jet ride back to New Orleans, leaving tomorrow. She wished she could just book the next flight. But now was no time to start taking risks.

She eased around another curve. More animitas stretched out in front of her. So many dead to mourn. She felt the weariness that the adrenalin had been keeping at bay seep into her. All she wanted was to end this. To see her father.

What would happen to Ash when it was over? Would they still be friends? Was that what they were now? It was hard to imagine spending time with him under normal circumstances. She wondered if he'd be different.

M glanced in the rearview mirror. A dark gray van had moved up behind her. As it got closer, it sped up, gluing itself to her tail. Annoyed, M hit the accelerator. The van kept pace. The lane in the other direction was empty. There was plenty of room for it to pass.

It didn't.

The hairs at the back of her neck prickled. It had been about five hours since she took the Set piece from the jaguar temple. Could the cult of Set have tracked the signal this fast?

Her Hyundai Sonata didn't have great pickup. And it wasn't like she could race the van all the way to town. There were no turn-offs. Just the two lanes with nothing around.

A plan. She needed a plan. There was a sharp curve coming up. Maybe she could use that. She slammed on the gas, screeched around the curve, and let the car plough into the low guard rail. The airbag deployed, banging her in the face. Ignoring the pain, M grabbed the backpack, and scrambled out of the car.

Let there be one, let there be one! Yes! There was a shrine made out of a small dog carrier a little way down the road. As she ran, she heard the van crash into the rental car. She smiled. That should slow them down.

M reached the crate, yanked open the door, and thrust her backpack inside, muttering an apology to the soul of the person it belonged to. "I'll bring it back, promise," she whispered as she picked it up in both arms and struggled to climb over the rocky outcropping behind the group of shrines. She slid down the other side. At least she was out of sight.

This had to work. The shrine was a sacred space, a *portable* sacred space. The Set acolytes would know she was nearby, but wouldn't know where. She took a breath, forcing herself to be still for a few seconds, to make sure . . . no throbbing noise. No signal. The shrine was doing its job.

M began fighting her way through the brush, wishing she could use her scythe, but it was impossible while carrying the animita. Her body was already aching and bruised from the struggle to get the Set piece, but she ignored the fresh pain caused by walking over the rough ground. Every second mattered. She heard shouts in the distance. How long until they figured out which direction she'd gone in?

She pressed on, expecting to hear someone coming after her. When she mounted a crest and saw a village—with people—stretching out below her, her eyes stung with tears of relief. She blinked them away, assessing the scattered groups of villagers.

Those three guys, she decided. With a little charm and a lot of Ash's money, they looked like they could be convinced to give her a ride to Flores. As she started toward them, she glanced over her shoulder again.

She wasn't being followed. Yet.

CHAPTER 22

M climbed out of the cab and adjusted the huge duffel bag she wore over her shoulder. She'd bought the biggest one she could find at the airport and managed to jam the dog kennel shrine, her backpack—and the last Set piece—inside.

The flight had felt endless, and there hadn't been a flight attendant to make her all the lattes she wanted on this one. But she was finally here, back in New Orleans, and all she wanted was to get to Ash. Her gut was still telling her he'd meant it when he promised to wait. Fear had made her doubt herself, doubt him, but he'd be there.

She swung open the gate to the cemetery and rushed to the mausoleum, the duffel repeatedly banging against her side. She opened the narrow doorway. She had to clutch the bag in front of her to step inside. "Ash?" she called, placing the duffel on the floor.

He wasn't there.

He wasn't there.

He wasn't there.

A few empty water bottles lay on the floor, but Ash and the backpack containing the Set pieces was gone.

Fuck. Fuck, fuck, fuck.

He'd betrayed her. He'd looked right at her, and lied, lied so well that every instinct told her he was being honest, even when he had every reason to deceive her.

What was wrong with her? Two minutes before she left him, he'd told her he lied to people who'd known him since he was a child, lied to his oldest friend, lied so well he convinced them he wanted back in the Set cult, an organization he despised. Ash was a master manipulator, and he'd made her trust him.

"Stop." She told herself quietly. "Stop," she said again with more force. Just because Ash wasn't in the mausoleum didn't mean he wasn't in the cemetery. Maybe he was out walking around. The mausoleum probably made him feel claustrophobic, and it had been a long time since they'd gotten the piece from Papa Ozee. He probably thought it was okay to go out.

Taking a deep breath, she stepped back outside, beginning a thorough search. She walked up and down each row of graves and mausoleums but didn't find him.

Maybe they'd just missed each other. Maybe he was back in the mausoleum. M was struggling to stay calm and explore all the possibilities. But her heart felt like it was beating double time. She could feel it in her throat, her wrists, her ears, even her fingertips.

She wanted to run back to the mausoleum, but she forced herself to walk, to at least pretend she might see him. When she reached the mausoleum and opened the door, the stone structure was still empty.

M went back in anyway, hoping she'd find a note. But there was no message. He might have tried to call her in Guatemala and not gotten through. She'd been off the grid for a stretch of hours.

But he would have kept trying until he reached her. She walked back outside and slumped down, leaning against the mausoleum wall. Hopelessness surged through her. She'd been wrong about him. Wrong about trusting her gut. Wrong about her ability to read people. Ash had probably been on his cell to Philip the second she left.

It was over. She'd done everything she could to save her father, and it wasn't enough. She'd failed, and he would be killed.

M took out her cell.

M: You there?

MIKE: Here.

The answer came almost instantly, as if Mike had her phone out, waiting.

M: Found the last piece. Got back to the cemetery and Ash was gone. You were right.

MIKE: Don't assume.

M: What else am I supposed to think?

MIKE: Maybe someone came after him?

MIKE: Any place you think he'd go or would leave a message?

M: Maybe one place. Let me check and get back to you.

MIKE: Godspeed.

They hadn't been in New Orleans long. There was only one place Ash might have tried to leave a message—Papa Ozee's. She shouldered her duffel and left the cemetery. The Set cult would be using every resource to get the pieces. Who knew how many people they sent to New Orleans following the signal. Maybe Ash's hiding place had been discovered. Maybe he'd escaped and found another sacred space. Or maybe he'd been captured by Bob and Liza.

His parents, who beat him. When he'd told her about them, all she could think was how awful they had been to him. Maybe she should've been thinking about how much he must hate them, how focused he must be on revenge, on destroying them and their god.

No. Stop. She began to walk faster. She and Ash were partners, a team. She'd trusted him. She shouldn't doubt herself—or him—now. What she should be thinking about is what she could do to help him. If the cult of Set had him, he was in as much danger as her father. More. Dad still had value, because she had something they wanted. They couldn't bring their precious god back to life without the last piece. And they would know her father gave them leverage over her. There would be no reason to keep Ash alive.

Papa Ozee's shop was just down the block. She jogged the last steps, the dog kennel shrine bouncing hard against her shoulder. She wrangled the large bag through the door.

Her eyes began to burn. There were traces of smoke in the air, and the scent of sage filled the room. When Papa Ozee appeared from behind one of the crammed shelves, M saw that he held a smoldering bundle of herbs tied with purple string. "I don't want that object back in my place," he told her, eyeing the duffel. "I told you it doesn't want to be here."

"I don't have it with me," M said quickly. "I just wanted to know if my friend Ash came back. The British guy I was with last time."

Papa Ozee's expression told her he didn't believe her, but before he could answer, there came the soft sound of beads clicking together and Veronica came into the room, wearing another gauzy caftan, this one of the palest violet. "When I was walking to work the other day, I saw him getting into a taxi over by the city of the dead."

"The cemetery, you mean?" M asked. "Was he alone?"

"No. He was with a man. Maybe fifty or so," Veronica replied.

M felt like she'd been sucker punched. There was no way one man could get Ash into a cab against his will. So he'd gone freely. Philip. The man must have been Philip, or at least someone from the Eye.

"Aww, cher, did he run off on you?"

M ignored the malice in Veronica's tone. "So he hasn't been here? I thought he might have left a message for me."

"No," Papa Ozee said, turning away to wave the smoking herbs around a display of books. "But Veronica stole his phone."

Veronica shot him a look that was equal parts surprise and anger. Then she shrugged. "He dropped it on the sidewalk, and I took it. It's nicer than mine."

"Give it to the girl," Papa Ozee ordered her.

Veronica stepped behind the counter and picked up her bag. She rummaged around in it, pulled out a cell, and tossed it at M. She barely managed to catch it. Her fingers had started to tremble.

M didn't bother replying. She got out of the shop as fast as she could without knocking over anything with the duffel, then she leaned against the peeling wall and hit the texts icon.

She opened the top one, and began skimming the conversation. The day was sweltering, but M felt as if all the heat was draining from her body, leaving only a cold ache. Message after message confirmed her deepest fears.

ASH: I can handle her. You'll get the pieces as soon as I get them.

ASH: You'll spook her if you show up. She thinks we're working together. Let me finish it alone.

ASH: We're getting close. Be patient. She trusts me now.

She couldn't bring herself to read any more. Ash had played her.

Of course he did, she thought. *He played everyone, his parents, his friends, everyone in the religion he grew up in. He's a zealot. He would do anything for Horus.*

Fury blasted through her, burning away the hurt and despair. She didn't need the Eye to save her father. And she certainly didn't need Ash.

She took out her cell and hit speed dial. When Liza answered, M didn't bother to say hello.

"I want to make a trade," she said. "The head of the Set animal for my father."

Tall flowers in fuchsia and pale pink brushed against M's legs as she strode across the field that ran beside Mike's convent in Thailand. She was alone. She'd practically had to tie Mike up to keep her from coming, but M didn't want her there. Using this place was as close as M was willing to let Mike get to the cult of Set.

When she reached a spot near the dirt road leading to the convent gates, she stopped. All she could do now was wait.

A fat bumble bee buzzed lazily around one of the cosmos, and M felt a pang of regret. It was so beautiful in the field, so peaceful, and she'd invited something evil here. Liza had pushed M to come to the Set compound, as if M wouldn't realize how easy it would be to kill her and her father if they met there. She really had never noticed how smart M was, even after living with her for almost a year.

M had countered with meeting in St. Patrick's Cathedral in New York City. She'd liked the idea of a sacred place where witnesses were guaranteed, but Liza refused to meet there or on any sacred ground. They'd gone back and forth until they'd agreed on the field outside the convent.

The bumble bee flew off. M pulled the duffel higher on her shoulder and used one arm to press it tightly against her side. The hard plastic of the kennel shrine bit into her ribs, but she liked knowing it was there. The cult of Set had one piece; M had one piece. She didn't know which—if either—would have the stronger power of attraction. If it was theirs, her piece would fly to join it from who knew how far away. That's why her piece wasn't leaving the shrine until she saw her father. If Liza thought M bringing a portable sacred space to the meet-up was a violation of their deal, screw her.

M wished she had a way to destroy the piece. That would have given her the advantage. If they didn't hand over her father—bam, she'd blow up the piece and they'd never be able to resurrect their god. They'd never risk it. But they both knew that destroying the piece was impossible.

She kept her eyes on the road. After what felt like an eternity, a sedan rounded the corner. An SUV and another sedan followed.

"Here we go," she muttered. She glanced at the open convent gates. Could she sprint through them fast enough if the deal went south? A flash of movement in one of the convent windows caught her eye, and she grinned. A figure in a black-and-white habit stood there—and in every other window facing the field. Whatever happened, she'd have a whole bunch of nuns as witnesses.

The cars pulled to a stop about thirty feet away. Bob and Liza stepped out of the first car and started toward her— alone. M cupped her hands around her mouth and shouted, "Don't come over here without my father. Or I'll never tell you where the piece is."

"You said you'd bring it," Liza called back.

"You said you'd bring my father," M answered.

Bob flicked two fingers in the air. The back door of the SUV slid open, and her father stumbled out, flanked by two bodyguards, each holding one of his arms.

Dad. It was Dad. Standing in the field, his sandy hair a mess like always, his greenish eyes locking onto hers. He was there, he was alive. Until this moment, she hadn't let herself believe it fully.

M let out a cry of joy. "Here's what you want. Take it and get out." She flung the duffel bag deeper into the field and raced toward her father.

The car had stopped. It felt like they'd been driving on a dirt road for a least a few miles. There shouldn't be a stoplight or even a stop sign out here. It was time for Ash to make his move.

He rolled onto his side, and winced. He was sure at least one of his ribs had been cracked during the beating he'd been given when they found him, and his vision was still blurry from the kick in the head he'd gotten from someone wearing heavy steel-tipped boots. His lack of food over the past few days didn't help.

The cult of Set knew it was harder for Ash to use his power when he was weak. It was something his parents had figured out—and used against him—when he was a kid.

But he'd had a lot of training since then, training that had taught him how to go deep beneath the pain to a still place within. There he could call on Horus and invite the god's power into his body.

It didn't take long, not anymore. With a few deep breaths, he felt the presence of Horus inside him. He wouldn't be able to wield it for as long as he could when he was fit, but it should be enough to get him out.

Ash focused on the trunk and directed all the power he could summon at it. With a screech of metal against metal, the door rolled up like a sardine can being opened. He didn't allow himself to cry out as he hauled himself up and half fell onto the ground, even though the movement blasted agony through every nerve.

He blinked rapidly to clear his vision. A field. Followers of Set, running toward some kind of big bag in the grass. His father. His mother. Hugh.

M.

Clinging to her father and staring at him with incomprehension. What the hell was she doing here? The Set acolytes must have left people behind at the cemetery. They must have grabbed her the second she got back.

"M," he managed to croak, his mouth dry and rough as sandpaper. "I'm sorry. They found—"

She took a step away from her father, moving toward Ash. "You weren't there. That girl, she said you got in a cab with a man. I thought—I was sure it was Philip. The texts . . ." He saw the moment the truth hit her. The confusion replaced by devastation.

Seeing her horror, Ash instantly understood. The cult of Set hadn't taken her. She'd made a bargain. When he wasn't waiting at the cemetery the way he'd promised, she assumed he'd taken the three pieces to the Eye.

She had just traded the final piece of the Set animal for her father. Now the cult had them all.

She hadn't trusted him. Not after all they'd gone through. She'd looked at him and seen what his parents saw, what pretty much everyone saw. A liar. Someone disgusting, repulsive, not even human.

He turned away. He couldn't look at her.

"Ash!" she called, a plea in her voice. He could hear her pain, but before he could decide how to respond another voice rang out.

"Ashwin!" His father's voice boomed across the field. "I wanted you to be here to see this. I want you to witness the power of the god you chose to reject."

Avid expectation lit his father's face. His mother's eyes blazed with anticipation. Hugh's lips were moving in what Ash was sure was prayer. In moments they would see their god.

Philip had been right. Ash should have brought the very first piece back to the Eye. Keeping just one piece safe could have prevented this. Now it was too late. For millennia, the Eye had kept Set from rising, and now it was all Ash's fault they had failed.

The Asim stepped out of the SUV, holding a large piece of flat stone in his hands. Ash recognized it immediately. It came from the ruins of one of the temples at Ombus and was used every time an offering was made to Set.

The Asim didn't even glance at Ash. The last time they'd seen each other was when Ash first arrived at the compound last year, saying he wanted to rejoin the cult of Set. The Asim had interrogated him for several days before allowing him to stay. Using the stillness Philip had taught him, Ash had fooled the Asim. He would never be forgiven for that.

Ash's parents, Hugh, and the woman who was the Asim's second-in-command each took a canopic jar from the van and followed the Asim into the field, walking single file. Ash knew Hugh had moved up high in the organization, and he couldn't help feeling a strange burst of pride. His best friend was a true believer, utterly devoted. Ash was glad that the association with him hadn't hurt Hugh's position.

They stopped when the Asim set the stone slab on the ground. His second gestured to another Set worshipper Ash didn't recognize, and the woman approached, anointed the slab with oil, and retreated.

Ash's mother opened the jar she carried, reached in, and reverently removed one of the Set pieces. She placed it on the glistening slab and stepped back. Ash's father opened his jar. As soon as he removed the Set piece it flew from his fingers. It melded with the first piece with a sharp click.

Ash had to stop this. He tried to open himself to Horus, but using the power to get out of the trunk had exhausted him. His body couldn't be used as a vessel, not without time to regain his strength.

M let out a moan of despair, finally running over to him, her father right behind her. None of the Set acolytes seemed to care about them anymore. "I thought you took the other pieces to the Eye. I thought they were safe," she cried. "I'm sorry. I'm so sorry. I should have trusted you."

"No." He wasn't going to let her believe that. "It was as much my fault as yours. If I'd told you the truth from the beginning—"

"You did more than anyone should expect from you," Dr. Engel interrupted. "You betrayed your family to try to save us all."

"They weren't my family anymore. Not—" Ash began. A sharp click jerked his attention back to the field. The third Set piece had attached itself to the other two. Hugh opened his jar, reached inside, and pulled out the fourth piece. It ripped itself out of his hand. A streak of black, another click, and the Set piece was almost complete.

"The last piece is in that bag." M's voice was oddly quiet and calm. Perhaps she still didn't believe. But the throbbing noise from all the pieces was so strong that it felt as if the earth itself was vibrating.

The Asim knelt beside the bag. Ash started for it, but one of the Set acolytes shoved him back.

M reached out and laced her fingers with his. "Can't you use your power?" she whispered.

Ash shook his head, red spots exploding behind his eyelids. "Not without some rest," he admitted. She reached for her father with her free hand. Ash searched for something to say to her, there had to be something in these last few moments they had together, the last few moments they had in the world.

The sound of a helicopter pulled him away from his thoughts. He jerked his head up. It was Phillip. It had to be.

"The Eye!" he told M. "They're here." Maybe they could stop what Ash had allowed to happen.

But the Asim was opening the duffel. He reached inside, and had to fling himself facedown on the ground when the last piece rocketed free and slammed home, joining with the rest of the Set artifact. Fusing together for the first time in thousands of years.

Philip was too late.

Ash had failed him. He'd failed the Eye. They'd taken him in and he'd vowed to devote his life to keeping the world safe from Set—and he'd failed. He'd failed M. He'd failed everyone. Most of all, he'd failed Horus. He'd failed his god.

He pulled his hand from M's and strode away. He didn't deserve to stand with her. Not when he was to blame for all of this.

The Set animal was complete. The god of the underworld was coming.

CHAPTER 23

The sky darkened. The air, then the ground, vibrated with a sound so low it was almost inaudible, like the sound the individual Set pieces made, only amplified a hundred times over. It invaded M's entire body, hammering at her skull, the delicate bones of her ears, and every joint that connected her frame.

The tiny blood vessels in her eyes began to pulse, and when she looked at her father, she saw that a splotch of blood the size of a dime had appeared in one of his eyes.

Her stomach cramped as the vibration moved deeper inside her. Everyone on the field and the road doubled over, struck by the same overpowering force. M forced her head up. She needed to know what was happening.

The Set animal, so small, so insignificant looking, was shaking. It began to morph, stretching out and up until it loomed seven feet over the ground. The skin of its body went from shiny black to the golden brown of human flesh. The head sprouted hair. There were elements of jackal, fox, and even aardvark in the length of its snout in that face, but it was wholly alien. She'd seen carvings and statues depicting Set, but nothing had prepared her for this. Even with the god standing so close that she could smell the human sweat and animal musk, she could hardly make herself accept what she was seeing. She couldn't look away as it stood there, tail thrashing around massive legs as if it had a will of its own.

M tightened her grip on her father's hand. It felt thin, bony, and when she looked at his face she saw that his skin had a gray tint and his cheeks were hollow. He stared at Set with an expression of weariness and defeat. But when he looked back at her, his eyes filled with the love she'd always seen there. He squeezed her hand back. At least they were together again.

The horrible sound fell silent, and M slowly straightened all the way up. Set stared around the field, eyes darting as the god took in everything. He threw up his arms, tilted his head back, and gave a long howl of joy and triumph. The wind whipped up as if in answer, bending the flowers almost horizontal, tearing huge hunks of grass out of the ground.

M could hardly bear to look at him, all the little hairs on the back of her neck and her arms standing up in primitive revulsion. But Bob and Liza, along with the other worshippers of Set, stared at him with ecstasy on their faces. Tears of rapture streamed down Bob's cheeks. It sickened her. These people had taken her father from her and let her believe he was dead. Bob and Liza had lied to her every single day. They'd abused their own son. And all for this *demon*.

Raw rage flooded through her. Without pausing to think, she dropped her father's hand and charged at Bob, fighting her way through the magical wind churning around the giant god. She flipped out her bo staff and slammed it into Bob's kneecap. He staggered toward Set, and reached out to his god to stop himself from falling.

The wind lashing around the god jerked Bob off his feet. Bob bucked and twisted in the air, then with a string of sharp cracks, his bones began to break. He shrieked as a bloody piece of broken tibia tore through his pants. One of his arms flopped as his shoulder shattered.

M covered her mouth with her hand and stumbled back in horror. Set didn't seem to notice as Bob's neck snapped and his lifeless body continued to circle in the gale. Instead the god appeared to be grinning with his mutant face. He flexed his fingers and stretched, reveling in having a body again.

She turned and ran to Ash, yelling into his ear so he could hear her over the wailing wind. "I didn't mean for that to happen. It just— The wind grabbed him." Ash hated his father, but seeing him die in such a hideous way . . . she couldn't even imagine what he must be feeling.

Ash pulled her close. "He wanted this. He wanted to reincarnate Set. He made the choice."

"What do we do? How do we stop this?" She looked up into his face.

It had gone slack.

Cold dread swept through her body. "Ash?" He still held her close, but his eyes were blank, staring through her as they had when they were hiding behind the Buddha. He didn't recognize her.

M shook him. "Ash!" Her voice came out shrill with fear. He pushed her away, like she meant nothing to him, like he didn't even know who she was.

Then he turned and strode toward Set.

Ash was paralyzed, yet his body was moving, legs taking long strides, arms swinging. His mouth opened and a shout erupted from his throat, the words in an ancient language, but one Ash understood immediately—"Today I avenge my father."

Set whirled toward him and let out a rush of snarling barks, then raced toward Ash. Toward *Horus*. In the past,

Ash had directed Horus's power as it flowed through him, but now Ash was nothing but a spectator in his own body. The god had taken him over completely. Ash couldn't even blink. Everything was controlled by Horus.

God channeler. He had never understood, until now, what that truly meant. He was nothing more than a vessel, a tool for Horus to use at will.

His body rammed into Set's with a hideous thud, Ash helpless as Horus and Set both crashed to the ground. Set immediately grabbed Horus's—Ash's—neck with his teeth. Everything in Ash wanted to react, to protect himself, but his body wouldn't obey his commands.

Horus wrapped his hands around Set's throat and squeezed, choking him. Ash could feel the thick fur under his fingers, the ridges of Set's trachea as Horus crushed it. Set began to wheeze. But instead of releasing Ash—Horus—Set tightened his jaws, digging his teeth deeper into Ash's throat.

With a bellow, Horus yanked, pulling Set off his neck— along with a chunk of Ash's flesh—and hurled Set across the field. He landed with a thud that shook the ground, but was on his feet again in seconds.

Ash felt blood pumping from the gash in his neck. Could Horus feel the agony in Ash's body—or was that Ash's alone? If the god had the capacity to feel pain, it didn't slow him down. He charged across the field at Set. Set responded by running straight at Horus, then launching himself in the air, jaws wide and dripping foam.

Power ripped through Ash's body, more than he'd ever channeled. His nerves were like wires conducting high volts of electricity. Horus leapt impossibly high, meeting Set far above the field. When their bodies collided, a boom of thunder sounded, and the blue sky darkened, the fluffy white clouds going black.

Ash expected to feel his body slam back into the ground,

but the two gods grappled in midair. The scent of ozone, sweet and pungent, filled Ash's nose as a ball of lightning formed in Set's hand. He smashed the ball into Ash's skull, and for a moment all he could smell was his own singed hair.

Horus pushed himself away from Set, flying backward through the air. A ball of lightning formed in each fist, Ash's flesh crackling, and Horus hurled the balls at Set. One ball went wild and hit the earth a few feet from Hugh, the impact knocking him to the ground.

Ash's instinct was to rush to his friend, no matter what had happened between them, but he couldn't act. He wanted to search for M, but he could only see what Horus chose to look at.

Set hurled another lightning ball and it hit Ash on the shoulder, with the harsh burn of dry ice. The blast sent Horus into a roll. He plummeted toward the ground, hit the grass and skidded across it, then sprang back to his feet. Power burned through Ash as Horus formed a lightning ball between his hands, letting it grow bigger and bigger until, with a grunt, he launched it at Set. It was a direct hit that knocked Set out of the air to the ground.

Horus gave a shout of glee. The battle was all he cared for.

M pulled her father away from the SUV. One of the blazing balls the gods were throwing had smashed into it and the gas tank had exploded. Someone was screaming. Shrieking. But before M could act, the sound abruptly stopped.

"Are you all right?"

Mike was running toward them. "What are you doing out here?" M demanded. "You promised to wait inside."

"Two of the people I love most in the world are out here." She gave M's dad a fast, hard hug. "I see the rumors of your death were greatly exaggerated."

"Well, for the moment anyway," her father agreed.

"I can't believe what I'm seeing," Mike said, gesturing toward the battle. "But I'm not going to think about it right now. How can we help Ash?"

"That isn't Ash," M told her. "He's being controlled by Horus. Ash is a god channeler, and now I know what that really means. But it's still his body. That thing ripped a chunk out of Ash's neck." She thought it had stopped pumping blood, but the front of his shirt was soaked with it. It looked like half his hair had been singed away. "I don't know how much longer he can survive." She had to shout the last words. A series of rhythmic booms had started up.

"What is it—Horus—doing?" her dad yelled.

Ash—Horus—held an enormous fireball, much bigger than the ones he'd been throwing, and was slamming it repeatedly into the ground. With each blow, the earth rose in response, gathering itself into a heap, then a mountain. She shot a glance at Set. He'd taken up a position about halfway across the field. His hands were spread wide, but M didn't see anything between them. He wasn't making another lightning ball. She didn't want to wait to see what was going to happen. She had to find a way to stop this.

The repetitive booming stopped, but a low rumble continued, and there was an underlying hissing sound. Mike brought her hands to her chest, and M saw she held her rosary. "Dear God. It's made a volcano."

The top of the mountain had started to smoke, and the entire thing was trembling. M saw her little dog carrier sticking out of the earth about halfway up. The animita.

"A sacred space!" she exclaimed. "We need to create a sacred space!" Sacred spaces made the Set animal fall apart, and it was the only thing she could think of. Would it work on an incarnate god? She didn't know, but anything was better than standing here.

"I'm not sure that's possible," Mike said.

"Bali. People create their own sacred spaces there all the time." Hope rose up inside her. Maybe the idea wasn't completely insane. "And it worked on the Set pieces. They fell apart every time Ash and I walked by one. The pieces were falling apart and coming together every dozen feet. The voodoo guy made a sacred space of his own too. A cabinet."

The odor of sulfur permeated the air. "It's going to blow. We have to try, or everyone here is going to die," M urged.

Mike knelt on the ground and began to pray, fingering her rosary beads. M hesitated, realizing that she didn't have a god to pray to. How was she supposed to create a shrine?

She thought of the animita again. Some of the shrines were dedicated to Mary or other saints, but some were just remembrances of the person who had died. The one she'd used had a collection of things that must've been special to the deceased person, nothing religious, but it had deactivated the Set piece.

M pulled her mother's Swiss Army knife out of her pocket. "It's intent that matters, whatever's sacred to you will work. I'm making a shrine to Mom," she told her father. "You make something too. Let's try to get a few points around the place where they're fighting. The convent takes up one whole side—if we can trap them between that and our new sacred spaces, the Set artifact might fall apart again."

Her father nodded, taking his wedding ring off his finger, then removing the chain that he always wore around his neck. It held her mother's ring. "I love you, Dad," M said, then she ran, heading for a spot on the other side of the field.

"I love you, too," she heard her father yell after her.

M tried to keep her focus on the plan. It was the best thing she could do to save Ash and everyone else. But she jerked to a halt when she saw the funnel of a tornado rise up from between Set's palms. That's what he'd been making.

He flung out his arms, and the tornado spun free, growing as it moved. M managed to circle around it before it got too large. When she was on the far side of the volcano and the tornado—and the gods controlling them—she threw herself to the ground, flipped open the knife, and thrust the largest blade into the earth. She rested both hands on top of knife handle. She wasn't sure what to do next, but closed her eyes, blocking out the destruction.

A memory rose up in her mind, one of the strongest she had of her mother. M lay in bed, not at home, someplace else. She was maybe five years old. The bedspread was cream with nubby flowers. Mommy sat next to her, wearing a kimono, her hair damp. She smelled like lemons and shampoo. She smiled at M as she pulled the blanket up over M's lips and lightly placed her hand over M's eyes. "I think you have your dad's nose."

She took her hand away, moving the blanket a little higher, so only M's eyes were showing. With one finger, she traced one of M's eyebrows. "Your eyes, though . . . They're shaped like mine, but the color, that's all you. I love your eyes." She pulled the blanket down a little. "I love your nose." She gave M's nose a little tap.

"And I really, really love . . ." Mommy paused, grinning, and M started to giggle. "Your toes!" Mommy grabbed M's feet through the blanket and began to tickle. M laughed until her tummy ached.

The memory sent warmth through her. She could feel it flowing from her hands into her mother's knife. "I love you, Mommy," M whispered, then opened her eyes. The volcano had begun to erupt, steaming lava sliding down the sides. The tornado spun around it, trying to destroy it. Bits of the molten lava were caught up with the vicious wind, then were flung off, out across the field.

M shoved herself to her feet. Keeping her head down, she

ran to a spot on the field she thought would be opposite from her father. She couldn't see him. The volcano blocked her vision. If she made a shrine here, they'd have one on each side of the battleground. Would that be enough? She had to try. What could she use for her new shrine?

Her hand went to her necklace, the way it so often did when she was trying to make a decision. Instantly, she knew what this shrine would be. Her father was still alive, but that didn't mean she couldn't honor the love between them. It was the most powerful force in her life. She'd gotten this far because every time she felt like she was trying to do the impossible, she thought of her father and kept going. She'd refused to let him die. She wasn't going to let him die now, either. Not him, or Ash, or Mike.

M pulled off the necklace and dropped to her knees. She closed her eyes, pressing the necklace into the earth with her hands. Her eyes pricked with tears as she thought of the moment she'd seen her father stumble out of the SUV— alive. Relief, and joy, and love had taken her over. M felt the power of the memory flow into the necklace, the necklace that had hidden the map, the map written in what had become a secret language for M and her father, the map she'd used to try to rescue him.

A shout went up like the wailing of a thousand sirens, and M's eyes flew open. Set was teetering. Blackness slid up his legs, obliterating the human skin. When the blackness moved over his knees, Set stumbled. By the time he hit the ground, the blackness had taken over his shoulders and was crawling up his face.

The tornado died, bits of lava raining to the ground. A piece flew at M. She dove to the ground, rolling away from it, then she scrambled to her feet again, her eyes finding Set. His body, now completely stiff and black, began to shrink.

Then splinter. Until all that remained was the five small pieces of the Set animal.

People rushed at them. A man snatched one up and raced to the helicopter that had landed near the convent gates. Seconds later the helicopter was in the air. The Eye had gotten at least one piece. M wasn't sure which side had gotten the others. But one was definitely safe, and that's what mattered.

Set was gone.

And Horus . . .

Ash! M's heart skipped a beat. What had happened to Ash?

Ash stared at the place where Set had just stood. All he wanted was to see M, to know she was okay, but Horus still controlled his eyes. The god's frustration and anger and disappointment coursed through him. Horus wanted to continue the fight.

The god let out a roar that vibrated Ash's throat. He turned in a circle, as if he couldn't accept that Set wasn't on the field somewhere, hiding from him. Ash got a glimpse of M, too brief, but enough to know she was alive. He saw Philip, too. His expression, one of awe and rapture, was exactly like the one Ash's father had worn when he looked at Set.

Ash felt Horus's control loosen, just a little. Without Set to fight, the god didn't have as much use for Ash's body. His power wasn't ripping along Ash's nerves, because he didn't have an enemy to hurl the power at.

Now was his chance. Ash used all his will to push the god out of his body, fighting against Horus's out-of-control emotions. But Horus still dominated every part of him.

I can't battle him, Ash told himself. *I'll never win.* Ash tried to let himself fall into a pool of stillness, letting the sights and sounds and feelings he was receiving from Horus pass by without impacting him.

When he felt calm and clear, unaffected by what the god was experiencing, he let the pool of quiet gently expand, picturing it growing wider and deeper, picturing the color as the cool green of M's eyes.

He could hardly sense Horus's emotions now. The protective pool around him was too vast for them to reach him. He pictured the water deepening and spreading out, out, out, out, until it became an ocean, until it became his world, until there was no room in Ash's body for both the water and Horus.

M stared at the closed door. One of the nuns had been a field medic before coming to the convent. She was in there with Mike, taking care of Ash. Was he even alive? The image of his mangled neck and limp body flashed into her mind again and again.

Philip jumped up from the chair across from the sofa where M and her dad sat. "I'm going in."

"No," she and Dad told him, speaking as one.

"We're all waiting here until Sister Juana gives us the okay," her father added. Philip gave a long, hard glare, then sat back down and began scrolling through his phone.

M checked the clock. They'd been waiting in the common room for almost an hour. She shifted a little, so her shoulder rested against her father's. He wrapped his arm around her.

She noticed that his juice glass was empty, and reached for it.

"I don't need any more," Dad said.

M studied his face. He looked better than he had on the field, but not enough to suit her. "How about some soup? I could get—"

"I'm fine. Being here with you is all I need," he insisted.

"I can't believe I'm really sitting next to you." It was at least the fourth time M had said it.

"I never doubted it would happen."

"Liar."

"Nope. I got a good feeling off Ash. I could see he was a kid who wanted to do the right thing. Even if his idea of the right thing didn't quite match mine." He glanced over at Philip, still engrossed in his phone. "I was impressed he'd hung on to basic decency, after the way his parents . . . He told you about that, didn't he?" M nodded. "I thought his integrity, and *your* stubbornness and knowledge of the map, would be my get out of jail free card."

M raised her eyebrows. "So you knew I wouldn't just hand over the map? That's what you told me to do!"

"I'm your father. Of course I knew. But I didn't think Ash would agree to team up with you, so I left it up to you to convince him."

"Threaten him, you mean," M said. Her father just smiled in response. "You sure you don't want soup?" she asked. "Or I could whip up some thousand-year—"

The door swung open, and Sister Juana and Mike appeared. "Well?" M demanded, a queasy mix of fear and hope swirling through her.

"He's starting to come to," Mike answered. "He's asking for you."

The light hurt his head. Ash tried to pry his eyelids open. He needed to see, to prove he was still here, somehow. Dark spots swirled through his vision, until he could focus enough to make out M, her father, Philip, and Mike gathered around him. He took a deep breath, the air painful in his throat.

"Are you okay?" M cried. She lightly touched the bandage someone had put on his neck wound.

"Are *you*?" Ash struggled to sit up so he could get a better look at her.

"It might be a good idea to stay down for now," Mike told him.

"Is Horus still with you?" Philip demanded, speaking over Mike.

Ash closed his eyes, feeling for the presence of the god, from his toes to his fingertips to his head. "He's gone," Ash breathed, relieved, cracking his eyes open again.

Philip began firing questions. "What did you learn from him when he was within you? Did you get a sense of what he wants? Did he have instructions for us?"

"Enough," Dr. Engel said firmly. "The boy's been injured. He's exhausted. If your god had remained within him much longer, Ash would be dead. We're staying here tonight." He looked over at Mike, and she nodded. "Then I'm taking him and my daughter home."

"You're nothing to the boy. I've taken care of him for the past six years. Who are you to take him anywhere?" Philip protested in a cold tone Ash was overly familiar with.

"All you've been taking care of is the conduit for your god," M snapped.

"The responsible thing to do is for you and your group to go find out how much destruction that battle caused," Dr. Engel continued. "There could be people out there who need help."

Ash struggled to understand what was happening. Dr. Engel barely knew him. What he did know was that Ash had lied to him and led his daughter into a death trap.

"Ash, we need to get back to London," Philip said, ignoring the others. "We have plans to make. The Eye managed to get three of the pieces when Horus destroyed Set, but the cult escaped with two."

"I'm not going with you," Ash rasped. There was more he wanted to say, but M's father was right. He was exhausted.

"The Eye—" Philip began.

"You and the Eye can go stuff yourselves," Mike announced. "You need to leave my convent now."

Philip opened his mouth to speak, but seemed unable to come up with a response. He turned and rushed out of the room in a huff.

"I've decided Horus isn't the sharpest knife in the drawer," M said, firmly shutting the door behind Philip. "Setting off a volcano is a terrible plan for saving the world."

"Not what he wanted," Ash said, the desire for sleep almost overwhelming him. "All he cared about was fighting Set. There was nothing for the people he killed. He didn't even notice them."

"Nothing for you, either." M looked like she wanted to punch something. "I don't get it. The whole point of the Eye was to stop Set from becoming incarnate because he'd destroy the world. Horus was supposed to be the good guy. But Horus seemed like he was trying just as hard to annihilate the world as Set was."

"Collateral damage," Ash explained. "Horus wasn't trying to obliterate the earth. He just wanted revenge. He wanted to kill Set, and the world was something he could make a weapon of."

"I think the followers of Set and the followers of Horus both misunderstood the prophecy," Dr. Engel put in. "You know, facts can be forgotten over so many years, and stories—"

"—get twisted so much their real meaning is lost," M finished for him.

He smiled, his eyes crinkling. "Right. The prophecy was that the battle between Set and Horus would continue until the end of time, until the earth was destroyed. But that didn't mean Set would demolish the world if he managed to beat Horus. I think it meant that the battle itself would obliterate the planet and all of us."

"So maybe whoever managed to trap Set in the statue didn't do it because they thought Set was evil," M said slowly. "Maybe they did it because as long as Set wasn't there for Horus to fight, the world would be safe. If they'd found a way to contain Horus, that would have worked just as well."

"This is making my head ache," Ash admitted. He felt like he was in free fall. Nothing could be counted on. Nothing was stable. He'd devoted so many years of his life to Horus because he thought Horus was on the side of right, while his parents and Set were on the side of destruction. Now he didn't know what to believe.

"We'll let you rest," Dr. Engel said. He and Mike started for the door. M pulled a blanket off the foot of Ash's bed, dragged a chair over, and settled herself in it with the blanket wrapped around her.

"M?" her father said.

"I'm staying," she told him firmly.

He smiled. "I know better than to argue with you when your mind is made up."

"I'll make us some tea," Mike said.

"But no food, please," Dr. Engel joked as they left the room.

Ash glanced at M. "You don't need to stay. I'm fine. And you won't be comfortable in the chair."

"Haven't *you* figured out yet there's no point in arguing with me when my mind is made up?" M asked, grinning. Then her smile faded. "I'm so sorry, Ash. When you weren't at the cemetery I panicked. I saw your texts with Philip, and I assumed you went back to the Eye. It didn't even occur to me I was giving Liza the final piece of Set. I thought it was the only way to save my dad, but what I did almost killed him, and you, and everyone else."

Ash shook his head weakly. "I lied to you, almost every day we were together. How were you supposed to trust me? I'm the one who should be telling you I'm sorry."

"Well, I forgive you, if you forgive me," M said.

"You forgive me?" He felt astonished. "Even after reading what I said to Philip? I was lying to him, too, sort of . . . I don't even know what I was thinking anymore." Everything seemed like a blur now, all his beliefs wrong.

"Of course I forgive you. You said we had a deal, and you kept it. You didn't betray me for the Eye. You saved my dad, and, oh yeah, the world," M told him. "But next time, we don't split up, agreed?"

"Agreed." A grin broke across Ash's face. Maybe he did have one thing he could count on, after all. He could count on M. "Wait," he said. *Next time?*